HE WOLF IN THE ATTIC

PAUL KEARNEY

First published 2016 by Solaris
an imprint of Rebellion Publishing Ltd,
Riverside House, Osney Mead,
Oxford, OX2 0ES, UK

www.solarisbooks.com

UK ISBN: 978 1 78108 361 1

A CIP catalogue record for this book is available from the
British Library.

Designed & typeset by Rebellion Publishing

In memory of my father,
James Francis Kearney,
who showed me what it was
to be a good man.

Author's Note

DURING THE COURSE of this narrative I have striven to follow faithfully the geography and history of the places described therein, but I have also taken certain liberties with space and time. I know the distance from Idstone Hill to Wayland's Smithy; I have walked it more than once. And I know that my fellow Ulsterman, C.S. Lewis, found his faith some months before his appearance in this text. I hope that the reader will forbear from comment if he or she finds that I have skewed dates and places a little in my telling of Anna's story.

PART ONE
Jericho

I form the light, and create darkness;
I make peace, and create evil:
I the Lord do all these things.

Isaiah 45:7

1

ALL DAY, PA went on, and it was raining outside in buckets and bowls, the kind of rain that makes another life for itself on the ground – it grows up and gathers together and starts gurgling everywhere. I like that rain – sometimes – I like looking at it, and thinking about it, but it's nasty really.

I like to hear Pa talking, and better still when he reads to me as it's growing dark and the lamp-smell is warming up the room. It reminds me of that other time long ago, before Oxford and England.

But when he stands on that dusty stage and speaks and raises his voice over their heads in the hall, I hate it so much. I don't want to shake hands with them as they file in and out, like they were a congregation and he was their priest. They all have such sad eyes. Even Pa can't change the hopelessness in them.

TALKED TO PIE today for a long time and tried to make her dance, but she's lazy. She'd much rather sit in the crook of my arm and watch things. I could scold her for being so lazy, but that would be *Hypocrisy*, which Pa hates, because he says I'm as lazy as Pie, and I hate the rain even more.

I'm getting too big for Pie, Pa says. I like it when he tells me I'm growing up, but I won't let her go. She's my best friend, if a friend is someone you can tell things to, and sit quiet with, and hug in the dark of the night.

He doesn't like her. She still has the burn marks on her from that last terrible day, when we were hemmed in between the fire and the sea. The day Mama died.

WELL, ALL RIGHT. In this country there are galoshes and things, which can be fun; I love rubber boots (and umbrellas – especially in the wind), but in the by and large of all that, the weather here is not nice.

I remember the warm rain coming over the hills behind the city; they were blue in the distance, and then yellow with sun and dust up close, and the crickets shimmered in them like an invisible gossiping little crowd. And the rain was warm, and swept across the land and upon the sea like a vast hanging music, dark and bright and silver, like God had made a painting.

Pa tells me I have no memory of anywhere else but England, and really doesn't like me talking about it. He gets angry sometimes, and has that look in his eye, the bright fire where bad things burn. So I go quiet, and he lays his hand on my head – sometimes – and it's all right again.

I am getting big. I got new shoes last week. Except they weren't new. They belonged to Miss Hawcross's niece, who must have very big feet. But I stuff newspaper into the toes and they're quite all right, except when they get wet. I wonder if she is a pretty girl, whose shoes I wear, and if her toes feel something when I wiggle mine in her old shoes. That would be nice. We could talk to each other, make up a language of twitching toes, and compose long letters while walking down the street.

Miss Hawcross says I have a mind like a dragonfly, which I thought was a fine thing, but apparently it's not; and she snaps the ruler across my knuckles when my dragonfly mind wanders, sometimes soft, like a joke, and sometimes hard, with the edge. She is very old, thirty at least. Pa told me once that she loved a man who died in the War, and that I must be good and meek and kind with her. I think of that when the ruler cracks against my knuckles, and I look at Pie and smile knowingly.

So, I KNOW all this stuff – and so much I know is supposed to be useful but isn't, like algebra and the gerund and how the subjunctive works and who was the king with all the wives. And the other things, the important ones – I am not allowed to mention them. As though the dragonfly is walled up in a quiet garden and flits around all the dead flowers, and can tell what colour they were when they were alive, and the names they had and how they smelled...

I do remember – and even the priest says you don't have to forget a sin. You are sorry for it, and then it's forgiven.

God forgives you. Our God, anyway.

But I remember what happened to us between the fire and the sea, and sometimes I think Pa hates it because the things I remember are not for me to be forgiven, but for him. And he can't forget or forgive himself. That's why he never sleeps, and why he drinks so much. He told me once that there are no memories at the bottom of a glass.

But even I can recall as clear as anything our lives back then so far away, in the lost city, when it was warmer – hot, lizard hot – and that bright, bright light had the dust-herb smell in it.

Nothing smells like that here. The only smells at this time of year are unpleasant: the drains, and the omnibus. The people on it when they are damp.

But I remember looking up at another sky, it was so blue and bright, and hot – I remember the stones burning under my legs, and something else in the light, that bright, bright light. I remember…

The rain taps the glass, like a polite little man wanting in. I wish there was less noise in the house. I wish… I wish we had some more peace, Pie and me. I wish Pa would talk to me like a person again, and not like I'm some dog he is training.

I like dogs too. And cats. And horses. I think we had a horse once, but we never had a dog. I would have remembered that.

I remember the horse galloping past us that day through the crowd, knocking people down. It was all on fire, flames streaming from its mane, and its eyes so wide and white with the agony. It galloped past us, and I never saw where it went.

I want to stop having to look at all these people who come into our house – it's not our house, really, but we do live here – and they sit down on our chairs, and talk to me in the old language and they think I understand what they're saying, but sometimes I do and sometimes I don't and I don't want to anyway. And when they troop through the door I stand sometimes where the glass is, and watch them come in, and the way they wear shawls over their head, and even the set of their faces – no-one in Oxford is as lined and brown as these people are – and this is not who I am or was or will ever be.

Pa told me that. I would never be the same. I kiss Pie, and am so *so* glad. Pa loves me more than anything else in the world – he told me so, a long time ago – and so everything is all right. I suppose everything is all right.

LORD JESUS CHRISTOS. *I say your name. Lord God please don't send me to hell. I am not a good girl – I know that – but I love my father and my mother (but she's dead), and I love the wrens in the garden and the irises when they come up blue. Lord Jesus I try to be a good neighbour to everyone. I really do. But can you please kill all the Turks? Because they murdered my mother and took our home. And they need to be punished.*

This is Anna. And thank you. Thank you very much.

AFTER I PRAY, I always feel much better, because I am told God is always listening – Miss Hawcross told me so. I hug

Pie until I'm sure it should hurt but it doesn't. I hug her so hard – until I think I can almost smell the sea again, and I think that if I open my eyes I might just be able to look at that line of blue – that other blue you don't get here – I heard Pa once call it kingfisher-blue. *Halcyon*. Somewhere out on the horizon, it's still there. I think Pa misses it something awful. I think the Turks took it from us because they wanted it for themselves.

I LOOK OUT at the rain, and think it cannot be the same world as the one I can still see in my head. All the colours have faded away.

PA SAYS WE mustn't live in the past. We have become English now. But we were Greek once, like Homer and Helen and Heracles. He used to tell me stories of Achilleos and Odysseos, but not any more. Was Troy a real place? He won't tell me. He looks out the window at the rain, as I do, and refuses to say. But I know we were Greek once, and Agamemnon was our king, and then he went to Troy and rode away on a great wooden horse and left us.

And somewhere out on the sea – Pa once told me the sea at sunset is as dark as wine – Odysseos still sails his ship, looking for us, trying to bring us home.

I miss Mama. I don't remember her at all but I miss her – isn't that odd? She smelled of lavender. And we had green basil growing in pots at all the windows, to keep out the flies. And it smelled like – like the best of summers. Like a land of dreams should smell.

And I hug Pie as I think of it, while the rain keeps tap tap tapping at the glass. We live in Jericho, in the city of Oxford, in the kingdom of England. And that is home now, and ever will be, until Odysseos returns.

2

I DON'T KNOW why that fat Henry wanted so many wives, I tell Miss Hawcross crossly, and for a moment I think she almost smiles. She is a small woman, with very thin ankles but a big... I'm not supposed to say it, but she has a big *bosom*, and looks like a puffed up little grey pigeon, with her hair up in a bun and a cameo brooch at her throat.

I see girls on the streets with short bobbed hair, and I saw a picture of Louise Brooks once outside the nickleodeon on Walton Street, and she looked so impossibly beautiful that when I got home I tried to cut off my own hair – it is as black as hers, and just as sleek when it's wet – but Pa caught me at it and belted me until my nose bled. He gripped the hank of hair I had cut off as though it were something precious I had thrown away, and then he had to trim the rest of it anyway, to make it all the same length. It still wasn't a Brooks bob, but it comes down to my shoulders now instead of the small of my back.

The children down by the canal still shout at me and call

me a *dago*, so I don't suppose it made much difference. It would be lovely to be pretty and elegant and sophisticated, and to smoke a cigarette in a long holder.

I bet if big fat Henry hadn't been king, he wouldn't have had so many wives. He was a wicked man, but sad, too I suppose. How awful, to never find someone you can truly love, so you are always looking for her your whole life. And cutting people's heads off when they turn out to be the wrong one.

He was a great king of England, Miss Hawcross says, and I am to learn all about him and his family if I am to pass as an educated young lady and not a scrawny guttersnipe. And She gives me the flat of the ruler after that, just to make sure I remember. She is very keen on the word *guttersnipe*. And *ragamuffin* too.

After lessons, I see her out the door, because that's polite, and watch her waddle down the street. A black straw boater she wears, when it's not raining, and little boots with mother of pearl buttons. I wonder if she still thinks of the young man who died in the War. I wonder if he would still like her if he saw her now, with her pinched lips and greying hair.

It must be terrible to be old, when you love someone who died young. They never change in your mind, and every day you see yourself grow away from that person you were when you loved and knew them. Until you are more of a shadow than they are, and the girl you were is altogether gone, more dead even than the young man on the battlefield.

If I loved someone and they died like that, I should wear black for the rest of my life, and a veil. I would never forget them, or let anyone else edge their memory out of my mind. Memories are important, like the bones of the mind. We build ourselves upon them, flesh and blood moulded around the pictures of what is past.

I look at Pie sometimes, and think she is a memory herself. How I got her; who gave her to me. Every time I look at her I can see him smiling.

Anyway, that's what I think. It is why I try so hard to never forget anything.

Pa is different. He wants to bury the memories and make himself someone else. It's why he shaved off his beard, and wears tweeds, and fights so hard to look and sound and behave like an Englishman.

'The English are a great race,' he told me once. 'But they have a deep down belief that they are the best of all peoples.

'You and I come of the blood that bred Homer, and Aristotle, and Socrates and Alexandros. Whatever they call you, remember that, Anna. Our people dug the foundations of civilisation itself.'

That was a long time ago, when we first came here. I do not think he would ever say such a thing again. But it makes me proud, and when the children down at the canal throw names and stones at me, I ignore them, for I am of the same blood as Achilleos. The English have their castles, and Buckingham Palace, and the Changing of the Guard. But we have the Parthenon, and the Iliad.

THERE IS ANOTHER meeting in the house tonight. If I hear the word *committee* once more I shall scream. I suppose I am a scrawny guttersnipe after all, because I have not the manners to sit still and smile at the people as they troop in, shaking the rain from their shoulders. These are the Greeks now, these poor folk who look like beggars from another century. There was a big debate last week, and they changed the name of the Committee they are all so fond of. Now it is not *Repatriation*, but *Resettlement*. And there is talk of hiring a steamship or something. It's all Greek to me.

IT'S DARK WHEN I creep out of the house by the back door, with the voices following me into the night. Ugh, winter; the light goes before the sun has a chance to get risen properly. I can see the gaslamps still on in the Lucy factory, up the canal, but when I climb over the garden wall, there is almost nothing but the blue deep dusk out to the west, over Port Meadow.

Behind me, Oxford is still busy and bright, and there are so many motor cars that they set up a hum in the night. This is where they build motor cars, this city, more than anywhere else in England. It seems strange, for there are so many days when Oxford is grand and beautiful and otherworldly, like a city created by a curious-minded king. The University did that. I think I shall go there, one day, and study something complicated and obscure just to show them I can, even if I am a girl.

But the land swells up to the west and there is a moon rising, low over the hills at Wytham. There are deep woods there, all damp and thick and full of deer and old trenches they dug to train the poor soldiers for the war.

I follow the canal to Walton Well Road, climbing the fences of other people's back gardens on the way, and then cross it and the railway, and step light as a…. as a cat… to Port Meadow, where all at once the world opens up, and the city is left behind, and the moon is riding higher and higher, a horned moon with clouds drifting across it, the light burning their edges silver.

It is enough to see by, but I go slowly, all the same, walking off the beaten path in the grass towards the faint light of Wolvercote in the north. Somewhere to my left is the Thames, a tiny river here compared to what it is like in London, but much cleaner I'm told, a country river.

It's cold, and the grass is wet, but I don't mind, and nor does Pie. I hug her to me under my coat, and feel the newspaper in the toes of my shoes become damp and start to squish and tear.

This is what Pa taught me once. You find the Plough, which is seven stars in the shape of a saucepan, and the outer rim of the pan are two stars called the Pointers. You follow their line up, and there is a bright glimmer that seems almost on its own, and that is Polaris, and it points north.

And Orion has three stars in his belt. And the Little Bear is like the Plough, only smaller. And that red flicker near the horizon in the east; that is Mars.

They are all here; all my stars. It has been a long time since the night was so clear and still, and my breath is a pale cloud in front of my face, so solid-seeming I almost think I could grab a handful of it and put it in my pocket. And the cold is getting deeper, seeping through my coat and setting chilly fingers on my bare knees, but I don't care. I tug Pie out of my coat so she can see the night too, and so I can hug her close to my face.

The world seems so not real at night under the moon and stars, with the streets and cobbles and motor-cars and heads-down hurrying people all taken away. Here and now, is the world as it was near to the beginning, when God breathed life into it out of the darkness, and brought it up out of the waters. Was that the second day? I think so. A world empty, before the creatures crawled out of the seas to set their footprints upon it.

I am shuddering with cold, but very happy, my dragonfly mind calm and still now, as though it has become frozen along with the settling dew. I almost feel as though I am floating over the fast-freezing grass.

I walk on, in a silver cloud of my own breathing.

Godstow Nunnery is up at the Lock to the north-east. We have picnicked there, among the ruins. I think it would be a grand place to be in summer, if you were in love.

Fat Henry destroyed it, but the ruins are perfect as they are, so I can almost forgive him. It would be... it would be truly something to picnic there with someone you loved, to hold their hand in the grass, and look up at the sky. I wonder if Miss Hawcross ever lay back in the grass at Godstow with her grey hair still brown, and held her soldier's hand under the sun before he went off to Passchendaele.

OUT OF THE dark a light leaps, yellow and small, like a candle fighting the wind. It's out on the Meadow to the north-west, near the river. I feel angry at once that the night has been invaded, that perfect tinsel-bright moon mocked by a stupid little campfire. I look at Pie, and pull a face. There is nowhere to be alone in this world, not even here, not for more than a moment.

But I creep forward all the same, curious as a cat. Pa told me once I look like a cat, with a pointy chin and big eyes. But I don't think a cat could possibly have a nose like mine. It's too long and crooked, and it steers my whole face like the prow of a boat.

I don't care anyway. Helen of Troy was beautiful, and look what a flibbertigibbet she turned out to be. Beautiful people are invariably boring, Pa says, because there is less of them to admire under the skin than there is upon it.

But Mama was beautiful; I'm sure she was.

I wish I could see in the dark like a cat. I am shivering, and I step in cow-pats as I creep towards the light. My shoes are so wet with the dew that I may just as well be barefoot anyway. Except for the cowpats. Yuck.

I would feel better if I had a knife. I have one at home, a little Watts penknife Pa used to keep for scraping out his pipe. But I don't think it's big enough to cut a Turk's throat.

Next time, I promise myself, I will bring a knife. It's best to be prepared for all kinds of villainy when out at night.

With my mouth open, I can hear my own heartbeat in my throat, a pulse, a rush, as though my insides were at the back of my teeth, crowding forward to look out.

The voices are louder now. Men, snarling and growling, a flash of anger. I grip Pie so tight that I am sure she will pop in my grasp. For a moment I lower my head to the ground and I feel a cold thrill go through me. I am no longer cold, but I am afraid.

I kiss Pie, and raise my head. It suddenly seems a very difficult thing to do. I wonder if they will see my white face glowing out in the dark, but a calm, reasonable voice inside tells me that they are blinded by the firelight. The night is blank to them, a wall of black.

'Look at you, you worthless gyppo shite. Call yourself a countryman. You nicked the guts, you bastard. We'll have to wash the thing now. Go take it to the river.'

A little carcass is flung across the fire by one of the men about it, to slap wetly in the face of another. This one jumps to his feet. 'If you had a knife worth the name and not one blunt as a tinker's thumb, I'd be able to cut clean. I'd have been better off using a fucking spoon.'

They are both on their feet now, a fat man and a thin one, the light glaring out of their eyes. Three more men are lying around the fire on bedrolls and blankets. I can see bottles glinting in the flame-light. I can smell the booze from here. It reminds me of the smell in Pa's study on the afternoons. It surrounds them all, like a bubble of violence all heated up by the fire. I know this. I have seen it before. Somehow I know what is going to happen.

'Go on Bert, teach the little bastard one.'

'Aye. Fucking gypos. Useless bastards. Show him how to use that knife, Bert.'

The fat man slowly pulls a length of shining metal out of his pocket. It is as long as my hand from fingertip to wrist. It certainly looks sharp to me. The thin one, dark and fine-boned, looks at it as though he has just seen a snake. He is much younger than the fat man, barely more than a boy.

'You would cut a fellow just for that?' he asks softly. And he is afraid, I can see it.

'I would cut a little squint like you as soon as spit.' The fat man edges around the fire, and there is a cackling from the others reclining on the grass. They sit up, pass a bottle around, and generally look as though they are about to be entertained.

'You thinks you are something special, boy, just 'cos we lets you travel with us and share a fire? You think we don't know your kind?'

'I got no fight to pick with you,' the boy says. 'Not if you are who you says you are.'

'What do you know about who I am?' the fat man sneers, and he flips the knife up in air and catches it again with a grin. All the men laugh, except for the dark boy.

There is a moment, still as a stone, when I think it will end at that, and everything will blow over. But suddenly the fat man utters a yowl, and comes springing round the fire, stepping on one of the others, who spits curses, and he lunges at the boy, pointing his way with the knife blade like a man lighting his way in the dark with a candle.

I thought the dark boy would run away – I want him to. But he stands his ground, side-steps, and with a grunt, he punches the fat man – Bert – in the side of the head, a slap of flesh which makes me cringe. The fat man stumbles, and the boy is so quick and deft that I do not quite see what he is doing. There is a tumble of shadow, a grunt, and then a high, thin wail of pain.

Bert is on the ground, very still. He is still breathing, because I can see his breath smoke. He groans.

The thin dark boy is standing over him. The knife is in his fist now, and he has the firelight at his back so that he is a silhouette. He raises his head, and is breathing very fast, the air sawing out past his mouth. He looks out into the moonlight where I am lying, and my heart seems to stop its rush in my throat for a second. Just for a second, I could swear that there is a light in his eyes, that they catch the moon and reflect it back, as bright as two coins of silver.

And then he throws the knife away, and I hear it clump into the grass just in front of me. I could reach out and touch it. And it is as though the blade is covered in fresh black paint, glistening under the moon.

My heart starts again, beating like the pistons of a train until I think it is going to burst. I cannot move. I look at the knife, and then up at the thin boy thirty yards away. The men around the fire are on their feet, shouting, and cursing, and a bottle is thrown into the flames to shatter, sending up a whoosh of light.

And in that light the boy is looking at me. He can see me. I am as sure of it as I am of the seasons and the sunrise. I cannot see his face, but I know those quicksilver eyes are on me. I can feel them.

Something comes out of my mouth, a sob of air, and with that I can move again. I see the fat man's friends all in a scatter about the fire, one kneeling at the body on the ground, two baying like dogs, the curses all melting together into a howl of hate and anger. But the dark boy stays in a half-crouch, staring out across Port Meadow towards me. I know he can hear the thumping of my heart.

I look at the knife again, fighting for breath. It is blood, not paint. The fat man is dying. The boy killed him. And now he can see me.

The calm, reasonable voice in my head cuts through everything, as clear as a bar of frost.

Run.

Up I jump, Pie in one hand, her limbs
off back the way I came across the open gra
air is biting at my lungs as I draw it in. So co
hurt. I cannot feel my feet, but I know they are
under me, fast, so fast. I have never run so fast in m
before.

The stars are so far and cold, and now away from that
horrible firelight the night seems huge and bright, and I
feel as obvious and visible as a ball on a billiard table. I
want to look back, but I cannot waste the time. But as I
run, I am sure he is following me, and I know his eyes are
alight, and I know also –

I do not know how I know this, but I am sure he is
loping after me on all fours, like a dog. I cannot see it, but
I know it.

And now the great meadow seems huge and unfriendly,
a place where I should not be. There is nowhere here I can
hide. And I gasp and hiccup as I run, my eyes set on the
light of the streets on the other side of the railway line. I
can taste the cinders of the trains in my mouth, and the
coppery taint of blood, and I feel as though I am going
to be sick, but I keep on running, the rime-dew crunching
under my shoes. Until I am at the bridge again, and the
gate there, black bars across my path.

I stop, I have to, and look back at last. I cannot hear a
thing, because my head is thundering so. And I know he
is behind me, grinning. He does not need a knife for me.

I hug Pie. She is damp and cold, but I am hot now. I feel
as though I am all aglow, and my breath could melt snow.

And the moonlit meadow is empty, as bright and bare as

is no-one near me, no-one
ngs in the dark.

voice in my head does not
now that.

s I do, Pie slips out of my
side of it, and Pie is on the
wn, and reach through the

I hear a sound, like that made by a little animal when it is dying. I do not even know it is me making it. The hand has my wrist in a grip I cannot break. When I tug backwards there is no movement. I think I can feel the bones in my arm creak, and the grip of the fingers burns as I try to twist free. I start to hiccup, and can only say, '*Please*,' and even in that moment, when I am so afraid, I am angry too, at how like a little child I sound.

The boy is there on the other side of the gate, and I can see his face in the moonlight, as clear as clear. It is wedge-shaped with a chin as pointed as mine and a long nose, and his eyes – oh thank you God – his eyes are not nickel-bright but dark and human and normal. But he will not let me go.

We stare at each other like that. Forever it seems, but it is only as long as it takes for a struck match to flare. He says nothing, but with his free hand he lifts Pie off the ground and puts her in my fingers.

Then he lets me go, and I pull my arm through the gate as though it were the bars at the zoo and the lion is on the other side.

We crouch there, and I feel a hot warmth between my

legs and I realise that I have wet myself, but I am still so afraid that it seems utterly unimportant. His black eyes hold me; that thin face, as lean as a lurcher's.

Then he stands up. And I cannot, but kneel on the ground by the gate hugging Pie, and I am breathing so hard I might as well be running again, except I am going nowhere. I can go nowhere. I know that now. Running will not help me.

The dark boy looks up at the moon, and I shut my eyes, for I cannot bear to see if his will brighten again with that awful beastly light.

And when I open mine again, he is gone, swift and quiet as a fox in the night. My wrist still feels his grip upon it, and my legs are rubbery and my toes are numb and the wet in my knickers is cold now, a chill line trickling down my leg. And I cannot help it, but I bury my face in Pie, and the air comes out of me in one big sob, and then another, and another. It sounds like the wingbeats of the swans when they fly low above the river.

THE FLICKERING GASLIGHTS are warm and safe and welcoming now, and the cobbles feel sure and sane under my feet. I am very cold, and I do not know what time it is, or how long I crouched by the gate hugging Pie. It is not late for grown-ups, for the pubs still have life and laughter in them, and there are people hurrying up and down, and motor cars, and the clinking of a milkman's wagon behind the clopping horse, and I am so cold. Oxford seems to exist on the other side of a thick pane of glass, and I am invisible behind it. I wish I was invisible.

I am shaking, not sure where I am going. I have come too

far, seeking the light, and am walking down the Woodstock Road, then St Giles, and I look up to see a sign hanging, an eagle with a little baby clinging to it. The sign halts me in my tracks, and I begin to cry. I don't want to, but I can't help it. I stand in the street and look up at the little baby being taken away by the eagle, and I think of the cold moonlight on Port Meadow, and the fat man's breath dying into the dark, and the knife with the wet paint on it, and I come to a stop.

The men coming out of the pub almost knock me down. They seem huge – well, one of them does. They stink of beer and pipe tobacco, and are both smoking pipes and pulling on their coats and talking loudly, and it takes a moment for the two of them to realise I am there, like a stray dog they have accidentally kicked.

I want to move on, to keep walking, but I am so cold and tired now and I just want Pa to scoop me up in his arms and take me to my room and light the lamp and put me to bed and maybe talk to me for a while like he used to. I want to hear him speak to me, and tell me that everything is all right. And I can't bear snivelling, but here I am, all a snivel, and I can't help it, and the calm faraway part of me is so cross about it but it can't do anything. And I have wet myself as well, like a baby, and I can't bear that either, and I wish – I wish –

'What have we here?' the big man says, teeth still clenched around the stem of his pipe. He seems enormous, with his flapping coat and scarf and hat and the pipe-smoke all about him. He has a fleshy, florid face, like a ham, but it is not a bad face, and his eyes are kind under the black brows. I can see that, even here and now.

His companion is more spare, a long, pale face under thinning hair. He is knocking the dottle of his pipe into the palm of his hand and he has sharp eyes, but they are not unkind either.

I look up at them, and try to say something, and I wonder if they can see the wet on my legs, and I have to fight the stupid crying again. But I am not a baby and I will not cry. There has been enough of that for one night.

I am about to speak, but the big man is kneeling in front of me now. He has taken his pipe out of his mouth and his eyes are searching my face.

'My dear, are you all right?'

And such is the sympathy and the concern in his voice that I can only shake my head, as dumb as Pie.

'Are you lost?'

I nod.

So does he, as though I had confirmed what he already knew.

'What's your name, girl, and where do you live?' the thinner man says, a little sharp, looking up and down the street. 'I do believe she's on her own, Jack.'

'Of course she's on her own. Look at her. She's freezing.' The big man touches my shoulder, and feels my shivers.

'You're a little icicle is what you are my girl. And out so late! Come now, is your mother nearby? You cannot be out on your own at this hour.'

I find a voice, but it is not my own. It is a little lost mew, disgusting to the calm, strong part of me that is listening inside.

'My mother is dead.'

Something in the big man's face changes at that. There

is a spasm of pain that crosses it, and his big hand grips my shoulder very tight for a moment. He looks in my eyes, and says quietly, 'That is a sad thing.' And just in that instant, I feel he understands me completely.

Then he straightens, and puts his pipe in his pocket. 'Well, this won't do, will it? We'll have to get you home. It's far too cold for little girls and their dolls to be running around the streets.'

The other man is retrieving his bicycle from where it leans by the wall of the pub. He looks me up and down. His face is not unkind, but there is a detachment in it.

'Children wander off all the time, Jack. I daresay her father or guardian is around here somewhere. In a pub, I expect. Try the Lamb and Flag.'

'You're a cold-blooded reptile at times, Tollers.'

'I'm a father, and I speak whereof I know. I take it she can look to you to be her Galahad.'

'She can indeed, since you are so set on being off.'

The thinner man mounts the bicycle. He looks at me, gauging. 'She's just become mislaid, that's all.' And to me, he smiles suddenly, and his face becomes different, almost mischievous. 'You'll be all right with Jack, my girl. He delights in taking on waifs and strays.'

'A low blow, Tollers,' Jack protests, but the other is already cycling off, the bicycle tick tick ticking under him.

'Edith is expecting me. I have my own waifs to see to, Jack. Good luck, and I will see you next week, God willing.' He waves a hand, throws his scarf about his throat, and dings the bell, and then is off down the street, the red glow of his dynamo fading.

The big man called Jack looks down on me. 'Forgive my

friend, my dear,' he says. 'He is a Christian, and believes charity begins at home. And often it remains there.' Then he snorts a laugh, and offers me his big, sweaty hand. And I take it.

3

WE WALK DOWN St Giles, hand in hand. Jack does not ask any more questions for a hundred yards. He has retrieved his pipe from his pocket and is puffing it into life again. Twice he is interrupted by groups of young men walking by, all beery and loud – students I suppose – who suddenly clam up as he approaches, and they utter a chorus of 'Good evening sir,' to which he nods, grunts and smiles.

'My acolytes,' he says with a grin as I look up at him.

'Do you work at the University?' I ask him.

'Yes, Magdalen. Now listen here –' He stops and looks down on me from within a little cloud of War Horse. I know the smell. Pa smokes it too.

'This just won't do. We have not been properly introduced. My name is Jack.'

'I am Anna,' I say. 'How do you do?'

He smiles again, and we shake hands.

'Now Anna, you must tell me where you live.' He

pauses. 'Is there someone waiting at home for you? Your father perhaps?'

'Yes Jack. Pa will be at home. We live in Jericho. Moribund Lane, down by the canal.'

'Well, that's not far then,' he says with some relief.

'Where do you live?'

'Eh? Oh, in Headington.'

'That's miles away! Do you drive a motor car?'

'Not I, Anna. I prefer to walk. It improves the digestion.' He is looking me up and down as he says this, and I lower my head. I suppose I am quite a mess, wet and stained, covered in cow poo and grass, the newspaper sticking in rags out of my shoes.

'You look as though you've been having quite an adventure,' he says thoughtfully, as we resume our walk. The Randolph Hotel is ahead, and the Ashmolean on our right. There are lots of smart looking people getting out of a motor car at the Randolph and the doorman is tipping his hat. One of the women has a sleek black bob, like Louise Brooks, and a mink stole around her shoulders. Her lips are painted red as apples.

To see her makes me happy and sad at the same time. I know now that I will never be that woman, or anyone like her. I will not dazzle or be sophisticated, and I will probably never smoke a cigarette in a long holder.

I saw a man murdered tonight. That I know. And the boy who did the murdering knows I saw him do it.

'Adventures are not what they are cracked up to be,' I tell Jack, and I hug Pie to me tight.

He takes his pipe out of his mouth and watches me as we walk along. 'Something frightened you,' he says.

'Yes.'

'Were you out on the Meadow?'

'How do you know?'

'There are not many places in Oxford where you can become so liberally splattered with cow manure, my girl.'

'There were men there,' I begin. And then I stop, and know that I am not going to tell this kind big man what I saw. If I do, things will happen, and I will lose control of it. For now, I want it to stay with Pie and me. I want to pretend it was not real, and that the dark boy with the knife did not have eyes that reflected the light of the moon in glows of silver-green.

Jack has stopped, and there is a different look on his face now. All seriousness, he asks me gravely, 'Anna, did someone hurt you?'

I shake my head solemnly. 'I ran away.'

He nods. 'That is usually the best thing to do.'

'It was not... it was not brave.'

'How old are you?'

'I'm almost twelve.'

'Then listen to me. Bravery is sometimes not enough. Courage is a dangerous virtue; it can get you hurt.'

'Discretion is the better part of valour,' I say, remembering my lessons with Miss Hawcross.

His eyes twinkle. 'Precisely.'

'So it was not cowardly to run away.'

'It was the right thing to do. These men – what were they up to, out on the Meadow?'

'They were...' I close my eyes for a second, picking carefully at the memory. 'They were cooking a rabbit over a fire.'

'Ah. Sometimes travellers of a certain kind pass through Oxford on their way to London, and they take a day or a night on the Meadow, or in the woods at Wytham. Especially since the War. Those are not places a little girl should be alone in late at night, Anna. No matter how brave she is.'

I know that now. And I am sure I will never want to carry a knife again so I can cut someone's throat, or daydream about being a soldier creeping up on the Hun.

'I won't do it again,' I say, a phrase I use a lot. 'But if Achilleos had been there, or Odysseos, they would have killed those horrible men, with sword and bow.' And as I spit the words out, I feel the heat rise into my face, and I wish – I wish it could be so. That the heroes of the Greeks could have been there, all armoured in bronze, with hard faces that held no fear. A stupid little knife would be nothing to their swords and spears, and the awful men around the fire would be dumbfounded, terrified, as Homer's heroes strode into the light with the moon at their backs.

'They might very well have,' Jack says, with something like surprise. 'I see you are classically educated, Anna.'

'I am Greek. I came from a city that the Turks destroyed when I was very little. One day we will go back, and throw the Turks out, and we will have our house again, with the balcony that looks out over the sea, and it will be warm summer. Always.'

Jack has a strange look on his face. 'I'll be... damned,' he says, very quietly, and his grip on my hand tightens for a moment. 'What a curious little bundle you are.'

We turn off Walton Street. It is darker here, and despite myself I shrink against Jack. I know these streets as well as my own hands, but everything seems different tonight, as though Oxford is a woman who has just unveiled herself, and the face revealed is not who I thought it was.

'It's all right my dear,' Jack murmurs. 'No-one is going to hurt you. You are quite safe.'

Our house is lit up and the front door is open. People are trooping out and Pa is in the doorway, shaking their hands as they leave. As Jack and I approach, he nods at us absently, and goes back to his handshaking. The meeting must have gone on forever.

I realise then that he did not even know that I was gone, and it barely registers with him that I am standing holding the hand of a strange man in the street. And for a tiny, little boiling second of time, I hate my father.

'What's your surname, Anna?' Jack asks me quietly.

'Francis. At least it is now. I think it was something else once.'

'And is that your father on the step?'

'Yes.'

'Jolly good.' Jack's black, bushy eyebrows have drawn together, and there is even more colour in his face. I realise that something has made him angry. He doffs his hat, and leads me up the three steps to Pa, shunting people out of his way like a train.

'Mr Francis?' Pa waves off the last clots of the Committee people, and looks at him, and then at me. Only then does it register in his face that something is out of kilter here.

'Anna – what the devil? Yes, I am George Francis.'

'My name is Lewis sir. I found your daughter on St Giles, in a state of –' But here I on tug Jack's hand, and as he looks down at me, without a word I plead with him not to say whatever is to come next.

'That is to say' – he gives me a tiny nod – 'I encountered your daughter and decided to see her home, since the hour was late and the streets were somewhat rowdy in that quarter. She is perfectly well, and if I may say, a delightful child. I hope you do not consider it untoward of me.'

Pa reaches out his hand, his handshaking hand, and it is engulfed by Jack's big paw. 'Why, not at all sir. I am most grateful to you.' He looks at me, and he has that hard set to his face as he takes in my appearance, the same as when I tried to cut off my hair. 'Anna, what have you been at? Go straight upstairs and draw a bath for yourself. You are in a filthy state.'

And to Jack, he says. 'Won't you come in, Mr Lewis? I should be happy to compensate you for your trouble with a drink, or taxi fare perhaps.'

'Not at all, not at all. I was passing this way at any rate, and I must be making my own road home.'

I squeeze past them, so very tired, knowing that I am in trouble again and that the adventure is done for now. I will cop it for this. I can see it in Pa's eyes.

The house is warm after the cold of the night, and the yellow light seems so calm and normal after the Meadow under the moon. I hug Pie, and feel like crying again, but will not. I will not.

Jack and Pa are saying their goodbyes. I start to trudge up the stairs. Even Pie seems heavy, and my feet are like two cold stones.

'Anna!' It is Jack's voice. I look back, and see he has raised up a hand in farewell.

'Say hello to Odysseus for me when he returns!' he grins, and winks. I can't help but smile back.

Then he is gone, and the door is closed, and Pa stands there looking up at me in the lamplight. I am in the shadow on the stairs, and I don't think he can even make out my face.

'Where have you been?' he asks simply, and he holds out his hands as though he is about to catch a ball.

'Walking. Port Meadow. There – there's a moon tonight, Pa.'

He walks slowly towards me. Up the stairs; one step, two. Then his hand cocks back and he slaps me hard across the face, knocking me down.

I climb back to my feet. 'I'm sorry Pa,' I say.

He nods grimly. 'Get upstairs. We will talk about this in the morning. I want you washed and in your nightgown in twenty minutes, Anna.'

I rub my face. 'Will you read to me tonight, Pa?'

'Go.'

And so up the stairs I climb, and Pie slips through my hand I am so tired, and I drag her by the leg as I go up, her head bump, bump, bumping against every step.

4

PEOPLE TALK ABOUT being in the doghouse after they have misbehaved. I have never understood why that should be such a bad thing. I love dogs, and would have no trouble at all cuddling up next to one in some little kennel. We could look out at the world side by side, and people would leave us alone. It would be a fine thing altogether.

Far worse is to be in a normal house, with running water and coal fires and lamplight, where it is warm and comfortable, but where you know that everything you do is being watched and weighed up and you must behave in a certain way, and spend your days under the grey weight of disapproval, and wonder if the cloud will ever lift and you will see a smile again.

I like things to be cut and dried and straightforward. If I have been bad, I want a belt on the ear, and then to be forgiven. Or a whack of some kind anyway – one that you can see coming, brace yourself for, and then know that when it is done, it is over. And afterwards it's all jam and buns again. Pa hits me because he loves me – I know that. And afterwards he is always so nice to me, and it is almost like old times. That is the way it's done and I am used to it. But things are different this time, it seems.

I tell Pie this, sitting in my room alone. I am confined to the house now, for how long I do not know. Like Rapunzel, only with shorter hair.

I am to stop calling Pa, *Pa*. I am to call him *Father* now. Which is horrible, and does not feel right in my mouth every time it comes out. But *Pa* is not genteel.

I am an ungrateful ragamuffin and wholly without discipline, and utterly unaware of the behaviour expected of my sex and station, Pa – Father – told me the morning after Jack walked me home. He was very quiet, very pale, but I knew just by the set of his face that he was as angry as I have ever seen him. More than that. I think he was a little afraid, or desperate even.

He has this way of raising up his open hands until they are at his shoulders, as though he were boasting about the size of a fish he caught. Then he lowers his head, and it looks as though he wants to cover his ears. He does that when he is not just angry, but sad as well. I have seen him do it in speeches in the hall down at Keble.

He did it to me that morning, and that quiet cold tone of voice came out of him like it was a stranger he was speaking to.

And perhaps I have not been attending lately, but as I stood all hangdog in his study I noticed as if for the first time that he is different, changed from what he used to be; and I do not believe that it is wholly my fault. It is to do with the Committee, and the Colonial Office – he has been down to London again – and I think, though he has not said it, that he has finally given up all hope of us ever going home.

If anything can possibly be left of home.

NO-ONE ELSE MADE it out with us, from all the friends and family we knew who were still beside us on that last day. Uncle Spiros, Aunt Eugenia; they just disappeared, and my cousins with them. Pa jumped into a launch as it was pushing off from the quay, with me in his arms – and it was sheer chance that it was a British boat and not one of the American or Italian ones. Otherwise we might be living across the Ocean now, and I would have an entirely different accent.

I could be riding a horse somewhere on the Great Plains, instead of stuck in a dark, damp old house in Jericho.

BUT THERE WAS no time to look at the flags on the boats that day as the sailors brought them up to the seafront, to choose which country we should end up in. Father put it very well once, in a speech. He said it was a case of the Devil taking the hindmost.

That is why we do not know where Mama is buried, or if she has a grave at all. The Turks had dragged her away earlier in the day, when we were packed on the roasting quayside; thousands and thousands of terrified people, with the water full of bodies in front of us, and the roaring of the great fire behind.

I wish I could forget it; the thunder-heat of the flames,

and the sound of the screaming as the Turks took away the young girls and the pretty women, and shot and bayoneted the husbands and fathers and brothers who tried to stop them.

And Pa took me from Mama's arms when they came for her, and pressed my face into his chest until I thought I should suffocate.

When he let me look up again, she was gone, and the crowd was pressed tight around us and screaming, but I could feel his chest heaving under me, and the noise that came out of his throat was a dreadful raw howl, with no words in it, like an animal in agony.

THE LAUNCH WAS desperately crowded, and everyone was wailing and the sailors were armed with revolvers – I remember them being waved in our faces, and the sharp crack as they went off. I think they made me cry even more with fright, for I was very little. And they took us out to a towering battleship, a castle of steel afloat out in the harbour among a dozen others.

So many flags were in the harbour that day, so many great warships. And they did almost nothing to help the poor people who were burning and drowning and being killed by the Turks back on the quays. A few boats were sent in, but for the most part, they sat there and their crews watched.

The last thing I remember about that day, before Pa carried me into the depths of the great ship, was the towering pillar of smoke that was looming over the city. It was majestic, immense, greater than anything I ever thought men could create, and at its base, the flames pummelled the smoke and boiled and burst and cast a far-off roar. I shall never forget it, not if I live to be ninety years old.

I USED TO think it might be that Mama was still alive – it might be possible – but when I said this to Pa later, in Oxford, he looked at me as though I had gone mad – I was very young – and that was the first time I think he ever hit me hard, across the face, and there were tears in his eyes as he did, I remember. I was so shocked I did not even cry, and he hugged me straight after, and said he was sorry. So very sorry.

That was a horrible thing, to see him weep, and I hate to think on it.

But we cannot choose what we remember and what we forget. All the lovely bright moments of our lives get forgotten except for remnants here and there, like the leaves blown from a tree in the autumn, and the terrible things, they stick with us forever, as bright and raw as the day they happened.

When we first came to Oxford we went to Liturgy at the Greek church off the Banbury Road. I loved the smell of the incense, and the singing was glorious, but so sad. As though everyone were in mourning. But it was beautiful too. The priests all have long beards and look like wise men straight out of the Bible, and the icons are all agleam with gold, until the face of the Madonna and the baby Jesus can hardly be seen; they are shadows surrounded by gold and jewels, not real people at all.

It seemed right and fitting to me, the dark music, the

shadowed saints. As though God understood what had happened to us.

The Mother of God lived her last years not far from our old home, and St Paul wrote letters to the Ephesians, who were the people who lived there back then. I saw Ephesos once, all tall white ruins and poplars and cypresses as shapely as paintbrushes.

All that is gone now, just history in a book. But it was a real city. And the people in it were as alive as me. I lived there once upon a time, in that place which is now no more. We had been living there for three thousand years before the Turks came, Pa told me. And now it is as far away as a fairy story.

There are so many echoes and shadows of memory I should like to have kept as clear and bright as fish in an aquarium. Not the horrible last days, but all that went before. But the pictures I want to keep are fading. The more I try to hold on to them, the fuzzier they become. And dreary old Oxford grows more real by the day. Perhaps that is part of growing up, this forgetting, and the pain of remembering the wrong things. If so, it is a hateful part.

FOR THE NEXT few days I read newspapers, which I never normally do. Father gets the *Times* and the new local paper, the *Oxford Mail*, and I read both; even the advertisements for Palmolive soap and Bovril and tooth powder – every page. There is nothing in the *Times* about murderous gangs of marauding tramps, and there is nothing in the *Mail* about a body on Port Meadow. Skullduggery. Murder by moonlight. Not so much as a paragraph.

I am oddly deflated, and there is a squirming part of me that is disappointed. Such a happening – such a horrible event should have been noticed and set on record by someone, anyone.

Except that the anyone should really be me.

So ANYWAY, HERE I am, stuck here. *Confined to barracks* is what the soldiers call it, and the barracks is the house we live in, father and me. I know most of it so well now that I could walk into any room on the lower floors blindfold and not bump into a single thing. The furniture is ancient, from the last century mostly, and it is not ours, but came with the place.

The house itself was built so long ago that it has no gas, so we use oil lamps as though Victoria were still Queen. And there is a hand-pump and a huge black range in the basement, and the stairs have no carpet on them and are very steep and narrow.

Father rents the place from a man called Matthew Bristol, and I have heard him call Mr Bristol a *greasy little oik* under his breath. I know Mr Bristol as a short man with cheekbones sharp as the corners of a box, a waxed black moustache, and a bowler hat which is green with age. He has very pale eyes, as pale as a robin's egg, and he almost never blinks, but his mouth smiles all the time, as though it has been frozen open.

Sometimes he appears unannounced, unlocks the front door and walks straight through the house without so much as a by-your-leave, which infuriates Father. And once he pinched my cheek and stroked me behind the ear when Father wasn't looking and I wanted to bite his fingers off, except they were yellow from smoking cigarettes and smelled horrible.

The trouble is we never seem to have enough money. Always, Father is hunting around for spare sixpences and thruppenny bits at the end of the month when Mr Bristol makes his visits, and there are usually a few bread-and-dripping days around that time, and no milk for tea.

I like bread and dripping, but it gets tiresome after a while, and I begin to fantasise about eggs and bacon, crisp green apples, and toasted cheese. Toasted cheese and cocoa is the best thing to have in the world when the fire is lit and it is raining outside.

When we first came here, Father had investments which he could count upon to *tide us over*. It was just as well, because we brought nothing more to England with us than the clothes on our backs, and by the time we made Portsmouth most of what I was wearing had been given to me by the dear sailors, and they made us up ditty bags and sewed me some cotton nightshirts and were awfully nice, so that I almost forgave them for not blowing the Turks to smithereens with their big guns.

So, Father had money back then, and took on the tall house in Moribund Lane, with its narrow garden that backed onto the canal, and iron railings at the front. And we had a cook and a maid. Cook was a tiny red-faced woman who used to like me to tell her stories of Greece while she worked in the basement kitchen. It was always so lovely and warm there, and she would never fail to make me a cup of tea which I would sip very politely at the big wooden table, since I was the lady of the house. Her name was Mrs Bramley, and I miss the warm kitchen – we cook over a miserable little spirit stove now and the basement is grey and cold most of the time.

We had a maid too, whose name was Elsie Blythe, and she was much younger than Mrs Bramley, and she set the fires and did the ironing and made the beds and brought Father his breakfast in the front room, kippers sometimes, and poached eggs all runny. And I remember how baffled she was by Father insisting that olive oil be set out at every meal so he could dip his toast in it.

Father used to go walking alone in Wytham Wood and forage for wild garlic, and he would rub it on toasted bread and drizzle the bread with oil and salt, and the smell was straight away like something out of a lost memory. No-one in England likes garlic or olive oil, and now even Father has stopped eating it, and dines quite like an Englishman, and fries his bacon in lumps of suet, which is nice enough but not the same.

I miss Elsie. She was young, and pretty, and always had time to sit and chat with me and Pie. She had such a pale face, with big blue eyes, and her hands were always red and she would rub her knees as she sat with me and talk about the boys she was seeing. There were no young men left in England, only old crocks from the War, she used to say, and laugh. And she told me once that even a one-legged man could have a lot of lead in his pencil, and if she met one with a fat pocket-book she would be a maid no more. Not that she had been a maid for a long time. And she would nudge me and wink as she said this. She had a lovely throaty laugh, and I always liked to laugh with her, even when I could not quite understand what she was on about.

So it was all rather jolly back then, with me and Pie and Pa, as I was still allowed to call him, and Mrs Bramley and Elsie always coming and going, and the house seemed less dark and empty, and there were fires lit in every room in the winter, not like now, when they are only in the study and the front room, and I creep from pool to pool of lamplight with the cold shadows in between.

It seems that some of Father's investments didn't work out, or else the Turks took them, or perhaps they just got lost down the back of a drawer or something, because all of a sudden, Mrs Bramley and Elsie were *let go*, and they both kissed me the day they left, and bobbed to Father, who was very stern and cold, but I could tell he was upset too. And Elsie cried, her nose as red as her hands. And the door closed on them, and Pa and I were alone.

THAT SEEMS A long time ago now, and Pie and I are quite used to the silence and the shadows. We sit and read E. Nesbit, or Charles Kingsley, or Daniel Defoe (I love *Robinson Crusoe* – how splendid it would be to have an entire island to oneself!). And we explore the canal, and Port Meadow, and Binsey, and sometimes when father is in London I walk all the way to Cowley village and back, just so I can cross and recross Magdalen Bridge, and stare up at the beautiful tower. There are so many beautiful places in Oxford. If only the weather were better! And I like seeing the students in their silly mortar-boards and flapping gowns, and the dome of the Radcliffe Camera (how can a building be called a camera? – no-one has ever explained), and the Bodleian, where they have all the books in the world.

But most of the time, in winter at least, Pie and I stay close to home. Father does not like me wandering around Oxford anymore, not since I got chased down Walton Street by a crowd of the local children who threw stones at me and shouted names and I got home crying and with a lump on my head. I think I still spoke English with an accent back then, and they called me a dirty Jew and other things, but I'm not Jewish, and what if I were anyway?

Now I speak the same as everyone else, my Greekness quite gone, and I am glad and sad equally. And Father hired Miss Hawcross to educate me in how to be an English girl, though I would still quite like to go to school like normal children, and perhaps once they got to know me they would not think I was just some dirty foreigner anymore. But they don't frighten me as they once did, as I am quite tall now, and I stand my ground and clench my fists and tell them to go to the Devil, and I am very good at throwing stones and hitting what I aim at. But Father does not know that of course. He says only guttersnipes call names and throw stones.

But at least the house is mine to explore. The upper rooms were closed off when we let Elsie and Mrs Bramley go, and I was told to keep out of the top floor, because of the dust and so on, and now up there the rooms are full only of a dim silence, with white sheets draped on all the tatty old furniture, and the air is always damp. It is a ghostly place, in a way, but I am not afraid. I have seen worse things than ghosts, and if one were to appear to me, I should have so many questions to ask of it that it would have no time to groan and moan and shake its chains.

THERE IS ONE place in the house where I have never been, because Father has expressly forbidden me to go there. And also because it is difficult to get to. But I have thought on it a lot lately, ever since the meetings of the Committee started to become more frequent. The house has become busier, but not in the good way that it was when Elsie was lighting fires in every room of a morning, and all the drapes were pulled back to let the light in, and the lamps were lit all over the place. This is different, the cold busyness of a bus station or a waiting room, with strange faces and loud voices.

Last week, I was creeping about the lower landing, and I found a man using Father's chamber-pot, while still talking loudly to the people downstairs. He was not ashamed or taken aback when he saw me and Pie, but grinned a little sheepishly, and went about his business before replacing the sloshing pot by Father's bed.

'All full up down below,' he said, and he rubbed my head as he passed me on the landing, so close I could smell the whisky on his breath.

It was at that moment that I knew I had to find a place all of my own in the house, or I think I would go mad.

ABOVE THE SILENT rooms on the third floor there is an attic. I know this because I have stood outside and studied the house, the way you study a person's face to tell if they are telling the truth or a lie. There are no proper windows, but there is a skylight on the street side and another on the garden side of the roof, and why put in skylights if there is nothing to light? So there is a space up there where I have never been, and it would be so remote and private from the rest of the house that as soon as I have guessed at its existence, I know I must go there. I will make an expedition of it, or a secret mission. I will be Odysseos, creeping about the hut of the Cyclops.

I pick my moment carefully, and set my plan in motion. It would not do to get caught. I am deep enough in Father's bad books already. I wait until there is a dull blue day when he is off to London, and after Miss Hawcross's lessons are done.

SHE STAYS ON a while on afternoons like these, to keep an eye on me while Father is away, but I can tell that she doesn't like to be sitting silent with me in the dank old house, with no noise but the occasional crackle of the fire in the front room and the ticking of the clocks. Outside, the winter dusk is falling fast, and I am pretending to read *The Coral Island*, but I have read it many times before – it is one of my favourites – and I am not focussing on the words, but peeking at Miss Hawcross over the top of the book, and exchanging glances with Pie, and every so often yawning so wide that the faked yawns become real, and Miss Hawcross catches them and covers her mouth to yawn herself.

She is knitting, but not with much attention, and the clacking of the needles has slowed. I tell her I think I shall go up to bed, and yawn again. She nods, clearly relieved. 'Your father should be back soon, Anna. I believe I shall make my own way home, while there is still a little light.'

She pauses. 'I shall see you up to bed… Are you… are you all right in the house by yourself?'

'Quite all right,' I tell her, and smile brightly. 'I have Pie, and my book, but I am tired anyway. I can get myself to bed, Miss Hawcross, really I can. Let me see you to the door.'

She gathers her things, her black boater and cloth bag, and she pins the hat in place on her head with a stab of pins. 'I suppose that's all right.'

As I see her out the door, she turns and looks at me. Her breath is steaming yellow in the light of the hall. 'I shall see you tomorrow then.'

I nod. She seems a little unsure about going so I smile again, and close the door firmly on her. Then I listen. There is no sound for a long moment, until finally I hear her heels tapping down the steps, like the sound of her knitting needles, only sharper.

'At last,' I say to Pie. I do not have a desert island of my own to roam, but for a while at least, the house is mine.

I GLIDE THROUGH the upstairs rooms like a ghost, touching the sheeted furniture so that the dust rises off it in tiny glowing mites that float in the very last of the day's weak sunlight. Already, the street below is in blue shadow, but if I look out of the windows here I can peer over Port Meadow to the hills beyond, Botley to the left, Wytham to the right, and the light sinking fast behind the rising ground, winter-red, a bloody sun falling behind blue-grey hills, and the night above it swooping in.

I shiver a moment, and hug Pie, and wonder if it would not be better to be down below in the firelight. But the thought makes me angry, too. Angry because after all this time I am still unprepared. I must search for matches and a candle, and waste more of this precious solitary time.

I find them in the basement, though the candle is only a stump; and by that time the night has truly fallen, and the lamps are all unlit and cold except for the one in the front room, and the fire is sunk to red coals, and the rest of the house is heavy with the dark, and the loud ticking of the two clocks we keep wound. And I almost falter again. But then I think of the Greeks, cooped up in the dark of the wooden horse under the walls of Troy, and know that I have it in me to do this thing.

Pie agrees. (She always does.) I light the candle, wedge it in a holder, and up we go again.

I talk to her as we ascend the stairs, but on the topmost flight I run out of things to say, and the candlelight seems very weak against the loom of the shadows.

I know these rooms, all of them. Not so well as the lower floors of the house, but I am no stranger here. All the same, I cannot think where the entrance to the attic might be. I scan all the ceilings, ignoring my shadow as it capers candlelit across them, but there is no hatch or door up there. It really is quite infuriating. And for a while the puzzle of it makes me lose all fear.

The clocks strike six, far below, and I know that time is slipping away from me. I stamp my foot in frustration, and do my round of the third floor rooms again.

And that is when I spot it. Hidden behind a tall, shrouded cabinet, there is a crack in the wall. As I prod the candle closer, it becomes the outline of a low door, one even I should have to stoop to enter. It has a recessed catch of brass, and looks as though it has been painted over at least once.

I shove the cabinet aside. Things tinkle within, and there is the thin thump of something delicate toppling, but I am undeterred by such trifles. The dust makes me cough, and rises like smoke in the yellow candlelight. I grasp the brass half-moon catch and pull on it. The painted-over door will not budge.

Here at least, I am prepared. I have my knife with me this time. Not a weapon, but a tool, I say firmly to Pie, and there is a difference. There must be a difference.

I run it along the line of the little doorway, the paint scoring and flaking off under the blade. Once or twice the knife goes astray and scores the door itself, leaving a quite horrible looking scar. But it is too late to back out now, I tell Pie. And I keep going.

Only to stop again a second later, listening.

Just for a moment, I thought I heard something, a sliding thump, something… moving. It came from the attic above.

'Rats,' I say to Pie. 'But I'm not afraid of them. They're cowards, and I have a knife, after all.' The tool that is a weapon.

Faint and far away, the clocks below strike the quarter hour.

I grit my teeth, and say through them, 'Fortune favours the bold, Pie,' and I continue with my work, the hard white lead paint springing off in scales, until there is movement in the door, a kind of give that was not there before. My knuckles are sore and my fingers too. I have paint chips under my nails and in my hair. I look at the candle. There is still an inch of it left. I put three fingers through the half-moon catch, and pull with all my might.

There is a squeal of wood on wood, and it is open. All at once, a breath of air brushes past me, as cold as a grave, and

I shiver. The hour seems much later than it is, and the tall old house seems to have somehow withdrawn in the dark, as though something in its very fabric had changed with the opening of the little hidden doorway.

'What rot!' I say aloud, but I know my voice shakes, and seems far too loud for the silent, shrouded room.

I retrieve Pie, fold up my knife, and peer through the little door.

Wooden steps leading up, steep and stark.

'Here we are, Pie,' I say, and I tilt her head back so that her black glass eyes close in agreement.

I crouch and enter the little staircase. One step up, then two. I look down at the black hatch of the door and have a sudden terror that it will slam shut behind me.

'Rot,' I repeat through gritted teeth, and as I ascend the stairs I keep the words coming, one with every step.

'Balderdash. Bosh, tosh, bunkum and bilge…' The words run out. But 'Bollocks!' escapes from my mouth as the steps come to an end, and there is another door, the twin of the one below, the brass of its handle dull in the shaking light of my little candle.

'Rats won't hurt us. They'll run away,' I say to Pie, to keep her spirits up. 'The trick is, not to let them know you're afraid.'

This door has never been painted over, and it swings open easily, but creaks horribly as it does, making me jump.

There is that breath of chill air again, as though a deeper winter has hold over this room, and beyond that, a smell in the air, musky, animal-like. It is quite pungent.

'Rats,' I whisper to Pie. And I make my face grim and resolute.

I straighten up, my candlelight leaping upwards on beams and braces, exposed brick, curtained cobwebs, and blocks of black shadow. I brace myself for scurryings and squeaks and little eyes gleaming in the dark, but there is nothing. No rats, despite the smell. Just a heavy stillness, and that hanging bitter cold.

I step forwards, raising the candle high. It gutters as I do, and I see that I am directly below the skylight. It is the one which faces west, towards the Meadow, and to my surprise I see that it is not closed, but raised and open, with one of its four panes broken. No wonder it is so cold up here.

No clock chimes can be heard in the attic. Even the sounds of the streets below are absent. There is nothing but darkness and silence and cold.

'This is very disappointing,' I say to Pie with a sigh, and I make my voice loud, looking around me as I say it. I am the mistress of this house – Mrs Bramley told me so. But I cannot shake the impression that I am not alone up here, and all the little hairs on the back of my neck are standing up, like the pelt of an alarmed cat.

The attic is full of junk. There are old broken-back chairs, and boxes, and racks of ancient-looking clothes that smell damp and dreary. I can see a feather boa, and an enormous hat, wide as a tray. I pick my way over the creaking floorboards, the shadows giving way before me.

'Bosh.' I say loudly. 'Bosh, tosh and balderdash.'

Some of the clothes have just been piled up in a heap on the floorboards, and they smell too. They look almost like a nest, but it's hard to tell. I look them over and see that they are covered in grey mould.

The candle is almost flat with the holder now, and spilling veins of wax at an alarming rate.

I don't know what I had thought to find up here, but it was more than this neglected, waiting emptiness.

A treasure chest, perhaps, or a cavalry sabre, or a madman's diary... or even a doll. But there is nothing, not so much as a book to read. Just that rank smell.

'It must be the damp,' I say to Pie.

I can see the slates of the roof, the beams and joists of old and massive wood which support them. Buttresses of brick stick out at regular intervals, and as I pick my way through the rubbish and the boxes I see the mummified body of a little mouse on the floor, and feel a pang of pity for it, to have died up here all alone.

'That's what smells I suppose,' I say. Though it seems too small to account for the stink.

'We shall open all the skylights and air the place out,' I tell Pie. 'Bring up a lamp, and some books, maybe even a stool or something. It could be cosy, I'm sure of it.' I don't think Pie is convinced.

I look up at the yawning broken skylight again. There are stars beyond, a glimmer of them. The catch is too high for me to reach. I would have to pile up the boxes, and they all look fragile, like sandcastles which have dried out and will crumble to the touch. It will have to stay open for now.

Newspapers, from another century, yellow and mottled. Here a pair of gloves, the leather stiff as biscuit. A belt, gnawed by little teeth and rippled with mould. A pair of broken spectacles. And some photographs. It is too dark and the candlelight too uncertain to make them out with any clarity, but I see stern faces and stiff collars, muttonchop whiskers, a pot plant. In one there is a sleeping baby, and for some reason it makes me shiver to look upon it.

I wonder who they were, these strangers in the photographs, and if they live yet, or if they are among the dead now. I suppose they must be. There is no life up here, nothing that was made in the century I know.

But perhaps the baby in the photograph is still alive, quite old by now, all grown up and with children who have children. Perhaps they have chased me down the street and called me names.

They belong here, these faded faces from the past. And I do not.

I return to the doorway that leads below. The candle flame is bright, and tall as a willow leaf, but it has not long left.

'At least it's quiet,' I say to Pie. 'It would be different in daylight, of course. And no-one would ever find me up here.'

No-one would ever find me. If I sat up here I could be as forgotten and alone as the dead faces in the photographs.

I shiver again. I think of the noisy, incessant chatter of the ground floor rooms when they are full of strangers, the way the voices echo through the house, my father's among them.

I know now that he will never read me a story at bedtime again. He has given up on all the stories. All he wants is his Committee and his Scotch and a daughter who will not embarrass him and who will keep out of the way.

The attic is a place apart from all that, a lost and forgotten space, like Calypso's Island.

'I am not afraid of you,' I say to the brooding room, the silent, listening house.

And with that, I leave the attic to its cluttered emptiness, and clump back down the cramped little staircase again, the shadows leaping around me like dancers as I go.

5

It snows on the Friday, and I am driven half mad by the sight of the fat flakes falling, dark against the lighter sky. I am in the front room, and Miss Hawcross is waving her ruler about with more than her usual testiness, and it cracks down on the table in front of my nose time after time.

'*Un, deux, trois, quatre, cinq, six, sept,*' I say obediently, all the while looking out the window at the world beyond as it slowly transforms. Is there anything more magical than snow? I am aching to be outside in it, and the local children are out scraping up snowballs and hurling them at each other, as loud as a flock of crows.

'*Huit, neuf, dix, onze, douze, treize, quatorze –*' Fifteen escapes me. I am watching the flight of the snowballs and wondering if I could throw one that far. I know I would be accurate. I am a very good shot with a stone.

Miss Hawcross smacks the ruler down on the table three times. '*Quinze, quinze, quinze!*' She is quite red-faced. 'You are impossible today Anna!'

I lower my head. 'Sorry Miss Hawcross.'

'Ignore what the hooligans outside are at and attend to your work. Life is not all about playing in the snow.'

'But it almost never snows,' I complain. And in a low tone I mutter, 'Why can't I be like them?' Looking out at the laughing children in the street.

'You must not confuse yourself with the likes of them, my girl. Do you want to be a disappointment to your father? Because you are going the right way about it. You must improve yourself if you are to maintain any kind of station in this world. Otherwise, you will end up in the street outside with those hopeless urchins, and believe me young lady, it is a hard and cold world out there.'

Something in her voice takes me by surprise. There is a catch of emotion to her tone, and as I meet her stare, I see that Miss Hawcross is in deadly earnest.

'Is that how you see yourself, Anna?' she asks me, more quietly now. 'A scallywag of the streets, scraping by hand to mouth? For that is what they are. Poor little beggars who would pick a pocket as soon as wipe their nose, who are destined for the workhouse and a pauper's grave. Do you see them, laughing? Half of them are barefoot in the snow, and the other half will not see a hot meal tonight. The lucky ones will grow up to black boots or wield a spade. The girls will sew, or pick flax, or do laundry until they are worn to nothing but rags and bone. They are not even refined enough for service in a decent house. This is what a proper education will spare you from, Anna.'

I cannot keep her gaze, but look down at the French words on the primer before me. 'What use is French to me?' I murmur.

'It supples the mind, it adds accomplishment. It marks you out as a cut above the common herd. As do mathematics, history, grammar. You must apply yourself to these things here and now, Anna. There is no other time or place for you to learn them. The world is changing all around us. Ever since' – she falters a little – 'Ever since the War, there are no more certainties in life.'

She looks away, and her voice lowers. 'The War swept everything away – you are too young to know what is cost this country. Nothing can be counted upon to endure anymore.' She seems almost to be talking to herself. For a moment, I feel quite sorry for her, and I set my hand on the fingers that clasp the quivering ruler.

'I am so sorry Miss Hawcross. I will try harder, I swear I will. I am sure you have the right of it.'

She smiles at that, and for a tiny instant we are not teacher and pupil or child and grown-up, but just two people talking to one another, and I see the young girl who loved the soldier and saw him go off to France all those years ago.

But more than that. For some reason her words go straight to the deep, calm part of me and sting me there.

And I am almost dizzied by a sudden knowledge, as cold as snow down my spine; that I, too, will grow up one day like everyone else, and look back and miss the years gone by, and the things I could have done, should have done. And growing up is suddenly not something to be impatient for, not all jam and buns and doing as one pleases. It is precisely the opposite. And Miss Hawcross is trying to tell me that, even as the moment passes and the lines settle heavy in her face again and she returns to the here and now and the stupid little words in stupid French.

So I turn my face from the window, and block out the sounds of the skylarking children outside. And the words I speak are still meaningless, but I no longer have any problem recalling them.

'*Quinze, seize, dix-sept, dix-huit, dix-neuf, vingt…*'

So SHORT, THESE days, the sun hardly to be seen between dawn and dusk. When I finally manage to get out of the house the lamplighters are at work though it is not half past four in the afternoon, and all up and down Walton Street the gas is flickering yellow, and the snow is still falling in the arc of the gaslights. It is ankle-deep now, and it has laid a hush over the city. It creaks underfoot, a sound I love, and I have one of Father's old woollen scarves wrapped round my neck many times over and a wool Monmouth cap which flops down over my ears and neck. I am quite comfortable. And the magic of the snow has driven Miss Hawcross's words to the back of my mind. But it has brought other things back to the fore.

I have left Pie indoors, because I want my hands free, and I am alone in the street but for the lamplighters, and the snow has fallen so thick and fast that already the footprints of the children have become mere dents in it, fuzzy and misshapen. It is almost a silent world, and above the city the sky is blank as frosted glass, and the flakes coming down are as big as feathers loosed from a pillow.

And I am not afraid, not in this white, soft night, not even though Pie is all toasty inside and I am quite alone. I will not be afraid. I have been up to the attic in the dark, and faced down the rats, and the pale faces in the photographs, and I am still a girl, no matter what Miss Hawcross might say, and I want so much just to leave my footprints in the snow and taste the flakes as they fall upon my face, soft as kisses.

Father has relented, after I pleaded with him, hopping from foot to foot in his dark old study. He had been drinking Scotch, and was elbow deep in Committee papers when I made my move. I am becoming quite cold-blooded about it.

So I am allowed outside again, but under strict rules. Father has given me one hour, and he will be timing me with his Breguet watch, he says. I did not even point out to him that I have no timepiece of my own. He wrapped me in his scarf and set the shapeless old hat on my head, and watched me in a spill of lamplight as I left the house – but he is gone now, and I am unwatched and free. And I know where I am going.

There is a Committee meeting at five, and I know that Father will get caught up in it, and the time will pass and he will not pull the beautiful Breguet out of his waistcoat pocket because he will be talking and talking and talking. And so my single hour will be longer, and as long as I can be mouse-quiet when I come back, I am sure that I can swing half as much again. More perhaps. And if I get a belt out of it for being late, then what does it matter?

That is what I tell myself as I stand there in the softly falling snow. Because I have decided to return to Port Meadow, and I do not truly know how much time I will need. Nor am I entirely sure what I am looking for there.

69

THERE ARE MOTOR-CARS crumping past slowly, flinging clods of snow from their wheels, the rubber window-wipers whirring back and forth like busy metronomes. Here and there people go by, as faceless as stones, bundled up, heads down. I do not understand why grown-ups hide their faces from the snow, as though they are afraid of it.

It tickles my nose, and seems to have a life of its own as it falls steadily, the air breathless and still. Even in my galoshes my sock-bound feet are cold, and I walk faster. I have a longing to roll in the snow, to grasp it in handfuls and plaster it into snowballs, snowmen, all those marvellous things which are impossible to create on ordinary days. I am Anna Francis, wanderer, adventuress, and I feel that the snowy dark is smiling on me because it knows the love I have for it. I am a creature now of shadows and the dusk

A train passes under the bridge at Walton Well Road, and the air is filled with the taint of soot, and I see the sparks fly out of the engine like fiery-fairies released from an iron cage. It hurtles north, dragging the wagons with it, a black roar, a goods train, clanking and clicking off into the gathering night to some other city of the Empire.

Port Meadow is not moonlit tonight, for the snow has swallowed up the moon and stars, but it is bright and empty all the same, and the snow is thicker here, and a thin breeze starts up to blow it in tumbling powder around my knees and ankles. The air is so cold it crackles in my nose, and my breath has iced my father's scarf around my mouth. I stamp my feet hard to keep the feeling in my toes and launch out across the Meadow with resolute strides, like Shackleton in the Antarctic. My knife is in my pocket, but I do wish Pie were here to talk to. The Meadow seems a lonely place. I think most people have gone home from work early today.

It will soon be midwinter, and I have heard people passing on the street say that the snow and the cold are unseasonal, too much for the time of year. Christmas will be here soon, but we don't celebrate it anymore, and it means nothing to me, except that Father will sometimes let me listen to the carols on the wireless, and he will drink wine at dinner instead of his usual Scotch, and then he will withdraw to his study as usual. And often he gets me something, a book, or a coat, neither new to anyone but me. We do not even go to the Greek Church anymore for Midnight Liturgy, which makes me a little sad. As though we are both children with our faces squashed up against the glass, staring into a brightly lit room we can no longer enter.

'Bah, humbug,' I say aloud. Who needs Christmas when you have snow?

I clutch my ribs and trudge north. There are no stars to light my way tonight, and no distant campfire jumps into life out on the meadow. I might as well be on the steppes of Russia, one of Napoleon's lost army trekking home.

I had almost thought to find something here, some remnant – a skull perhaps, grinning out of the snow like that chap in Hamlet. But there is nothing. Murder does not change the land itself. I cannot even be sure that I can find the same spot again, though I have dreamed of it since.

'Perhaps he was not dead,' I say, hopefully. Perhaps I dreamed the dark boy's shining eyes. He gave me back Pie, after all. And he did not start the fight that night, Fat Bert did.

I keep walking, faster now, to keep up the warmth in me. I am past Binsey, past the Perch where I have drunk lemonade in summer. Soon I am in Wolvercote village, and the lights are shining out of the houses, and the road leads west, across the Thames, which is black as tar without a gleam, and past the Trout inn with its weir, and more lights, warmth, voices, a different world from the one I am in.

There is no colour out here, just black and white and shades of grey. Godstow Nunnery is on my left. Wytham ahead, and beyond, the black loom of Wytham Great Wood on its hills. This is where I knew I would come. I cannot even say why, but I know that I must go into the woods tonight.

I climb a fence, snagging Father's scarf as it hangs from my neck. I unpick it in the dark, breathing hard, the snow as thick as a wedding veil in front of my face, the flakes smaller now, and a sting in them as the wind picks up. The grass is rougher, in clumps and tussocks that try to trip me up, and the trees rise before me like the walls of a castle.

I stop on the edge of the wood, listening. Nothing but the sigh of the wind, and the rush of it through the tall trees. I wish Pie was here, and grasp the knife in my pocket.

I am in England. There is nothing in the woods that can harm me, just as there was nothing in the attic back home. Father has walked these woods, looking for wild garlic, and the soldiers were here training in the War. This is not the wilderness. There is no witch in the wood, nor goblins nor bears either.

'*Un, deux, trois*,' I murmur, and step into the Great Wood.

THE WIND DROPS at once, down below, though it keeps coursing through the trees overhead like the sound of the sea. I look up, and can see the branches moving across the grey sky. It is darker here, but I can still see my way. I have become used to the night, and my eyes are wide open, taking it all in.

The forest floor is covered in dead bracken and brambles, lean as wire. I pick my way through it, always uphill, and I am warmer now, puffing, even hot under Pa's big shapeless cap. I knock snow from the brambles as I advance, and tear myself free of the thorns. The undergrowth is worn down by winter, but it still rears up like a cloud all around me, blocking my way. I am about to give up and turn back, when all of a sudden a path opens out in front of me, paler in the gloom, a white lane through the trees. I stumble onto it, scratched and breathing hard. I bend down and look close at the ground, like Hawkeye, and I see tracks in the snow, cloven marks left by deer that have punched through the snow and left frozen slots in the earth below.

Happier now, I follow the track as it curves and meanders like a stream round the foot of the trees.

The woods are lovely, dark and deep...

I read that once, somewhere. It seems to fit here, as though there were power in the words.

'Dark and deep,' I whisper aloud as I stride along, faster now. I feel almost as though I am here for a reason other than my own, as though the trees themselves have something in store for me. I wanted to get clear of Oxford, the Meadow, the sounds of the city and the walls of the house. And my father, too. I wanted to leave them all behind and just be myself for a while. Anna Francis, intrepid explorer.

It seemed all so very simple when I left Walton Street, but now it as if I have stumbled into quite another world, in which I am not even a spectator. I am barely here at all. The woods ignore me, and I feel oddly at home in them. There is no fear in this dark. After that last day on the burning quayside of the city, there is not much more to fear in life at all. The very worst thing has already happened.

That is what I tell myself as I make my way deeper into the woods.

FOR A WHILE, I think it is my own heartbeat I hear thumping in my throat, a soft rhythm. But after a while I realise that the sound is beyond me, in the trees up ahead where the land rises. The path is narrower here, the brambles and dead bracken starting to choke it, and when I look up I can see the sky darkening beyond the treetops, and here and there the glimpse of a star.

The cloud is clearing, and it seems with that the cold deepens, and the snow begins to crunch under my feet like barley sugar between the teeth. A light grows in the forest, soft and silver. The moon must have risen, and though it is nothing like full it seems incredibly bright. The snow seems to take on a glow of its own, glittering like crushed glass. And still, I hear that strange thumping beat off in the wood ahead. A drum, tapped lightly, now slow, now fast.

And I hear a woman laugh.

The sound is shocking in the moonlit wood, a noise that

does not belong there. It brings me up short, breathing hard, my heart beating as fast as the drum.

And there is light, a yellow flicker of it in the deep part of the trees.

Another fire, another night of moon.

Now I am all at a stand. I want to go back. I do not want another adventure in the night, with a knife at the heart of it. But I am angry at myself for the fear I feel now. I am angry in general, at father, and Miss Hawcross, and the bloody Turks, and the memory of running across Port Meadow and wetting myself like a baby. The anger is stronger than the fear.

I start walking again, but now I leave the path, and pull Father's old cap around my head like a hood, and move at a crouch, zigzagging through the trees towards the far flickering light. The knife is cold in my pocket. It feels ugly to the touch, and there is no reassurance there.

Closer. And now I see that the fire is bright and tall, much bigger than the one that was on the Meadow. And the drum is being tapped light and fast. And the woman's voice starts up again, but now she is singing, a rippling, soaring song in a language I do not understand, and yet it is familiar too. Her voice is beautiful, and the song is old and foreign and like nothing I have ever heard in England before, sometimes almost tuneless, sometimes as piercing and beautiful as a sunlit shard of ice.

Closer, the trees hiding me, the moonlight fading as the firelight grows, until at last I hunker down behind a mound of snapping ochre bracken, and I can take it all in.

There are perhaps a dozen people around the fire, some sat upon bedrolls, as comfortable looking as though they were lying down on sofas in a warm room. I see the shine of the flames on metal pots, on earrings – the men as well as the women – on jewellery, and there is a lovely savoury smell. A big blackened pot is hung over the edge of the fire by a single bent branch and a stout woman with a blue headscarf is stirring it.

An old man taps a little drum he holds between his knees, his big brown hands almost hiding it, and another woman with long skirts and a fringed shawl is singing the beautiful song. She is very pretty, with eyes as large and dark as a horse's, and heavy eyebrows. She looks something like the people who come to the Committee meetings – foreign, eastern – but there is none of their defeat in her face, and her teeth are white and perfect. I feel a sudden rush of memory, as though I had seen her before somewhere, but it passes as quick as a bursting bubble.

They look so similar, all of them. Dark, lean men with sharp faces, dressed shabbily, with kerchiefs tied round their necks, their trousers out at the knee. Some of them are barefoot, despite the icy cold. The women are better clad, the older ones with bright headscarves and dangling necklaces that glitter and gleam in the firelight. They have long rings in their ears, and the one tending the pot has a jewelled chain sparking low on her forehead, hung with little coins that jingle as she moves.

Somehow, these people remind me of the long-lost city where I was born. They are exotic, out of place here in the cold northern wood. I can tell just by looking at them that they are from so far away.

As I am.

Something else, moving in the firelight. I thought it was

low-hanging branches but now I see that dangling from the trees surrounding the campsite are lots of little shapes made of twigs, and as I frown and study them I see that they are all the same. They are stars, five-pointed, bound with roots – crude, but rather lovely too. And somehow disquieting here in this place. These people have ornamented the trees, hanging these symbols up like somebody decorating their drawing room. How odd.

I hear something close by in the briars, a rustle, and I turn.

And right beside me the thin dark boy with the wedge-shaped face is crouched, the firelight playing on his long nose and lighting up his eyes.

I start to leap away with a sharp cry that I cannot hold in, and once more, I feel the hard grip of his hand as he seizes my arm, harder even than before.

'No, no no!' I hear myself scream, though I am barely aware of anything except his face, and the eyes.

The singing stops. There is a spatter of exclamation around the fire, words I do not understand. With my free hand I reach into my pocket for my knife, but it takes two hands to open it, and he is holding my other arm fast.

'Leave me alone!' And I punch him with my free fist, my knuckles lighting with pain as I strike his cheek. He growls, and grabs my other arm, pinioning me, throwing me on my back in the bracken and the snow. I try to kick him, but he sets his weight atop me and crushes me down. I struggle harder than I ever have in life before, but he is far too strong. Our faces are mere inches apart and I raise my head to try to bite him, but he butts me back with his hard skull, and lights go off in my head and I taste blood at the back of my throat.

'Luca,' a voice says, 'let her up.'

It is the young woman who was singing. I blink away the tears and see that they are all standing around us now, silent. The dark boy looks at me, and all of a sudden he gives a grin and lets go my wrists and springs up, and I am lying there in a circle of strangers on the edge of the firelight, and overhead the moon is bright and fat and the trees are black as veined coal beneath it.

6

THEY LOOK AT me as though I am some insect which is set upon a pin, like those I have seen in the glass cases of the Pitt Rivers in Oxford.

A quick gabble between them in a language I don't understand, and then the older woman, with the coins on her forehead, says;

'What you doing spying on us, girl?' Quick and sharp. There is more authority in her tone than I have ever heard in Miss Hawcross's, and I answer at once.

'I wasn't spying.'

'I calls it spying,' she snaps, and to the dark boy she says, 'Bring her to the fire Luca. Gentle, mind.'

Luca holds out his hand to me with his head cocked on one side. I slap it away. 'I can get up by myself.'

No knives at least. They stand around studying me again.

'Just a child,' a young woman says in English. 'No harm here, Queenie.'

And to me she says, 'Come to the fire me dear. No-one will hurt you.'

I rub my throbbing head where Luca's skull clipped it, and decide that I have nothing to lose. It would be just too absurd to turn around and run away now. It would be childish. And I am not a child, whatever they say.

'All right.'

The warmth of the fire is very welcome, as I have begun to shiver; and the smell of the food in the pot is something to relish, whatever it is.

'Sit by me,' the young woman says with her bright, white-toothed smile. She is really rather beautiful, and her black hair falls in long curls down her back. I sit beside her on a lumpy bedroll of canvas and old carpet, and about the fire the others resume their seats, except for Luca and one of the older men, who talk quietly in their unknown language. Luca looks at me, then nods to his elder, and without another word he sidles off into the dark woods as quietly as a fox, to disappear in a twinkling.

What a sneak, I think, and I rub the bump on my head again.

'Is you alone?' the older woman, Queenie asks me, hands on hips. Her eyes are dark as sloes and she has a strong face, as broad as any man's. The coins glint on her forehead. She looks like a figure from some strange faraway past.

'Yes.'

She studies me a second, and then grunts, and leans down by the fire. She ladles some of the stuff out of the cooking pot into a battered pewter bowl and it is passed around the fire to me. The young woman retrieves a beautifully worked wooden spoon out of her skirts and places it in the bowl.

'Eat, me dear. You look half starved.'

I am hungry, and though I cannot see what it is I am eating, I begin scooping it out of the hot bowl with a will. Some kind of beef stew, and there is wild garlic in it, and thyme, and the taste transports me for a moment to another, warmer world. I wolf it down while they all watch, silent as the trees.

'Where be you from?' Queenie asks me in a softer tone.

'From Jericho, in the city,' I answer between steaming mouthfuls.

Queenie frowns. 'That ain't right. You ain't no more English than me, my girl. I sees it in your face. You is from somewheres far south o' here.'

'I am Greek,' I tell her. I look around the fire as I say it, and I realise with something of a pleased shock that I must look just like these people here. I am dark and olive-skinned with brown eyes and black brows, just like them.

'Are you Jews?' I ask them.

Queenie laughs, a rasp of humour, and it travels round the fire.

'We'm of an old and wandering folk girl, a tribe as ancient as you Greeks – or the Jew-folk too, comes to that. The ignorant calls us Romani, but we ain't the same as the travellin' people, though we has dealings with 'em. Egypt is where our kind hails from, in the old, old part o' the world.'

'Then what are you doing in England?' I am quite unafraid now, with the good food in me and the warmth of the fire and the beautiful smiling girl leaning against me.

'What is you doing here?' Queenie darts back.

I set down the empty bowl, and decide that the truth

cannot hurt. 'The Turks drove us out, and killed my family and took our home.'

There is a buzz of talk at this, the men speaking among themselves. Queenie gives me a long hard look. I can't keep her eyes. There is something in them that is as sharp and shrewd as a black crow.

She gives a snort, and then turns back to the fire. Kneeling down, she sets some more sticks upon it, placing each one as carefully as though it were made of glass. Then she blows softly into the heart of them, and the flames lick up and dance yellow and blue, and the heart of the fire glows bright and hungry. She waves her hand through the flames as though she is caressing them, and it seems for a second that the light jumps up brighter to meet her fingers.

'I was askin' what you are a doing in this here wood, creeping up on us like a little stoat,' Queenie says. 'Care to tell us that, Greek girl?'

'I... don't know,' I say, keeping carefully to the truth. 'The moon and the snow... I had to get out in it. And there was something about the woods that just drew me in.'

Queenie looks up at that, and I see her glance at the moon. One of the older men, the one who had exchanged words with the boy Luca, rattles on harshly in their language, shooting suspicious glances at me as he does. I don't like him. He has grey whiskers, and looks like a bright-eyed rat in a flat cap.

Queenie frowns. 'There's more you ain't told us, child.'

The girl beside me tightens her arm about my shoulders. Now it feels less like affection, and more like a restraint. 'Speak up dearie,' she hisses to me.

My heart is thumping fast again. They all stare at me.

Who are these people, so strange and foreign, and why are they out in the woods on a night like this? The fear comes back, cold enough to make the food I have just eaten turn to a cold lump in my tummy.

'I saw that boy before,' I say, reluctantly. 'Luca. I saw him on Port Meadow weeks back. He was with some other men, and they had a fight.'

I wish I had Pie to hold. Their eyes are all so sharp and cold now, and the firelight almost makes them seem to shine yellow, blank as glass.

'You saw what happened then,' Queenie says.

'I didn't tell anyone, I swear,' I say, gulping. 'Fat Bert started it. He had the knife. The boy was just fighting back. I won't tell anyone.' I feel the tears hot at the back of my eyes. There is no warmth in the fire now, and I am crushed by the darkness of the great wood around me, and the dark night, and the loneliness of it, here in the middle of these people. They could bury me here under the trees in a corner where I would never be found.

'She's shaking like a shitting dog,' one of the men says, and laughs horribly.

'Shut your mouth, Job,' Queenie snarls. She has long brown teeth from which the gums have pulled back, and they look almost like fangs.

'I believe her,' the girl with her arm about me says. 'There's no harm in this one, Queenie. A proper little flat she is.'

'T'ain't for you to say, Jaelle. Job, call the boy back in, and we'll get his word on it.'

The old rat-faced man raises his head, and gives a yipping series of barks which make me jump, so high and sharp they sound. Then he shrugs, and begins filling a clay pipe, all the while shooting looks at me, at Queenie, and at the others around the fire, who sit as silent as a jury in a trial. Some of the men nod at me, but the women are all slab-faced and hard.

After a few minutes, Luca is there again, breathing fast. Steam rises from the open neck of his shirt, and his hands are covered in dirt, as though he has been scratching in the ground with them.

'What's the matter?' he demands, quick and sharp.

'This one saw you on the Meadow that night not a moon past when you had your trouble,' Queenie tells him.

'I know. I told you.'

'So? What thinks you? Did she blab, or leave it be, like she says?'

Luca stares at me. 'She's just a little 'un, Ma. Ain't no harm in her. She even had a doll with her.'

'That makes no matter boy.'

The girl, Jaelle speaks up beside me. 'Why would she be here if she had run to the peelers?'

'She might be leading them on us,' rat-faced Job says, puffing on his clay pipe, eyes narrow as coin slots.

Luca laughs. 'She ain't leading no-one nowhere. The wood is empty but for us. I been coursing it like a hare. She's on her own, Ma, I'd take an oath on it.'

Queenie holds my eyes with her own black stare. 'Luca is my boy, and I taught him never to lie, 'cept to flats and peelers. What about you, girlie. Do you lie?'

'Sometimes,' I can't help but say.

Queenie cackles. 'Well, there's truth at any rate. My boy didn't mean to kill no-one, Greek girl, and was like to have been cut himself if he hadn't done what he did. Even by law, what he did wasn't wrong, though no judge would ever let it go at that.'

'I saw it,' I say. 'He didn't start it. It wasn't his knife.'

'No, it weren't.' Queenie looks at me with her head cocked to one side. 'Our folk has enemies you know nothing of, girl.' Then she raises her head, and it is almost as though she is sniffing the air. When she meets my eyes again I can't keep her gaze, but drop my own.

Finally she throws up a hand.

'She ain't lying. Whatever she saw or didn't see, the girl is straight, just a babe in the woods. And unless I miss my guess, there's old blood in her. I can smell it plain as paint. Let her be, Jaelle.'

The girl at my side looses her grip on my shoulders, and I half-see something disappear into the folds of her skirts, a shine of metal barely glimpsed before it is gone.

'I knew you was all right,' she whispers to me, her white teeth close to my face.

'She can't be staying here all night though,' Queenie goes on thoughtfully. And she turns back to tending the pot above the fire

'You no home to go to?' she asks without turning round. 'People to miss you this time o' night?'

'We have a house in Oxford, Pa and me. We're all that's left,' I say, and as I do, I feel a moment's panic as I think of Father looking at his pocket-watch, and I wonder how long I have been gone, and how I am ever going to get back through the dark woods on my own, for I have been quite turned around by events, and I cannot even tell if I am facing back towards Oxford, or into the heart of Wytham Great Wood.

'Time a girlie like you was warm in bed,' Queenie goes on. 'The deep wood is no place for your like. Not tonight.' More sharply, she says; 'Luca, see her home. All the way, mind!'

'Aw, Ma!'

'Do as you're bid. She don't know which way she's turned. I seen rabbits in a trap with more sense.'

'I can find my own way home,' I say, stung by her words.

'Not this night, you won't, girl. The moon is up, and the snow is deep, and will be deeper yet before morn.' Queenie turns to Luca.

'This is no place for such as her. And if she's missed, then there'll be questions asked, and things kicked up that are better left buried. You see her to her doorstep, and no mischief on the way neither. You hear me boy?'

Luca nods sullenly.

'Then be off, the pair of you, and keep the moon at your backs, and move quick and quiet.'

'I know what to do,' Luca says, and he jerks his hand at me.

'Come on then, you. Time's a passing.'

I stand up, and the girl Jaelle rises with me. 'You be careful now dearie,' she murmurs, and her dark eyes take the light of the fire and seem to shine with it, and her grin is very white and not altogether pleasant.

I turn to go, and the rest of them around the fire all watch, and say nothing.

'What are you doing out here?' I ask Queenie on an impulse. 'Out in the cold and the dark?'

'We'm living life as we see fit to do it, dearie,' she replies. 'We've been this way since your folk was young, and the

86

Christ-man was unborn, and the world was wide and full o' marvels. This is what we is, and like as not this is how we'll die.'

There is a murmur around the fire at her words, like the Amen at the end of a prayer. I stumble out of the firelight after that, baffled, and I am glad to be going but sorry to be leaving, all at the same time.

I look back once, and Queenie is still watching me as I go, standing as still as a stone. I think I see her shake her head.

But there is nothing to do except follow Luca's back as the moonlight takes back the night, and down the hill we go amid the black and silent trees, and the frozen snow crunches under my feet like burnt toast.

LUCA GOES VERY fast, and it seems that he glides by every grasping briar, and even his footsteps seem quieter than mine. Soon I am gasping, unable to keep up with that easy lope, and I have to beg him to slow down.

He looks at me as I stand panting before him, his face in darkness. 'Girl, you came to the wrong shop tonight,' he says.

We continue more slowly, always downhill, and through gaps in the trees I can see the lights of Oxford, but they seem far away, and the wood is dense and still and in the more open spaces the snow is deeper yet, still falling in skeins across the moonlight.

'My name is Anna,' I say to him, annoyed. No-one bothered to ask back at the fire, which seems strange, not to mention impolite. And Luca does not reply, but keeps walking, his head turning from side to side, up and down, as alert and searching as a deer.

'Don't you want to know where I live?'

'I knows where you live,' he says carelessly. I am dumbfounded.

'How –'

'I followed you home last time, on the Meadow. I saw you meet up with the big man outside the pub. I watched you all the way, girlie.'

'My name is Anna!'

'All right, then. Anna, watch where you put your feet. You make more noise than a lame cow.'

I have no response to that, but am outraged. I would much rather be called a guttersnipe. Luca's deft sureness in the woods is infuriating. I have always thought of myself as quick and agile, but he makes me feel like a clumsy toddler.

But there is clearly no point in talking, and I do my best to tread more carefully. Luca is following no path but his own, and so quiet is he that more than once I am sure I have lost him in the play of moonlight and shadow and drifting snow amid the trees.

In fact I come to a halt at one point where the wood is especially thick, because it seems he has completely disappeared. I feel a moment of cold panic, but then there is movement ahead, perhaps forty or fifty yards away in the wood, and I start off for it.

Only to be grabbed from behind. I utter a squeak before a hand clamps over my mouth and in my ear a hot breath says, 'Don't move.'

It is Luca. He has one arm around my chest and the other

is under my nose. It smells of soil and tree-sap and sweat. I can taste the salt of it as the fingers hold firm against my lips.

I struggle for a moment and he gives me a shake, like a terrier with a rat, and his hands tighten on me. 'Quiet,' he hisses, and I can feel his mouth make the word against my skin.

We stand like that, locked together. I can feel his breath on my ear. I know now that he is going to stab me. He brought me into the heart of the wood to kill me and dispose of the –

The movement I saw becomes more obvious. Someone or something is picking its way through the trees ahead and downslope of us. I see a dark shape move, brindled with light and shadow. A deer, I think, but it is the wrong shape, too low to the ground. And it has a bulk which is like nothing I have ever seen before. A black lion, a tiger, a panther. No, it is none of these, and yet it is a big animal of some sort, padding quietly through the undergrowth.

I catch a blink of eyes, silver green, reflecting back the moon, and I begin to shake. Luca holds me closer.

The thing veers off, and I swear I can hear it sniffing the ground as it draws away again. More than that; I am sure that at one point it rears up and walks on two feet, like a man, before dropping down again. But that cannot be right.

Luca and I stand stock still for a full ten minutes after it disappears, until my nose is running down his fingers and I have pins and needles from standing so still, and I am desperate to go to the toilet and the cold only makes it worse.

At last Luca releases me, but he takes my shoulders and turns me round, and lays a finger on his lips. I nod, wiping my nose on my sleeve, wishing more than ever that Pie was here to hug, or that Father would suddenly appear with a torch and a big revolver – or even that someone big and cheerful like Jack would turn up smoking his pipe, to rescue me again.

But there is only the dark silent wood, and the strange boy whom I know to be a murderer, but who may have just saved me from something unknown and terrible.

'What was that?' I say in a tiny whisper.

I see his teeth as he answers. 'No business o' yourn, girl. Just be thankful I was with you. Now let's be off out of here, lessen you wants to sleep under a tree tonight.'

I keep close behind him as we pick our way onwards, and at times I even reach out and seize the back of his coat for fear of losing him when the slivered moon goes behind cloud and the night darkens as though someone has just blown out the wick of a great lamp.

It seems an age before I see the lights of Wytham village through the last of the trees, and we finally come out from under the canopy and are crunching through calf-deep snow in open fields. It is the familiar world again, icy cold, white and stark, but a world I know. And the jagged ice-cold terror I felt in the woods slips back again. Into the half-denied space where what we have seen and heard cannot be true.

We climb a last fence, and are on the road once more, though it is almost lost in the snow, a tunnel between white blasted hedges. My toes are numb in my galoshes and I have fragments of briar and bracken clinging all over me by thorn and hook, and I desperately need to pee. We trudge along until I can bear it no longer and I am shuddering and shivering as I call on Luca to halt.

'Look away.'

'Why?'

'Don't be stupid. Just do as I ask.'

His eyes widen. 'All right then, but be quick about it.' And he stares resolutely at the lights of Oxford as I squat shaking in the snow, and the steam rises around my legs, and the sharp smell of it too, and my face is burning as I straighten and rejoin him but I am sure he cannot notice in the darkness.

We walk for what seems a long time, and I am barely aware of the distance, my numb feet setting themselves down one after another like the workings of a clock. At last, though, I stop shaking, and begin to feel more normal again.

'So Queenie is your mother,' I say at last to break the silence.

'Aye.'

'That stew was very good. What was it?'

'That were rabbit. Ain't you never had rabbit before?'

'I don't know.'

'Queenie can make rare vittles out of anything. She could make a stew out of rat if she chose.'

'Ugh. Who would ever eat rat?'

'Anyone, if they was hungry enough.'

That stumps me a little. We pass the Trout, which is lit up and has a few men propping up the bar inside as though the world were still normal and ordinary.

We walk through Wolvercote like two snow-flecked

phantoms. Luca seems not to mind the cold, and he is all the time looking at everything as though expecting something to jump out at us, whereas I have my face half buried in Father's scarf and the cold is searching every corner of my clothes. I am beginning to see how grown-ups can consider snow a tiresome thing.

'The pretty girl, Jaelle, is she your sister?' I ask at last, to chop up another of the silences.

'That she is,' Luca says patiently.

'And the others – are they all family?'

'Of one sort or t'other.'

'Why are you all living in the woods?'

He waits a while before answering. 'We's just passing by.'

'You were here a month ago, when... when I saw you that night.'

'Wasn't a month. Wasn't a whole moon just yet.' He spits into the snow. 'Sometimes we stays longer in one place than in others.'

'What about Bert? Did he die?'

'That he did.'

I can think of nothing more to say after that, not for a long while. The snow is blowing in clouds across Port Meadow, and we are not far from where Luca killed the fat man that night and I want to ask more but I am too scared and bewildered.

This boy seems so much older than me, so much in charge of things, so sure of himself. I want to ask him why his eyes lit up under the moon that night, and what happened to the other men on the Meadow, and why his family are camping out in Wytham Wood, but somehow I cannot.

And I keep coming back to the animal in the trees, and every time I think on it my mind gets as frozen as my poor feet, and I really don't want to know anything else, and in point of fact I am quite sure I know more than is good for me already.

And so I say nothing, but I can't help but look at Luca as we walk along, side by side now. He is rather handsome, in a pinched sort of way, and his long nose seems too big for his face. He is very thin, and I suppose he appears as though he could very well have eaten rat stew and enjoyed it, and I suddenly feel very slow and stupid beside him, and though he seems so much older, I really think he is not.

These thoughts take me all the way across Port Meadow to the railway line, and as we cross the bridge and the buildings of the city loom up all around us, the thought of the trouble I am in now rises like a sour taste on my tongue, and I am almost as afraid as I was in the woods when Luca held his hand over my mouth and the nameless beast walked past us through the trees.

'What time is it?' I ask him as we find ourselves back on Walton Street, with the snow blowing through the yellow cones of gaslight. There are not many people around, and the snow is packed tight on the road, pocked with prints of feet and dug into channels by the wheels of motor cars.

'Nowhere near the middle o' the night yet,' Luca says, sniffing the air as though midnight had a peculiar smell to it.

'Father will kill me,' I say.

'Does your Da know you're out?' Luca asks.

'He said I could have an hour. I think it's been three. Or four.'

Luca grins. 'Never heard o' time being doled out like that, in bare mouthfuls. There ain't no clocks in the woods neither.'

I am more hungry for time of my own than I am for food, I think. And I am suddenly furious at Father, who is so miserly with his own time and will not allow me to spend mine.

Is it that I just want to be alone, me and Pie in our own little world? I used to think so. After tonight I am not so sure. The woods, the people I met in them, they have me in a spin. I did not think that Oxford could be exciting, or that people like these even existed outside the pages of books. I almost tell Luca this –

But in the end I only sigh. 'I can get home myself from here.'

'Queenie said to see you all the way home, girlie, and that's what I aim to do.'

'Have it your own way then,' I snap. *Girlie*. Why can't he use my name? And I kick my way through the snow, arms folded, annoyed, wanting to get back at him.

'But if my father sees you, I bet he'll... he'll call the police or something.'

Luca glides along, and there is something ugly on his face. 'Why would he do that?'

'Because you're a stranger, and you talk funny, and... and your eyes light up at night, that's why!' *And you killed Fat Bert* I think, but do not say.

Luca watches my face as I stomp along, until I am uncomfortable with it, and somehow ashamed. As if he knows my thoughts.

'Well they do – I saw it!'

'You don't know what you saw, or half of what you see neither,' he says with disgust. 'You ain't nothing but a spoiled little brat that needs a good kick up the arse.'

'I'd like to see you try!' I want to say, but I am infuriated with myself. I am saying stupid things, and I feel so young beside him, and it makes me angrier still because I don't want to say I am sorry and yet I feel I should and I am not even sure why.

'Just you stay out of the woods, you hear me? Midwinter night is coming and they ain't no place for such as you.'

'I'll go where I like. You can't stop me.'

He throws up his hands in exasperation, a little like Father does when he is making a point.

'You want to wander the Great Wood, then you goes ahead, and see how much I care. You'll find things in there you don't want to see, girl, and it'll be on your head alone. But don't say that me and mine didn't treat you square, or try and warn you, that's all.'

'What could be in the woods that is so dangerous?' I sneer. 'Rabbits? We're not in Africa. There are no lions and tigers or bears, not in England.' And I am thinking of the shadow in the trees as I say it, and know how false my words sound. And he knows too.

'There's more to this world than what you folk see under gaslight, or through a window. My people, we wanders the length of the country all our lives, and we knows things the rest of you has forgotten, and we see things that ain't seen no more by such as you. So heed me girl.'

The corner of Moribund Lane is in front of us. We stand under the streetlamp there, white with snow, Oxford shrouded and withdrawn all around us. It feels more dark and cold here than it did in the depths of the wood, and all at once I feel close to tears, and hate myself for it.

'I don't want to go home,' I whisper. 'It's not home at all.'

Luca stares at me, exasperated. But then his face softens. I see pity in it, and I hate that too. He is right. I am a spoiled brat who knows nothing, and I have always supposed myself very clever, but I can only come out with the wrong things to say, and I want to make it right and I don't know how.

'Places ain't home,' he says at last. 'People is. Bricks and chairs is nothing.'

He drops his eyes, and again, he raises his hands the same way Father does. 'I leaves you here,' he says gruffly. 'I see your house, and there's light in yon window.' He reaches out and tugs a piece of dead briar from my scarf, the thorns ripping away one by one. 'Your Da is there, I suppose,'

I look at him. I am quite tall for my age, and he is short for his. I do not have to raise my head by much to kiss him on the cheek, but as I do he darts back as though I meant to bite him.

He rubs his face. 'What's all that about?'

'Nothing,' I say, and sniff. 'Tell Queenie her stew is very good. And thank her for it.'

'You be all right now?' There is colour in his face. I do believe he is blushing, and I feel as though I have won a tiny victory, but I don't know why.

'I'll be all right.'

'Then that's that.'

And just like that, he turns and walks away, back up

Walton Street. I watch him a while, and I see it when he turns around to look back at me, and I raise a hand. He just stares, then continues on his way.

And all of a sudden I feel more alone than I ever have in my life before, and my feet are like two lumps of clay as I trudge down the street towards the tall old house with the lamplight spilling out of its window into the falling snow.

7

AND OF COURSE the door is locked, and I had a feeling that would be the way of it. So I stand in the snow, and I listen to the voices inside.

Sometimes the lessons we learn take forever to be driven into our heads – like learning French – and sometimes a thing happens which can teach you that lesson in a second, a moment. So I stand and wait outside the door and don't touch the bell chain. For some reason I feel I am not the same Anna who set off from this same place just a few hours ago. She was a spoiled brat I suppose, just as Luca said.

I still want warm feet, and lamplight, and I desperately need to hug Pie in a snug fresh linen-smelling bed. But it is as though the quiet calm voice which has always been inside of me has suddenly taken charge, and it is not a strange other kind of voice at all.

It is me, and it has always been there.

The door opens at last, as I knew it would, and the Committee members begin to troop out, the warmth of the house blooming out into the night with them. The meeting went on late, as it always does, and Mr Paparakis goes by with his little moustache, putting his homburg on his head. And Mr Meronides, who wears too much eau de cologne and whose eyebrows meet in the middle. They seem disgruntled and preoccupied, and barely glance at me as I squeeze past them without a word, hidden by the passing overcoats. I am in the hall and almost at the foot of the stairs when I hear Father's voice, sharp as the crack of a whip.

'Anna!'

I turn around, and Father is glaring at me, and his face is blotchy and his eyes are red-rimmed. Even in the meetings, he keeps a tumbler of Scotch at his elbow these days, along with the piles of papers and his pipe and his fountain pen.

Then he is distracted again by someone shaking his hand, and says goodbye to Mrs Gallianikos in quite another tone, and smiles, and claps someone else on the back, and I sit down on the bottom step and pull off the old Monmouth cap and unwind the scarf from my neck, and now that I am in from the cold I can smell the woodsmoke on them, a fine, blue smell that instantly brings back the woods and the firelight. I wonder what it would be like to go to sleep staring up at the stars, and feel the snow land cold on my face with the bright warmth of a campfire beside me and the cold earth below, and the trees in the circle of my eyes overhead, moving with the wind. That would be freedom, to do that.

And for a moment, I understand Queenie and Luca entirely, and think that they and theirs are rather a sensible folk, to want to stay clear of desks and hallways and committees and heaps of papers no-one ever reads.

The door closes, and Father is alone in the hallway with me, swaying slightly. His rubs his hand over his eyes, and he seems very pale and I can see the skin of his head shining through his hair, which I never noticed before. I feel sorry for him, and that is a rather horrible thing – to feel sorry for one's own father.

'Where have you been?' he asks distantly, and he fumbles in his waistcoat for his pocket watch. He presses the stud on the side of the Breguet and it gives a series of beautiful little chimes, telling the hours and the quarters.

And I do not feel the least shame in lying to him. 'I walked around, and played in the snow. I went along the canal, and wandered Jericho. It was very quiet. I didn't speak to anybody.'

He looks at me. 'It's after eleven. All this time, Anna?'

'I don't have a watch, Father. I'm sorry. I forgot the time. But I'm all right.'

I stand up, and go to him, and hug him, smelling pipe tobacco and whisky and the old stale tweed of his jacket. 'I'm quite all right.'

He runs his hand over my hair. I can feel it curl into a fist for a moment, and I am sure he is going to belt me – I brace for it – but then the fingers relax again, and he sighs. 'I forgot the time too.' And he hugs me back. 'I should have gone looking for you.'

'I was not lost, Father. There was no need.'

'You can't be running around the streets of Oxford at all hours. And you smell of smoke.'

'There was a brazier lit somewhere. I stood by it to warm up.'

He lifts up my head to look in my eyes, and I can't help

wonder if he can see the lies in them. His own are watery, as if he has been crying, but it is only the booze. I know the look.

'You're half frozen,' he says with a snap.

'My feet are cold,' I admit, and I smile up at him, willing him to believe.

He shakes his head. 'This just won't do, Anna. I must be able to trust you. I said one hour, and here it is the middle of the night. Anything could have happened to you.' And he tugs me close.

'Christos,' he whispers. 'Don't you know you're all I have left?'

'I'm sorry,' I say. And I mean it. The way he hugs me makes me feel little again, and reminds me of the days when he would put me to bed and read to me, or tell me stories of Agamemnon and Achilleos as though they were people who lived in the world we knew, and could any day drop by for tea, leaving their spears and helmets in the hall and breezing in all brown and sunlit and full of life. But I know better now.

'We're never going home again, are we, Father?'

He shakes his head and runs his fingers through my hair. 'Oxford is our home now, *moraki mou*. We are not Greek any more.'

'Then why do you still have these meetings, with all the old Greeks?'

He pauses for a long time, until I think he will not speak again. When at last he answers his voice is as thick as though he had a heavy cold.

'It is complicated. Greece is still out there, Anna, but it is not the same as the country we knew. Our city was unique, and the people in it...' He trails off.

'Just by coming here, and talking about it, and remembering things; it is a way of keeping some part of it alive. Those people need that. They sit here of an evening, and recall the time that is gone, and the loved ones who are no more.' He swallows. I can see it in the thin flesh of his throat.

'Perhaps it is not altogether healthy. But it's a hard thing, to give up on a life. Harder still when you are my age, and all the happiest days of that life are dead and gone forever, and youth gone with them.'

'We can still be happy, Father. We're still together.'

He shakes his head, and smiles. '*Kori*, I have had my love and happiness, my life's share of it. There is nothing more to come now but the fading of the memories, and yet more loss. All lives reach a point in their years where there is only sorrow to be had, and the joy has all been given or taken away. Grief is the price we pay for having loved.'

He raises my head in his hands.

'You have the look of your mother, always had. She was from Anatolia, and she lived in a little village in the hills. When I first met her I was not much more than a boy, and she was barefoot and illiterate, but she was the most beautiful thing I had ever seen.' He smiles. 'I took her away from there at a gallop in a two-wheeled trap, and I thought her father was going to shoot me for it, but your grandmother blessed us both, and told him that God had meant me to find her.' He looks away, and his eyes are full of real tears now. 'She had a voice, such a voice. When she sang the nightingales would stop to listen.'

There is agony on his face, and he has broken out in a sweat. His hands tighten on my face until it almost hurts. Then he lets me go and pushes me away, wiping his eyes.

'It's time you were in bed now. Go on up, and take the lamp with you. I shan't be needing it tonight.'

I want him to keep talking, to tell me more about my mother, but I know that it would be of no use now. He walks into the front room and lifts the oil lamp and hands it to me. I stand in the hall with it, the heat rising from the glass, and watch as he shuffles back into the darkened room, scarlet with the dying of the fire.

Then he turns. 'Where is your doll?' His voice has changed. He is quite sharp now.

'I left her behind. She's in my room.'

A grimness comes into his face, all red light and black shadow.

'Good. It's time you left childishness like that behind. We must all of us grow up sometime. We can't hold on to things, no matter how hard we try.' And his face clenches up like a fist. 'That is something you will learn, soon enough.'

His shoulder strikes the door with a stagger as he closes it behind him, and I stand alone in the hall with the light in my hands. For a mad instant, I wonder what would happen if I took the lamp and dashed it against that door; whether he would even care.

At last, slowly, I begin climbing up the stairs into the darkness of the snowbound house.

I LIE LATE in bed on the Sunday, listening to the bells of Oxford. I love the sound of them. Somehow there is hope and reassurance in the peals tolling from one church after another, as though it were the city itself calling out to those who lived in it. I lie in my bed with Pie in the crook of my arm, and I stroke her head as Father stroked mine, and I think of Wytham Great Wood, and the Romani, and of kissing the boy Luca. That is the first time I have ever kissed a boy, and I wonder if he liked it. I think of my mother, barefoot in some mountain village far across the world in miles and years, a girl like me who could shame the nightingales with her singing, and I wonder how she died. I hope it was quick. I hope she went to God in an instant. I hope she is with him now, singing still.

LORD JESUS CHRISTOS, this is Anna. And I know I do not talk to you as often as I should, and when I do I am always asking for something. But all the same, could you please help my father, and bring him back to the way he was, and make him drink less of that horrid Scotch. And try to make him happy.

Amen. Thank you.

I TALK TO Pie as I lie in the warm bed, and tell her about the forest, and the people in it, and the stew from the pot, and the pretty girl, Jaelle, who put her arm about my shoulders. And I tell her of Luca walking me home, but I do not mention the beast stalking the trees in the night, because I do not want to frighten her, and besides, it seems almost like a dream now, in the bright morning with the church bells tolling and the sounds of motor cars in the streets below.

And Pie listens to me with wide black eyes.

FATHER STAYS IN bed late on Sundays these days, especially after a meeting, so I get up and dress and splash water over my face from the basin in the corner, and run a brush through my hair, wincing and hissing as the knots and tangles come out of it. I stare at my face in the mirror, and study my long nose and wish it was smaller, and brush my teeth with the green tooth powder. I wish I was beautiful, like Mama was. It's all very well to say beauty is under the skin, or in the eye of the beholder, but no-one would say no to being prettier if they had the chance, so it is all rot.

It is another bread and dripping day, being closer to the end of the month than the beginning. But I cannot face it. I drink water out of the brass tap, stuff down a crust of bread and cheese, and then Pie and I are set up for the morning. I listen at Father's door on the landing, and I can hear him snort and breathe as loud as a horse on the other side of it, so I leave him a note saying *I have gone for a walk*, and with that I have a clear conscience.

The snow has been trodden on and is broken and crunching and dirty, and my socks are damp in my paper-stuffed shoes, but it is bright and sharp and still, the world wide awake, and the streets full of people. Everyone is going to church, and the children are all buttoned up in their Sunday best with pink knees and new collars, and some of the students are trying to ride their bicycles in the frozen ruts with their gowns billowing out black around them, and there is a snowman standing at the corner on Little Clarendon Street with a hat and scarf, and coal for eyes, and it makes me happy just to look at him.

I keep walking, hugging Pie close and staring all around me. I wonder if Luca and his family ever come into the city and walk up and down the streets like normal people, or do they stay in the wood and sit around the fire and eat rabbit all the time. I wonder how they brush their teeth in the morning, and if they ever take a bath. What a strange way to live. But on a morning like this, it does not seem a bad way of doing things, though they must miss clean sheets and pillows every so often. And I could not live without reading books. Though I could happily get by if I never saw another word of French, or those horrid letters in algebra that are supposed to add up to something but never do.

The High seems busy to me, despite the snow and the fact that it is Sunday. There is a beggar sitting swathed in rags in front of St Mary's church, and people just walk past him as though he is not there. I smile at him, and he looks up at me out of a red, bearded face, and does not smile back, but stares blank as a stone, and something about him makes me feel cold.

But I forget him as I walk on in the bright bustle of the day. Even on a Sunday, Oxford is noisy. I've heard Father lament the fact that there are so few horses to be seen on the roads now, and motor cars are everywhere with their din. I think the horses are another reminder of Father's youth, but even I can remember a time when it seemed there were far more of them, and when you crossed the road you had to watch where you put your feet. But the world is changing fast it seems.

It was the War that did it, so Miss Hawcross is always saying. There is no decorum these days, and young people are quite out of control. And I grin as I think on it, and wonder what she would make of rabbit stew in the woods with the Romani. Their world has not changed, it looks like, not in years and years. Mowgli would be quite at home sitting at their fire.

I find myself on Magdalen Bridge, and jump up a little so I can lean on the balustrade and look down into the half-frozen Cherwell. The punts are all stacked up for the winter and there are fans of ice spread out from the banks, and fragments of it bumping slowly along in the lazy current.

I have been here in summer, when the river is a raft of boaters as people take their sweethearts and friends out in punts with hampers and parasols, and the river is brown and thick and slow, like sun-warmed treacle, and the stone itself is warm against my skin, like a reminder, a little echo of the fierce bright light and heat I knew in our old home, and the balcony that looked out not on a sleepy Oxfordshire river, but on the Aegean Sea, where Agamemnon launched his galleys, and Don John fought the Turks at Lepanto, and Nelson led his band of brothers to beat Napoleon at the Nile.

Now if only that history were the one that Miss Hawcross taught me, I should be so much more interested in it than in which queen got her head lopped off by horrible fat old Henry.

I cross the road, crunching in the brown, frozen ruts, and I jump as someone in a bug-eyed motor squeezes their horn at me. *Parp parp*! It is such a comical noise. No wonder old Toad loved it so.

I make my way into the Botanical Gardens, where there are some wonderful old trees and plants and things that do not grow in England, and which I love to smell to bring back the memories of that warm sea.

The Gardens are dishevelled now, and the colours are muted, as though the place is sleeping through winter, and as I stroll along with Pie it becomes quite quiet, and even the traffic noises seem to fade away, and the place seems almost abandoned. And there is another tramp here, asleep on a bench, little more than a mound of rags. I walk more quietly, suddenly reluctant to pass by him.

But further on, by one of the most interesting of the trees there is a lean man wrapped in a scarf and smoking a pipe. And as I look on he goes up to the massive trunk and pats it, as one would the flank of a horse. As though the tree were an old friend. And I think it is a strange but also a rather lovely thing to do, so Pie and I stop and watch him as he peers up into the bare branches. His face is familiar.

He turns, and sees me standing there, and gives me a nod and a rather shy smile. He has a thin, pale face, and I recognise him as Jack's friend, who rode off on his bicycle the night I met them outside the pub.

'How do you do,' he says.

'Very well, thank you sir,' I say politely. I can see that he knows my face.

'Have we met?'

'Your friend Jack walked me home one night.'

It dawns on him. 'Ah, the little girl, of course. I am glad to see you well my dear.'

'You like that tree a lot,' I say, stepping forward.

He shrugs slightly, takes his pipe out of his mouth and peers into the bowl a moment. 'I suppose so.'

'I think it's beautiful. I like trees too,' I say.

'Do you? That's splendid. So few do, these days.' He pats the side of the great tree again. '*Pinus nigra*, black pine. It's Austrian, in point of fact.'

'It looks like it has arms.'

He smiles. 'Yes, it does rather.'

'They pollarded the willows in Binsey last year, and they looked so sad afterwards, all stumpy and grumpy.'

'That's what they do,' he says, and his pale face becomes animated. 'They use trees without looking at them, harvest them as though they were mowing grass; and yet there's something in trees that is found nowhere else. They are the oldest living things. This one is a mere stripling, perhaps a century or two. But there are yews growing in English churchyards which were alive before the Normans came.'

I stare at him. 'But that's wonderful – imagine if they could talk!'

He laughs. 'Yes. But what language would they speak?'

'Their own I suppose. Tree language, all deep and slow.'

He looks at me thoughtfully. 'Now that's a curious idea. I like that.'

'I've been to Wytham Wood, and there are old trees there, and it's a curious place altogether,' I say a little breathlessly. 'I was there in the night, and it was like being outside England, like an older place where time is not moving so fast and there are memories in the wood, and you might see anything if the moon is right.'

He stares at me once more. He has a long, kind face and very bright eyes that seem younger than the rest of him.

'So Jack walked you home, eh?'

'Yes. And he knew who Agamemnon was. He is very clever.'

The man laughs again at that, throwing his head back. 'I shall be sure to pass on the compliment. He is waiting for me in the Eastgate.' He pauses. 'And what are you about on this cold Sunday afternoon?'

'Just walking. Father is still in bed, and so Pie and I are taking the air.'

'Pie?'

'This is Pie,' I say, holding her up. 'Her real name is Penelope, like Odysseos's wife, but she likes to be called Pie.'

'Charmed, I'm sure,' the man says, nodding at Pie. Then he does something no-one has ever done before. He reaches out and takes Pie's little cold hand and shakes it, rather solemnly.

'And you are?'

'Anna Francis. I live in Jericho, but I come from Greece. I am quite English now, though.'

'You look rather cold, Anna.' He considers a moment. 'Would you and Pie like to join Jack and me for a hot chocolate in the Eastgate Hotel? I'm sure he would be pleased to meet you again, and they keep a fire burning.'

I look at him. Hot chocolate! 'That would be very nice,' I say carefully. 'If it's not too much trouble.'

'No trouble. My name is Ronald, by the way.'

'Jack called you Tollers.'

'Yes, he does that. Come now, before your nose turns even more blue.' He looks me up and down, and a frown goes across his face, and his mouth clamps on the stem of his pipe. 'We must get you in front of that fire. A hot chocolate is just the ticket for warming up little girls. Come on – hop to it.'

He walks surprisingly fast for someone so old – he must be forty at least, and I have to skip to keep up with him. The tramp is gone from the bench and the gardens are all deserted now.

It is not far, but as we reach the door of the Eastgate I hear the din of all the people inside, and shrink back. I am apprehensive, and I cannot think why.

'It's quite all right,' Mr Ronald says quietly. We'll find a spot by the fire and you can watch them all come and go.'

I follow him inside, and there is a blast of heat and noise and smoke which quite makes my head swim, and I hug Pie tight to me. I have never been in a public house before, or a hotel, or whatever this is. But the warmth is very welcome, and I see Jack's big beefy face almost at once. 'Tollers!' he cries out in that booming voice of his from the middle of a crowd at the bar, and he raises a brown brimming glass to his mouth, then sets it down again as he catches sight of me.

'Well I'm blowed. It's little... little...'

'Anna,' Mr Ronald tells him. 'Order her a hot chocolate Jack, there's a good chap. She's half frozen. Join us by the fire. And a Burton for me, if you please.'

Jack bends over me. 'I remember. And how is Odysseos, my dear?' he asks, smiling.

'Very well sir,' I say. 'Thank you for –'

But the crowd comes in between us. I can hardly hear myself think, and stand there wondering where to go. Then there is a hand on my shoulder, and Mr Ronald is guiding me gently to the big fireplace where the logs are burning and there is space to sit on a low settle. Most people seem to be pushed up tight against the bar, and the room is full of blue smoke and laughter and the smell of beer, and I feel very small and out of place, but Mr Ronald stands over me and makes sure I am not jostled or trod on, and Jack joins us with two glasses and a steaming mug, and his face is shiny and broad as he hands it to me.

'Marshmallows!' he says. 'That's the key. 'One must always have marshmallows in hot chocolate. Tollers, the girl will melt sitting there, as will I.'

'She needs to warm up,' Mr Ronald says, sipping his beer and looking down at me. 'We shall be a trio of coalbiters, hogging the fire. How is your chocolate, Anna?'

It tastes like the best thing in the world.

'It's lovely, thank you.'

After that, Jack and Mr Ronald lean in close to one another and begin talking loudly in the way that grownups do in a crowd. They seem very obsessed with furniture, because they keep talking about a chair. I sit and feel the heat of the burning logs and my feet thaw out and my shoes begin to steam. I watch the people who are stuffed in the room like tin soldiers in a box, and wonder at the noise and the closeness of it all. Surely it would be easier to have conversation if it were quieter. But everyone seems to like talking loudly with their faces close together, and then drawing back to drink again, or puff on a pipe or cigarette. There are even a few women here, seated at tables around the walls, but everyone is quite old. I wonder if this is what grown-ups do when they reach a certain age, and if I will have to do it. It all looks rather jolly, but exhausting.

There is an old man with a grey beard by the door. I look away, and then look back, and I cannot shake the impression that he is watching me, though I never catch his eye. People come and go like a shifting flock of starlings, and when I try to pick him out again over the rim of my mug, he is gone and the door of the pub is swinging closed.

Out of the current of noise, I pick a sentence. It is Mr Ronald.

'… wandering about on her own. It's not right, Jack.'

'I know, but what can one do? I spoke to the chap, and he seems sound enough. We can't go putting our noses in.'

'Hmmph.'

I look up to find them both peering down at me. Jack seems slightly embarrassed. He drains his glass, and hands it to Mr Ronald. 'Your round, Tollers.'

'I declare, Jack, you gulp down the stuff as though it were lemonade.'

'*Bibo, ergo sum*, old chap. Now off you go.'

As Mr Ronald weaves his way to the bar, Jack sits down beside me on the low settle, and it creaks under his weight.

'Is everything all right, Anna?' he asks me, and he knocks out his pipe on the edge of the fireplace and begins refilling it from a leather pouch. There is sweat on his upper lip and he looks a little pop-eyed with the heat of the fire.

'Quite all right,' I say. 'Thank you for the chocolate – it was lovely.'

'Do you go to school?'

'No. But Miss Hawcross comes round every weekday. Tomorrow it is French again, and maths. She says I do not apply myself.'

'A governess, then?'

'I don't know. She looks after me sometimes when Pa – when Father is in London. But he doesn't go as often as he used to.'

'What does your father do in London?'

'He goes to the Colonial Office. He is trying to get us all home. Or he was. I think he has quite given up now.'

'Home – you mean Greece – Smyrna?'

It is quite a rum sensation to hear that name. We never speak it. None of the exiles do. It's like the way the Jews can't speak the name of their God. I nod slowly.

'Do you speak any Greek, Anna?'

'Not anymore. I remember words here and there sometimes, but I was very young when we left on the battleship, not more than five or six. It was a long time ago, I suppose.'

'The years are very grand and long when you are young,' Jack tells me, fumbling for his matches. 'As you grow older, so they dwindle, and fly past with much less fanfare.'

'I hope so. I'm tired of being a child. I want to grow up and be able to go where I please and stay out as long as I like.'

Jack lights his pipe, cupping the flare of the match in his hand and running the flame around the bowl. The pipe smoke is sweet and blue. He puffs a moment, looking straight ahead, but he is not seeing anything in the bar. I can tell.

'These years are the crucible of your life, Anna,' he says at last. 'The things that happen to us as children, they mark us all the rest of our days. That is why this time is so important. Do not wish it away.' He smiles through the smoke. 'I am an exile of sorts too. I was born across the water, where the mountains meet the sea. The land of our birth never truly leaves us.'

Mr Ronald returns with beers, and a plate with a thick-cut beef sandwich. 'I thought you looked a little peckish,' he says to me.

'Really, I can't –' I say.

'It's all right my girl. I had purchased it for Jack, but forgot he's a very picky eater. Prefers mustard with his roast beef instead of horseradish. Can you imagine?' He makes a face, and I laugh, and take the sandwich.

Apart from Queenie's rabbit, I have not eaten beef in weeks, and the taste is glorious, and I prefer horseradish too.

'You are very nice gentlemen,' I say with my mouth full, and I shouldn't, because it is not genteel, but I don't care.

'You are very welcome my dear,' Jack says, and he sets his big hand on my head for a moment. He and Mr Ronald look at one another.

'You should come to tea sometime,' I go on, still chewing. 'We have Earl Grey, and toasted muffins sometimes.'

'That would be fine,' Jack says.

Mr Ronald is consulting his wristwatch. He gulps at his beer. 'We'll be late for the service, Jack.'

'Oh, hang the service.'

'Even an infidel like you must make an appearance from time to time.' He looks at me. 'You will go home after this won't you child? I hate to think of you wandering the streets.'

'I like wandering,' I say, and look at Pie, wondering if I have done something wrong. 'I can look after myself. I have been to Wytham Wood in the middle of the night, and I was quite all right.'

'What on earth took you there?' Jack asks, astonished.

'I wanted to see the trees in the moonlight.'

They both laugh. 'What glory there is in being young,' Jack says. And to Mr Ronald, 'You go on, Tollers. I will see her part of the way, at least. Miss Francis is rather more engaging than the Chaplain.'

Mr Ronald nods. He stoops and holds out his hand. 'Miss Francis, it has been a rare pleasure,' he says as I shake it. 'And I quite agree with you about the moonlight on the trees.'

8

8

THE STREETS ARE quieter now, and the sun has hidden itself in cloud and Oxford is grey with cold, but the warmth of the fire and the chocolate stay with me as we walk up the High past all the grand colleges and churches. Jack is still puffing on his pipe and despite the fact that he is rather a large man, he strides along quickly in his shapeless old flannels.

'Walking stirs up the mind,' he says. 'I can see you and I are eye to eye on that one, Anna.'

'I like walking, and exploring. There's always so much to see. I should like to spend my life tramping all over the interesting places of the world, and reading as many books as I please.'

'I couldn't agree more my dear. A new book is an adventure in itself.'

'I suppose that's what you do – you read a lot of books?'

'Among other things. There's nothing like a good old sullen read, with a pot of tea and a good pipe to hand.'

'And what about adventure? Have you been to many places? I should love to travel. Oxford is all very well, but it seems to me there are so many other more interesting places in the world.'

'Ah, there you have me. I am one of those pitiful souls who would rather read about adventure than go out and look for it. Perilous things, adventures. They are invariably uncomfortable at some point, and they make you late for dinner.'

We walk along briskly, and I look at Pie. 'I had an adventure,' I say quietly.

'Port Meadow. Yes, you told me. It sounded a little too hair-raising for someone of your age, Anna. I do beg you to be careful.'

'No – after that. When I went to Wytham Wood in the moonlight. I met people there. I saw things.'

He looks at me somewhat sharply. 'What kind of things?'

I feel uncomfortable with Jack's stare, but I am bursting to tell someone, and have been for days.

'There were people living in the wood, all sat around a fire eating rabbit stew, and singing. Some of them were quite frightening, but others were not so bad. I think I like them.'

'Gypsies, I'll warrant,' Jack says, frowning, and he gives a *harrumph*. 'Listen to me Anna, it is all very well having a high spirit, and the urge to explore and so on, and I do not doubt your courage for one moment, but you must exercise caution, too. The greatest explorers are those who return safe and sound to tell the tale of their travels.'

'Captain Scott did not come back. Or Magellan either.'

Jack chuckles. 'Well, you have me there. But Amundsen

and Shackleton returned safe and sound, and Columbus had to get back to Spain before we knew that America was out there across the sea. Just think if he hadn't! What a pickle we would have been in.' He slows, and takes his pipe out of his mouth, stabbing the air with it. 'The Gypsies, or Romani as they are known, are an ancient people, and they have been with us since time immemorial; but they have their own ways and customs, and it does not do to cross them. The country has taken some shrewd blows this last year or two, Anna, and there are more poor and desperate folk abroad than there used to be. It is... it is a damned ticklish time for a young girl to be out on her own, even in the environs of a city like Oxford.'

He jams the pipe back between his teeth.

'Your father would tell you the same, I'm sure.'

'He has.' I am disappointed in Jack. All grown-ups are the same after all. I was going to tell him about the animal in the trees, but I won't now. I feel sure he would not like it, or not believe me. So it must stay between Pie and me, like the killing of Fat Bert, and the shine in Luca's eyes as they met the moon. It is a tiresome thing to have so many secrets after a while, not exciting at all. Like walking around with stones in your pockets.

We are at the corner of George Street, and the Randolph is just ahead. It has begun to snow again, and the flakes are thin, biting flecks which chill my face and legs.

'When is Midwinter?' I ask Jack.

'Eh? Oh, that would be tonight. Today is the shortest day of the year, and this will be the longest night. But Christmas will be here soon. I'm sure you're looking forward to that.'

'Yes,' I say, not really attending. I wonder what Luca and

his family are at, out in the woods right now. There was something about Midwinter's night that seemed special to them.

'There will be carols in Magdalen Chapel. Perhaps you and your father would like to come.'

'Why did Mr Ronald call you an infidel?' He stops in his tracks. 'I only ask, because it was what we were called by the Turks, and they were all very horrible, but Mr Ronald does not seem horrible at all, so I wondered why he used that word. You are friends, aren't you?'

Jack is standing in the street looking up at the sky, and the snow gathers bit by bit on his hat. He does that for what seems quite a long time, and then gently touches me on the shoulder and we resume our walk, more slowly now.

'An infidel,' he says slowly, 'is a pejorative – it is a rather nasty word used to describe someone who does not believe in the same God as you. But believe me, Anna, Tollers meant it in jest.'

'Oh, a joke.'

'Well, not quite.' He smiles around his pipe. 'Our friend is a Papist – a Roman Catholic, and he has always been faintly scandalised by my atheism.'

'What's that?' I ask, puzzled.

Jack sighs a little, and looks me up and down with his head cocked to one side. 'I don't believe in a God, Anna.'

'Really? How interesting. I thought everyone believed in God.'

'Well, most say they do, I suppose.'

'I pray to God all the time, but I'm sure He doesn't listen much. I never considered that He might not be there at all. I just thought He was busy, or that I was too wicked to help.'

Jack sets a hand on my shoulder as we walk along. 'If there were a God, He would not find you wicked, Anna, I am sure of that. And I pray too, from time to time. It is a thing I cannot help. It is a need that is embedded in us all. That is man's condition. He must always look to something greater than himself, be it a deity, or a king, or a myth. To believe that the world is just as we find it, with nothing of the numinous at its heart; that is intolerable. It simply throws the fact of our own mortality in our faces, and Man cannot bear too much reality, to quote Eliot.' Then he stops. 'Bless me, my dear, I've started to lecture you. Do forgive me.'

'That's all right.'

I like it when a grown-up talks to me like an equal, like a real person. It does not happen much.

'I know Pie is only a doll, but I love her, and she...'. I hesitate. 'She makes things better. So even if she is not a real person, I am glad she is here. It's like that, isn't it?'

Jack raises his eyebrows. 'My dear, you have it in a nutshell.'

'So, there is no God, but people feel better believing in Him.'

'Which would be a fine thing,' Jack says, 'if only they would let everyone else believe or not believe in peace. Belief leads to religion, and there we have the start of all the trouble.' He laughs. 'I am so glad Tollers is not here, my girl; you would have him spitting smoke by now.'

'Well, I don't care what people believe. I just want to be left alone,' I say.

'And I say Amen to that,' Jack replies gravely.

We come to a halt outside the windows of the Randolph. There is a Christmas tree inside, all lit with candles, and very well dressed people are taking tea, and waiters are moving back and forth with starched collars and silver trays. I rub my cold nose, and stare.

'That is not to say there is not beauty in belief,' Jack says quietly. 'The story has a power all to itself. And I for one love a good Christmas carol.'

We walk on. Somehow, looking in at all the people snug in the Randolph has made me feel colder, and though I don't much care about Christmas, I can't help feel that I am missing something, and I hug Pie close and bury my cold nose in her hair. Luca's people around the fire in the forest were out in the cold too, but they were together, like a family. I wish I had that. I wish the Turks had left us alone and we were all still together in the beautiful city by the sea.

'I had a brother once,' I tell Jack. It just spills out of me. 'He was tall, and dark haired, and he would throw me up in the air and catch me again, and he had big dark eyes. But he went away with the army to fight the Turks, and never came back. That was before we had to leave our home. I remember, though I was very small – just a baby really. Perhaps he is still alive somewhere. Perhaps he is even looking for us now. Father thinks I have forgotten him, but I never will.

'He gave me Pie, before he left. He was in his uniform. I remember – he looked so smart. She came in a box lined with pink tissue paper.'

We walk along in silence up St Giles, and Jack sets his

big hand on the back of my neck for a moment. In a thick voice, he says, 'You are a brave girl, Anna. As brave as anyone I have ever met.'

I cannot think why Jack should consider me brave, but I am enormously pleased by his words. And I cannot figure why I suddenly blurted out all that about my brother. Perhaps it was the sight of the warm people in the Randolph taking tea. It reminded me of the drawing room of the old house, and Nikos – that was my brother's name – standing stiff and tall before the mantelpiece, all in khaki, and with a big grin on his face.

We come to Walton Street, and the snow is quite thick now, and it is no longer the kind of day where I want to play at snowballs and run around in it. The snowman on the corner looks dingy and lost and has slumped to one side like a cripple. I feel sorry for him.

Jack kneels down in the snow beside me and takes me by the arms, staring into my face. I can smell the beer on his breath.

'Anna, if ever you are in trouble, or you are just in need of a friend, then you must come to Magdalen, and leave a message in the porter's lodge for Professor Lewis. Will you remember that now?'

I nod, wide-eyed.

'Do not let them fob you off or hunt you out. Stand your ground like I know you can, and tell them to find me.'

'I will, Jack.'

To my surprise, he hugs me.

'If there is a God, then I am sure that He is looking down on you my dear,' he says into my ear. He stands up again. 'I will leave you here. I don't want your father to entertain the notion that I spend my days promenading around the streets with little girls, intriguing though they might be.' He grins, and holds out his hand.

'Merry Christmas, Anna.'

'Merry Christmas Jack,' I say firmly, shaking it.

He lifts his hat to me, then turns on his heel and walks away followed by the ribbon of his pipe smoke, a faint blue trail in the falling snow.

9

THERE IS A storm that night, a great noisy wind that leaps up through the streets and whips the snow into a thrashing fog in which the gaslights are mere orange flickers, and the roads empty of traffic and people, and there is a great blow-down of soot from our chimney which sends it all over the front room, like black snow. We try to clean it up, Father and I, but after an hour he throws down his duster in disgust and we step down into the basement to make tea over the spirit stove and huddle in the lamplight with blankets over our shoulders. Above us, the tall old house groans and creaks in the wind, until I almost imagine it is swaying. It is like being in the hold of a ship while the masts and sails are battered overhead, and the sea swirls in great waves about the hull.

I hear a small, repetitive banging from far upstairs, and almost I think I must be imagining it, because Father appears not to notice. He sips his tea without much relish and scans yesterday's paper, while I read about E. Nesbit's sand-fairy, and wished I lived by the sea again where I could perhaps find one on some hot summer's day and persuade it to grant me wishes.

The basement has windows below pavement level, and we both look up at the sound of running feet, and an explosion of shouting outside. I see shadows flicker past in the snow and the gaslight, and the shouting seems awfully fierce. Father raises his face from the paper. 'What the Devil?'

We climb up the stairs and he opens the front door, holding me back with his free hand. As soon as the door is opened the wind seizes it, and wrenches it back, and in comes a freezing blast of snow and bitter air. Father swears in Greek and drops his blanket to grapple with the door, and I can hear the shouting outside, farther away now, and I peep out around the doorway, squinting into the snow.

Shapes and shadows, disappearing down the street towards the canal. The shouting fades away. Father pulls me back inside, glares out at the empty street, and growls, 'Drunken louts,' then slams the door shut again.

HE TUCKS ME up in bed later, which he has not done for a long time, and sits by my bedside fiddling with the candle for a while. I think perhaps he is going to read me a story, or better yet, tell me one – the way he used to tell me tales of Troy and the gods of Olympos, and make them come alive in the quiet room until I could almost picture the tall walls, the windy plain, and the hosts of warriors with their chariots and brazen shields and long spears.

But he sits there saying nothing, looking very gaunt in

the candlelight. His eyes have sunk into his head, and for a horrible second it seems almost that he has been transformed into an old, old man. Priam, mourning his dead Hector. I have never seen him look so worn and worried.

He takes my hand. 'Anna, do you remember your real name?'

I shake my head, and feel like my ears have pricked up like a cat's.

'I changed it when we came to England, the better to fit in. Nothing makes an Englishman's lip curl faster than a foreign moniker, believe me.

'Our right and true surname is Sphrantzes. You must remember that. We come from an old, proud family. Georgios Sphrantzes, my namesake, was the best friend of the last Emperor of Constantinople, Constantine himself. He was there at the fall of the city, and escaped afterwards, but lost everything in the sack. He ended his days a monk, and wrote the story of the great siege, and his sons who survived continued the fight in the Peloponnese until that, too, fell. Then they moved to our city, and there they lived and their line prospered and continued under the rule of the Turks. And that is us, our family, Anna.

He smiles, and is so far away as he does that I am almost afraid to touch him.

'They were not all bad, the Ottomans. I used to go hunting with Rahmi Bey, the Governor, and he was a good and decent man. We all lived in harmony for years, Greeks and Turks and Jews and Copts and all manner of faiths and peoples. There was tolerance. There was peace. But the War changed things. All the old friendships were lost, and our world came down in blood and fire, and it is utterly destroyed now.' He clasps his hands together as if praying. 'I tell you this that you should not entirely forget who you are.'

He bends and picks up one of my shoes from the floor by the bed. Shreds of damp newspaper are sticking out of it. He stares at it.

'England may be our home, but we will always have that difference about us, you and I.'

I am so surprised I cannot speak. But confused too. Father is always telling me that we are English now, and that our life is here. This does not sound like him. It sounds like an old, lost man looking back on a life that is over. I reach out and take his hand.

'I know, Pa,' I say. Perhaps I do. I do not mind being different so much, but I feel neither Greek nor English really. I am somewhere in between.

He smiles at me, and rises, before bending to kiss me on the forehead.

'You were always a sharp one,' he says. 'What are you reading?'

'*Five Children and It.*'

'Again? I will leave the candle with you so you can read on for a while, but don't forget to blow it out.'

He straightens, and listens to the storm that is blowing about the roof of the house. 'I am going downstairs now. I have some papers to look through.'

'Be careful on the stairs, Pa.'

'I will. And I told you to call me *Father*, did I not?'

'I like calling you *Pa*. But it isn't genteel, is it?'

'Not really. But we'll keep it between us and God. Good night Anna.'

He leaves the room, shutting the door behind him, and I hear him clump down the creaking stairs in the dark while the wind howls about the walls.

It is the middle of the night, the longest night, and I wake up in the dark with the wind still roaring and buffeting us like a drunken giant wanting in. There is that banging again, far above. I hug Pie close to me and listen to it, and will it to go away but it does not. And suddenly there is a different sound which brings me bolt upright in bed – the shriek of smashing glass.

I sit there in the dark, breathing hard, clutching Pie. I am sure I know what it is – the open skylight in the attic has broken again. It is that which has been banging all night in the wind.

I lie back down, and the banging still goes on, like a patient man with a hammer grimly striking the roof again and again. I wonder if Pa can hear it, but as it goes on and on, I am sure he is not in his bedroom, but has fallen asleep down in his study as he does so often these days.

At last I can bear it no longer. I fumble on the bedside table for the matches and strike one, then light up the candle.

'Jack called me brave,' I tell Pie. 'And I would not be much of an explorer if I was too frightened to climb up into that stupid attic.'

Pie looks at me with her black glass eyes.

'There's nothing up there but the wind, Pie. I will pile up some boxes and close that skylight, and even though it's broken, at least that dratted banging will stop.'

I sit there in the warm bed. I think of Pa's story, and can't help but be amazed by it. I am Anna Sphrantzes, and my family were friends with the last Emperor of Constantinople. It is so grand that it makes up my mind for me.

'You can come with me, and I'll show you how silly it is to be spooked by an open window, Pie.'

With that, I jump out of bed before I can think any more on it, and pull on my old woodsmoke-smelling coat. I fumble in the pocket for my knife, but it is not there any more. I search all the pockets, and scan the floor and the bedside table, and even the wardrobe, but it is nowhere to be seen.

'Bah,' I say. 'Who needs one anyway?'

The slippers I own are down at heel and floppy, so I go barefoot, the candle-holder in one hand and Pie in the other. I can see my breath in the room, and my toes are very unhappy about the cold floor, but I am above such things. Before I leave my bedroom though, I dart back and put the box of matches in my pocket.

I creep out on the landing. The house is wholly dark, and the wind is so loud it hides the sound of my feet on the creaking stairs as I make my way up to the third floor. I am so glad that I have Pie with me, and I kiss her as we go up, shivering a little and wishing I had thought of putting on my shoes, but they are still wet from the snow, and besides, it does not seem right to be doing that in the middle of the night – and if I had a dressing gown I would be wearing that instead of my old coat.

'It will soon be Christmas, Pie,' I whisper to her. 'Perhaps we will go to the Greek Church this year and hear them singing. And think of all the bells going on Christmas Day, how fine it will sound.'

The third floor is like another world, shrouded and mysterious and hidden. The white sheets that cover the furniture loom up one after another in the deserted rooms, and in the candlelight they look more than ever like creatures crouched and sleeping, and I pad forwards as quietly as I can, as though I am afraid of waking them, but at least the carpet is warmer on my bare feet.

I pull back a shutter and look out one of the tall windows. The street below is white as a tablecloth, and the snow is hurtling in clouds through the gaslight and the wind rattles the sash and when I set my hand against the glass I can feel the air push at it as though there is something invisible outside which wants in. For a moment, it feels as though I am the last person left awake and walking in the world, and it is all rather eerie.

I find myself wishing that adventures happened more in the bright light of summer, in a field, or by a bright river with the sun beaming down. But I suppose, as Jack says, they tend to be inconvenient things.

He called me brave, and so I cannot be afraid.

The cabinet is still pulled aside, and I can see the marks of my knife scored across the hidden door, as though something had been clawing at it. I set down the candle and grasp the latch and the brass is icy to the touch, and I can feel the air moving around the cracks in the door, as chill as winter in a graveyard. But I have been here before in the dark, and I know what to expect.

'Stuff and nonsense,' I mutter as I tug the door towards me. It grates and grinds as it did before and the candlelight flutters.

Now the wind seems louder, as though a layer of the

house has been stripped away and I am climbing into the bones of it. I go up the narrow, steep stairs feeling the old wood under my toes, and I wince as a little splinter pricks my sole.

'*Nil desperandum*,' I say to Pie. 'Don't give up the ship.'

It is so loud as I push open the top door into the attic itself, and the air is freezing, and the storm seems almost to be in the room with me. It feels more like outside than inside, and I stand one foot upon the other as the candle flame flaps and gutters, and I have to put down Pie to shield it with my palm. The rafters creak and groan, and as I stand there I hear the click and grind of the slates moving above as the wind frets at them.

And the smell is stronger than before, despite the air moving in the attic. It reminds me of wet dog, but is more powerful. I look up with a start as the skylight bangs again, and the candlelight catches the glint of broken glass in it and on the floor below.

The attic is a place apart, barely part of the house at all. It is an afterthought, a forgotten space. But it is no longer dead and still and silent. Tonight it seems shuddering and alive and somehow fierce, and the shadows of the candlelight are mad and leaping as sea waves in a storm.

I look down at Pie, and have nothing to say. My breath seems awfully heavy in my throat. I walk forward, and realise suddenly how stupid I am being. What of it if the skylight bangs all night? What is that to me? But I am here now, and I will not turn back.

I walk slowly across the creaking floor and feel the grit and dust under my feet, and find a place to set down the candle where the air will not whip out the flame. Then

I straighten to look around, to find something to stand upon.

And deep in the blackness of the corner, I see two lights blink, silver-green. Like those of a cat, but much bigger.

And there is a low growl in the dark, a sound which seems to reach deep into my bones and shake the marrow of them.

I stand there as though I have been turned to stone, and nothing will move or work. It feels like the whole world has squeezed down into this darkness, and I am caught in it like a wasp in jam. I hear a tiny whine, like that of a rusty hinge, and it is coming out of my mouth.

Oh Christos. I do believe in you, I do believe in you. I do, I do, I do.

The lights wink out, and the growl comes again, but now it is more of a grunt, and something big is moving in the shadow beyond the candlelight and I would give anything in life to be able to move myself, to turn and run back to the door, but I cannot turn around. I cannot even blink. And I think to myself; this is Midwinter. This is the longest night, and the greatest dark, and now I know why the Romani wanted me out of the wood, and I know what it was I saw in the trees. It is the same thing which is in the attic with me now.

10

INTO THE LIGHT it crawls, like the thing in the poem which is slouching towards Bethlehem. I can see it now, and it lifts up its massive head and looks straight at me, and the eyes are huge and round and they seem one moment green, and the next yellow, and there is the wet shine of teeth, such big teeth they are.

Finally I manage one step backwards, and then another, as stiff as though I had strings attached. There is a scream in me, shrieking out as loud as can be, but it is only in my head, and my throat has closed it down into that rusty whine.

And I hear it say, '*Wait*.'

I want my Pa here, and I want my Mama, and my lost brother Nikos with rifle and bayonet; but I am wholly alone, and Pie is lying on her back with her eyes closed, as if she does not want to see what comes next.

The thing raises one limb, and it has pale fingers – a hand – and it is palm up. And there is an arm, a perfectly

137

normal arm, and then a shoulder, and the head dips and comes up again, and it is smaller, but still covered in black hair, and even as I watch and the candle fights the wind in the attic and the storm does all its screaming outside, I see that it is a face, a real, proper face that is turned towards me now, and the face is one I know.

It is that of Luca, the gypsy boy, and there is blood on it.

He has no clothes on, and his body is very white except where a line of black hair trails down his spine from the nape of his neck. He coughs, a human sound, and spits blood into the dust.

'Don't go,' he whispers, and it sounds as though his mouth is full of glass.

My heart slows a little, and seems less likely to thump its way out of my throat. I look at the candle, then glance back at Pie, and finally make myself stare at him again as if my eyes need a second chance to take it all in.

He is shuddering, and I can see the muscles sliding under his white skin in cords and bunches. He levers himself up, and I want to look away, but can't now, and he sits in the attic in front of me hugging his knees, still shivering, and I see that he is covered in scratches and bruises, and one eye is swollen, and there is blood leaking slowly out of his nose and it is drying black around his mouth.

'What are you doing here?' I ask him.

'Hiding.'

'From whom?'

'The Roadmen. Have you a blanket?'

'No. How did you get in?'

'The skylight... I'm freezing.'

'I should call the police.'

'Don't – please don't, girlie.'

'You're... you're nothing more than a burglar.'

'I'm more than that, and you knows it.' He grinds his teeth to stop them chattering. 'Don't look at me. I got no clothes on.'

I can feel the heat rise in my face. 'You're in my house.'

'Don't mean you got to stare at me so. T'ain't decent. Is there nothing I can wear in these here boxes?'

'Look for yourself. I'm not going near you.'

'I won't hurt you.'

'You better not, or you'll be in big trouble.'

'I'm already in big trouble, girl.'

'My name is Anna!'

'So it is.' He stands up, and totters like someone who is drunk or exhausted, and begins fumbling in the old boxes that litter the attic. I look away, but something about him catches my eye, and as he turns his back I see that he has a tail, an honest-to goodness hairless little tail some six inches long sticking out at the base of his backbone, nestled in black fur.

I take off my coat and throw it at him.

'Those old clothes are covered in mould. Here. Take this and cover yourself up.'

'Thankee.' He wraps the coat about him and sinks to his knees once more. He touches his face as though it is someone else's and stares at the blood on his fingers, wincing.

Now it is I who am shivering. I sidle backwards and pick up Pie and hug her close, and am completely at a loss. But at least now it is a boy I am talking to, and not the horrible toothed thing with the burning eyes. It was here a moment ago; I saw it and I know it was real, and yet it cannot be.

'What are you?' I ask him in a low voice.

He looks at me with big, dark eyes, as human as my own. He seems a lot younger now than he did in the forest.

'I'm Romani, or kin to 'em, like you knows.' He looks away, wipes his nose with the sleeve of my coat. 'All right. I'm a skinchanger.'

'What's that?'

'It's what you just saw. I changes my skin every now and again, 'specially on nights of moon. I becomes the beast you saw.'

'Have you eaten someone?' I ask him, awed despite myself.

'I ain't eaten no-one. And we don't want to hurt no-one either, me and mine. But we got to fight back when others is a hunting of us. That's just plain sense.'

'You're a wolf in... in boy's clothing. That's what you are.'

'I suppose.'

'Who's hunting you?'

'I told you: the Roadmen.'

'Who are they?'

'You're a curious one, and no mistake.'

'This is my home. I'll ask all the questions I please.'

He licks his teeth. 'Fair enough.'

There is a silence. I am barely even aware of the wind outside now, so strange and enormous is the knowledge I have uncovered. Fairytales are true. The wolf is big and bad and I am talking to him right here and now. I start to shiver again. There are so many things I want to know that they crowd out my mouth.

'Just let me stay here a while, is all I ask. I'll be no trouble,' Luca says.

'Where is Queenie, and Jaelle and the rest? Are they here in the city now?'

He stares at me a moment, and then shakes his head. 'I'm on my own.' He runs his tongue over his teeth again, as though they are strange and new to him. 'I came down to... to the river, and they caught me there and sought to make an end of me, so I ran any ways I could, and ended up crossing the railway and the canal both, and they was close on my heels so I took to the rooftops. And I knew where you live, see, and... I knew the skylight was open. And in I climbed.'

'And in you climbed,' I say, amazed. I think of the shouting in the street Pa and I heard earlier.

'You wouldn't have a bite to eat on you by any chance?' Luca asks. 'I'm fair famished.'

'Don't you eat sheep and lambs and things when you're the wolf?'

'Ain't no lambs near here, girl.'

'We have bread and cheese, and tea,' I say.

'Can you bring me some? When you changes back, it fair takes it out of you. I feel as though my belly is cleaving to my backbone.'

I wonder what time it is, and think of all the long stairs down to the basement kitchen.

'You are a nuisance,' I say to him.

'I'm right sorry for that. I just need to rest up a while, and see out the night. The Roadmen are still out there somewheres, and I ain't no match for 'em when I'm like this.'

'All right then. But don't make a noise. It will take me a while.'

'Much obliged, Anna.'

I turn to go, pleased to hear him say my name, but as I do something occurs to me.

'Have you been here before?' I am thinking of the peculiar smell the attic has always had, and the open skylight.

'Not me,' Luca says. 'Not lately.'

'Huumph,' I say, and take the candle. 'You'll be in the dark.'

'Bless you, girl, I got no fear of the dark.'

Of course he hasn't. Because he is the fear in the dark, the monster under the bed. Luca is a thing out of stories, and he is here in my house wearing my coat. If that is not an adventure then I do not know what is.

THE WIND HIDES my footsteps on the stairs, and there is no longer anything to fear in the shadows beyond the candlelight. I grab a blanket off my bed, slip on my wet shoes, and in the basement I fold a loaf and a wedge of cheddar into the blanket and fill a jug of water. What with the food, the jug, the candle, and Pie, I am fairly warm and bothered by the time I climb back up into the attic again, and I am gone so long I wonder if Luca will be gone too by the time I get back, and if the attic will be its old self again, empty of marvels, and I will wake up from a sleepwalk with the night black and stormy and normal.

But he is still there. I catch his eye at the back of the attic, that green-yellow gleam which is so unnerving. I am perfectly composed however as I wrap myself in the blanket and set out the food for him.

He crawls forward – his face is swelling fast – and we sit

cross-legged with the candle and the jug between us while he gnaws on the cheese and bites off chunks of yesterday's loaf.

He looks up, mouth full, still chewing, and mutters 'Thankee kindly,' as I watch him eat. When he drinks from the jug the water trickles down over his chin and he is as noisy as a dog lapping from its bowl.

'Now you have to answer my questions,' I tell him.

There is blood on the cheese as he sets it down in the dust, and his face is black with it, smeared like jam.

'You sure you wants to know what I have to tell?' He asks. 'Could be you'd sleep better knowing nothing.'

'That's for me to decide,' I tell him.

He rubs his mouth. 'Awright then. Ask away.'

'Who are the Roadmen?'

He frowns, and for a second his face turns ugly. 'They's our enemies. Not all the time, but mostly. They wanders the country like we do, but they ain't kin to one another like we are. They got Chapters in every town in Albion and Albu, and in old Erui too, as well as in Gaul across the sea.

'They's wandering men mostly – tramps – but they ain't your average beggar. The Roadmen have been walking all the long and narrow ways of the world since the Great Stones was raised. They danced to the sun before the coming of the Christ-man, and on Midsummer's eve they dance to it still. I've heard 'em called many things. Queenie reckons they was the same manner of folk as us once, long ages ago. Druids, witches, or whatever you care to name it.

'Now we walk the same roads – but me and mine, we

dance to the moon, and this time o' year is ours – same as Midsummer is their time for feasting and whatnot. We is like two sides of a coin. They are the light; we's the shadow.'

'And they are hunting you.'

'They hunts us when they take a mind to, and when they have the numbers. It takes some sand to chase a skinchanger under the moon, and blood is spilled more often than not.'

'What about Fat Bert and his friends?'

Luca drops his eyes and pushes the cheese through the dust with his fingertip.

'They was just regular tramps. I was travelling with them a while, to meet up with the family. I been walking alone all over the old country in the west, but we tries to gather together for the Long Night.

'I should be with them now, up in the woods. No Roadman will go near a forest this night. But they caught me in the open, by running water where we is weakest, and so they laid chase on me, and steered me from the woods to the city. They are strong here. This is an old place o' theirn.'

'You make them sound like some kind of secret society.'

'That they are. In ages gone by they ruled the land, and the people in it. It was the Roadmen who carved the white horse on the hills, for the horse is their beast as the wolf is ourn. Wayland was their king, back in the time before time. It was he as first made the black iron, and they used that against us. They carry mistletoe, and hawthorn sprays too, and so ye shall know them. A mistletoe berry is sure poison to one of us.'

Something like a snarl flits across his face.

'Tramps and gypsies – that's what people call us all, but you folk got no idea of who we really is, or the ways o' the Old World – not no more. The Roadmen, they was warriors and priests back when the land was young, and they do not forget that.'

He shrugs. 'Queenie could tell you more of the history of it.'

'She said you came from Egypt,' I say, fascinated.

'So we did. We was the black dog that watched over the kings. Our folk were the guards who kept the doors of the tombs. But when the Christ-man came into the world we was cast out, and went a wandering. And the doors stand open with no-one to watch over them now.

'That's what I was told as a nipper, anyways.' Luca seems uncomfortable. 'Like as not it's all just story and such. But we are such as we are, and so are the Roadmen, and there ain't no denying that.' He looks at me. 'Once you know all this, there ain't no way to unknow it, girl. Queenie says you have the Old Blood in you, else I would not be telling you this, not for no hunk of bread and cheese leastways.'

'The Old Blood?'

'Our blood runs in many a one who don't know it. Your folk is from the Old World; even I can see it in your face.'

I am rather pleased by this, as though I have suddenly found myself to be a character in a wondrous story. And here in the old attic on the longest night of the year, it does not seem fanciful at all. Not after I have seen a beast turn into a boy before my own eyes. Anything could be true now. Anything at all.

And I feel as though the world has suddenly grown much

larger around me, full of mysteries I had not even guessed at. It is alarming and thrilling at the same time. Not like finding a Psammead in the sand, but nearly as good.

'Are you all like this, all the Romani?' I ask him.

'Not likely!' He snorts. 'No. And we ain't Romani – it's just what we is called by those as knows no better. And as for skinchanging...' He squirms a little. 'There's only a dwindling few as has the Black Change left in us. Job is another. It was he you saw that night I walked you out of the wood.

'Some has it a little, and can hear the beasts speak and see in the dark and smell out the stink of life. But most are normal folk, not much different 'n you. The skinchangers walk alone, most of the year, but this is our night. Before I came east to the city, it had been nigh on five moons since I laid eyes on old Queenie.' He lowers his eyes. ''Tis a lonesome life at times, tramping the roads, working here and there.

'I'm good with beasts. I know the working of them. I can plough a furrow straight as a plumb-line, and swing a scythe with the best of them. But when the moon rises full, I got to move on.'

'Why?'

''Tis hard to fight the Change, when the moon is up, when it's full and sometimes when it's new. I can come back from it, if I tries hard enough, but when it comes upon me, it's like... ' He colours and stops.

'Like what?'

'Like needing to piss. Like you are bursting full and there ain't nothing you can do about it but let it out. There, now ain't I genteel?' He scowls.

'I'm not some silly girl who will have a fit of giggles because you say the word *piss*,' I tell him crossly. 'Didn't I just see your bare bum and... and the other bits, and I never said a word.'

'Well...' He gathers my coat more closely about his middle and looks down as if to check nothing is hanging out. 'Well, there's no decency to be had.'

'Oh, stuff. So what do you want to do now? Will you change back into the wolf and jump out the skylight again?'

He shakes his head. 'I'm done with that until the sun sets again. T'ain't like turning on a tap.' He rubs his eye. It is swelling shut.

'Did they beat you badly?' It occurs to me that Luca must be in pain. He keeps touching his bloody face and makes small, writhing twists with his shoulders.

'They landed a few on me, I'll not deny it. Hawthorn sticks. But I gave one a bite he'll not forget.'

'Does that –' I dredge up memories of old stories. 'Does that mean he'll become like you, because you bit him?'

Luca snorts. 'No. Doesn't work like that. Truth to tell, I don't know how it works, or how my kind are made to be. We just are.'

'Would you eat someone, if you got the chance?' I ask him, and I pull Pie close to my chest.

Luca grins. 'Depends on how tasty they was.'

'Now you're making fun of me.'

'Am I?' Luca asks. His face sobers and he looks positively grim for a second. 'Girlie, I am right grateful to you for taking me in and the grub and all, but you don't want to be more deep in matters that are not your business than you have a need to be. None of the Roadmen saw me slip in here, and come dawn I'll make sure none see me slip out, either.

'If they think that a normal person is helping a skinchanger, they'll not take it too well. This fight is supposed to be between them and us, the folk of the Old World. And we don't drag no-one else into it if we can help it; that's the way things have always been.

'I wasn't looking to meet anyone up here in this attic, just needed someplace to lie low for a while is all. Best you forget you ever saw me.'

'I'm not afraid of a bunch of tramps.'

Luca shakes his head wearily. 'Ain't you been listening to anything I just told you? These ain't just tramps or beggars. And if you get in their books, there's nowhere you can go to be free of them. They have ears in the ditches and eyes in the water, it is said.'

'I'll call the police on them,' I tell him.

'Some of them are the police,' Luca sighs. 'This world ain't what it seems, Anna.' He reaches for the cheese, blows the dust off it and starts chewing again.

We sit like that for what seems a long time, while the wind howls in the rafters and the skylight keeps up its infernal banging.

'I'll get you some clothes out of the hamper,' I say at last. 'Pa doesn't send out the laundry more than once a fortnight. It'll be days before he misses anything. I can get you a shirt and some trousers, and socks I suppose.'

'I'm fine barefoot,' Luca tells me. 'But I am obliged to you.'

'There's nine inches of snow outside!'

He shrugs. 'I seen worse.'

I study him. His face is triangular, the nose long, the eyebrows thick above deep-hollowed eyes – a severe face, for a boy. There is no scrap of spare flesh on him – in fact he looks more gaunt than Pa. And his mop of hair looks as though it has never seen a brush. His nails are black-lined, and his knuckles seem too big for his hands. For all that, he looks more or less like a normal person, no more fearsome or strange than the children who throw names and stones at me down by the canal.

'Would you hurt me, if you were the wolf?' I ask him.

He stops eating, and stares at the floorboards.

'Most likely not. I still know things, when I'm in the beast's skin. I still can puzzle out what I'm at, and who is who and what is what – that's how I knew to come here. But it can't be relied upon wholly. There's times the beast takes over all the way, and I just ain't there no more, and it is just an animal. When that happens, no-one is safe from it.

'Job's been teaching me how to keep my own eyes when the Change comes, how to keep a rein on it, and turn back if I have a bad need to. The turning back is hard. Takes it out of me. I can't do it every time.'

'I'm glad you did this time.'

He smiles. 'There weren't no other thing to do. If I hadn't, you'd have screamed the house down, no doubt.'

'I would not!'

He studies me, and nods. 'Maybe not then. You are a rare plucked 'un, I can see that, and you nothing but a little nipper too.'

'I'll be twelve in a week!' I say hotly. 'How old are you?'

Luca raises his eyebrows. 'Bless you girl, I ain't right sure. I know I saw fourteen, but it's been a while since that.'

'How can you not know your age?'

'We thinks different, you and me. I sees time go by in moons and seasons more than years. I reckon I must be fifteen, or maybe a season more – two maybe. I don't know.'

'Will you be moving on again, now that Midwinter is over?'

'Most like. We'll head south when the year's turned, to the Old Chalk Road. There's many as gathers there, up on the Downs. We gots to keep on the move, our folk, or the peelers and the do-gooders start to creep around us like flies on honey. Seems they can't bear to see folk live their lives by their own rules. That's the nature o' the world.

'We gathers on the old high castle on the Downs. Used to be, there was a truce o' sorts in that place, for a while. Tis the Roadmen's sacred spot – but before that, it was sacred to us all. No-one wants to fight on ground such as that, 'tis holy earth.

'But when we leaves it, we all go our own ways again, and scatter to every corner o' the kingdom. That's the way it has been since there was men to move the stones and make the old roads.

'Queenie says everything gets smaller by the year. One day, there'll be nowhere to wander at all, no woods to light a fire in, just streets and highways full of motors and acres of houses like little boxes. One day, even the great stone rings will be cast down and built over, and there won't be nothing left of the Old World but memory.

'I hope I don't live to see that day, but if Queenie says it's comin', then it must be so. She has the Sight, and can look ahead of us sometimes, and see things as they are going to be.'

'I should hate to see that too,' I say.

'Why would you care?'

'I like the trees and the woods and the open country just like you do. I may not sleep out in them and eat rabbit, but I don't want to see the cities cover everything.'

Luca lies down on the dusty floorboards and pulls my coat close about him.

'I'm tired. Might be I'll sleep a while.'

'You don't have to leave in the morning, not first thing. No-one ever comes up here. I can bring you breakfast.'

'Don't you got no school to go to in the morning?'

'I don't go to school. Miss Hawcross comes and teaches me here in the house. And if the snow is still bad in the morning she will be late, and Pa is asleep in his study, and he always rises late when that happens.'

I cannot imagine that Luca is comfortable in this freezing room with nothing but my threadbare old coat, even though his eyes are closing already.

'Here,' I say, and give him my blanket.

He smiles, and wraps it around his feet and legs.

'I'll go get you some of Pa's clothes now,' I say, looking at the candle. There is not much life left in it.

'Mmmph,' he grunts, eyes closed.

'Will I see you in the morning?'

'Not likely,' he murmurs. 'Best not.'

'Luca, I want to go to Wytham Wood again, and talk to Queenie and sit with you all. I want to hear more of the stories. I'm not afraid. Luca?'

He is snoring quietly.

I pick up the candle, which is little more than a leaf of light in a pool of creamy wax. Then I turn and tiptoe out of the attic, the skylight still banging out above me, and the wind hurling itself at the roof like a thing demented. At the bottom of the steps, I push the cabinet back against the hidden door. It will remain my secret alone.

It is the Longest Night, the turning of the year, and it feels as though the storm is transforming the world around me with every gust of wind.

11

Something has changed. I wake up late in the morning – I know it is late by the mere fact that there is daylight in the room, peeping round the drapes. For weeks now I have been getting up in the dark.

The wind has dropped, but the house is not at peace. There are voices downstairs, and as I lie there I hear the front door open and close.

It is snug and warm in the bed with Pie next to me, and I have to try and run over yesterday in my mind again. The pub, and talking to Jack and Mr Ronald, and then Luca in the attic.

A day to remember. If only all days could be as interesting as that.

It is very late, and no-one has woken me up. Usually Pa comes in and out of a morning and sees that I wash my face and get dressed in time for my lessons. I suppose Miss Hawcross has cried off due to the snow, and I am to have a lovely, toasty lie-in.

Luca will be back in the woods by now, I suppose. I shall go up later in the day and check, just to be sure. Right now, no matter what I said in the night, I am quite glad that I am here in bed with Pie and not sitting on the cold forest floor in the snow.

Footsteps coming up the stairs. I am dozing off again... It must be Pa, come to wake me at last. I remember what he told me the night before, about our family, and that sends me to wondering in that delicious half-asleep way where all things are possible. I hope he will tell me more. I hope it cheers him up to think how grand our ancestors were.

There is a tiny knock on the door, not like Pa at all. Before I say anything, it is opened, and I am startled to see Miss Hawcross standing there. Her face is white except for a red nose, and she is still wearing her hat.

There is someone else behind her on the landing, because she turns to look back at them, and then nods.

'My dear,' she says, coming into the room, 'I looked in on you earlier and you were fast asleep.' She is kneading her hands together as if washing them, and her eyes are red-rimmed. She has been crying. I sit up in bed.

'But you have to get up now, Anna. You have to be very brave.'

Is it Luca? Have they found him? I say nothing, but stare at her, and hug Pie close.

She sits down on the bed beside me and tries to take my hand, but I won't let go of Pie. She is trying to say something, but seems to be struggling with the words. Finally, she just blurts it out.

'Anna, your father is dead.'

Her eyes are watery, and her fingers are very cold as she sets them on mine.

'No he's not,' I say, and rub my eyes, sure I am not quite awake. 'Don't be silly.'

'I'm so sorry my dear.' She tries to lean in and hug me but I back away until I am at the headboard.

'He's not dead. He tucked me in last night. He told me my real name. You're wrong.'

'I wish I was. It was I who found him this morning.' She gives a little hiccup, and her voice takes on a tone I have never heard before. 'The front door was ajar, the hall full of snow, and he was in his study. There is no mistake. Anna, you have to get up and get dressed now.'

There is a horrible hanging moment when I feel as though someone has silently slapped me across the face.

'You're lying!' I spit at her, and smack away her hand. 'He's alive – he's alive! My father is not dead – he's just downstairs – and you're lying to me! Why would you say such a thing?'

A tall dark shape enters the room behind her. It is a policeman. He has his helmet under his arm and a handlebar moustache and a silver chain and brass buttons.

'Now young lady. You must get a hold of yourself. I don't want to be seeing no hysterics. Miss Hawcross here will get you dressed, and then you must come downstairs and let us ask you a few questions.'

I stare up at him. The police are here in our house. A policeman is standing here in my room.

Then it must be true.

It cannot be true. I look back at Miss Hawcross.

'No,' I say, very quietly.

And this time when she takes me in her arms I do not fight, but bury my face in her big soft bosom, and smell her perfume, and feel the hard edge of her brooch on my cheek.

'I don't understand.'

I want to go back a few minutes, just a few minutes. To that moment before the door was opened. I want to have that second again, and keep it, and stay there in the warm bed with my father alive down below and the world all strange and exciting, but in its place. Everything as it was.

I want to stay in that part of the passing morning when everything was all right, and I am only a child I suppose, but I know right here and now that will never happen again, and I shall never have that feeling again.

THERE IS ANOTHER policeman downstairs. The hall is tracked with footprints and melting snow. Standing in it is Matthew Bristol, and he tips his bowler at me and looks me up and down with a smirk on his sharp-edged face. He has not waxed his moustache and it looks like a wet mouse on his upper lip.

Another man comes out of Pa's study, so that the hallway seems very crowded. He is wearing a pale trench-coat and is smoking a cigarette.

'This is her?' He sets a hand on my shoulder with the cigarette burning in it.

'I want to see my father,' I say.

'All in good time – Anna, isn't it? I have to ask you a few things Anna.'

I try to dart round the door but the other policeman catches me and holds me back.

'Don't let her in there, Brough,' the trench-coated man says. 'It won't do her any good.'

'I want to see Pa!' I yell, and I struggle, but the policeman has me held fast. 'There, there lass,' he says quietly. 'Do as the Inspector says, and we'll all be better off.'

'No,' I say, and I can hear the break in my voice, but I will not cry, not in front of all these strangers, and especially not in front of Mr Bristol, who looks positively bored and is not even pretending to be sorry, and I want to kick him for it.

'Let's go down into the kitchen,' the trench-coated man says, and the big policeman hands me to Miss Hawcross whose hands fasten onto my shoulders like chilled claws, and she steers me down the stairs to the basement. It is icy cold down there, and I can see my breath in front of me, and they make me sit at the big table where once I sat and had tea and talked to Elsie and Mrs Bramley, back in days that already seem impossibly distant.

The Inspector lights a second cigarette from the first and tosses the butt into the sink and then thrusts his hands into his pockets and puffs out grey smoke and looks at me, while Miss Hawcross holds one of my hands and strokes my hair. At least she has stopped blubbering now. I don't want to see her tears. It is hard enough looking after my own.

'Miss Francis,' the Inspector says, 'did you hear anything odd last night? People coming or going – the sounds of an argument perhaps?' He picks a speck of tobacco off his lower lip.

I shake my head, wondering even as I do if Luca has anything to do with this, or the Roadmen he told me about.

'It was blowing a gale last night. You can't hear much

from her room when it's like that,' Miss Hawcross says. I wish she would stop stroking my hair.

'The door was not forced,' the Inspector goes on. 'Was your father expecting visitors? I know that he has a lot of them, due to his... activities.'

'He's really dead,' I say slowly, as if I have to test out the words.

'I'm afraid so my dear. And it is my job to fathom out how it happened.'

I look at him. 'Did someone kill him?'

'It looks that way, Anna.'

'Was it the Turks?'

'What?' he looks at once interested and bewildered.

'They killed everyone else. Perhaps they came here to finish the job.'

'Turks?' He steps forward, but Miss Hawcross raises her hand from my head.

'It's not what you think. Her family Inspector, back in Greece in the early twenties...'

'Ah, yes, of course. So you said. But that is an angle we shall have to look into. This so-called committee, and the things he got up to in London –'

'Not in front of the child,' Miss Hawcross snaps.

'So you heard nothing untoward last night, Anna?' the Inspector asks me, ignoring her. He really is quite rude.

'Nothing. I was asleep.'

'Still, it's only up a couple of flights of stairs,' he says, looking hard at me.

I stroke Pie's hair. 'I was asleep.'

He sighs. 'Very well then. No witnesses. This is a nasty turn of affairs and no mistake.'

'I want to see him,' I say.

'I'm afraid that won't be possible just yet.'

I look at Miss Hawcross, and I am fighting the tears, and I don't want to let them go, not in front of everyone. It comes out as a cracked little whisper.

'Please. Let me see him.'

She looks at the Inspector. 'Let her.'

'I've no wish to be giving a little girl nightmares, Miss.'

'Not seeing can be worse than the sight of it,' she says. And I know as clear as day that she is thinking of her own lost soldier at that moment, and how she never saw him buried.

The Inspector stands there. He takes his cigarette out of his mouth and looks at it.

'Simkins.'

'Yes sir.'

'Let the girl into the study. One minute, mind. And make sure she doesn't touch anything.'

'Yes sir.'

HE IS LYING on the floor, on his back. The study is snowed over with papers, books torn off the shelves, drawers hanging out of the desk. There is a broken glass lying, and the whisky bottle is on its side, empty.

His eyes are closed, and so I will never look into them again. His face is peaceful, almost surprised, and one arm is flung out as though he is pointing at the window.

He is lying in a small muddled pool of blood which has soaked into the papers littering the floor. I cannot see where it is coming from at first, until I make out the wound in the side of his chest, the darkening of the waistcoat there. It was a knife did this. A knife killed my father.

And I think of Fat Bert on Port Meadow, and Luca flinging the knife away with the blood on it, black in the moonlight, and all these things seem to whirl together in my mind like horses on a merry-go-round. Perhaps the Romani boy did this, and if that is so, then it is all my fault.

I reach out and touch Pa's hand. It is cold and horribly solid, as though it is an effigy lying there, not the flesh and blood of my father at all. I cannot believe that the eyes will not open and he will not get up off the floor and dust himself down and check his pocket-watch.

The watch is gone, the fob hanging loose from his waistcoat. They robbed him then.

I tug on the chain, but at once the policeman behind me barks, 'Don't be touching that now, girl. That's evidence that is.'

Miss Hawcross takes my shoulders again – why will she not let me alone? She tries to move me away from Pa, but I fight her, and stay on my knees beside him.

'Why?' I ask.

There is another voice in the room, a hateful one.

'Keep a close eye there, constable. He owed me six weeks in back rent, he did, though he wasn't short of a few bob – all those weekends gallivanting round London with his trollops. If there's any cash left in here, I have a claim to it – I'm owed. I want that set down fair and square.'

It is Matthew Bristol, the landlord. He is rubbing a finger along his moustache as if petting it.

'No-one is touching nothing,' the policeman growls. 'This is a murder we have here, Mr Bristol.'

'All the same –'

'When the estate is wound up, you'll get what you're owed out of it, I'm sure. Now kindly step out of the room sir.'

Bristol backs away round the door, bristling. The policeman adjusts his helmet and whispers, '*Tosspot*.'

'That's enough now Anna,' Miss Hawcross says to me. 'Say your goodbyes, and come with me.'

I look at Pa one last time. I think of the day Mama was taken away, the day we stood on the burning quay with everyone wailing and dying around us. All that, he survived, only to lie here like this on a floor in Oxford, on a snowy Monday morning.

How pointless, all of it. I wish he and I had died that day too, in our own country, in the middle of family and people we knew.

I wish I was dead. If there is a God, then he has a heaven, and all the people I loved are in it together now, and they have left me alone down here on earth.

'*Herete*,' I say to Pa, remembering that word from an age and a world ago. Then I let Miss Hawcross tug me to my feet, and out the door.

DAYS PASS, AND they are at once agonising and slow, and a mere blur.

They take Pa away in a black van with double doors at the back, and the police go over the house, but they do not find the way into the attic.

Things are kicked over and left to lie, and there is wet on all the floors with the feet coming and going, and the fire is never lit, and at night Miss Hawcross stays in the box-room across the landing and she makes sandwiches and tea for everyone, but I cannot touch any of it. I spend most of my time curled up in bed with Pie, staring at the white light beyond the windows.

The snow melts slowly, and Christmas comes and goes without anyone noticing or caring. I lie in bed and listen to the bells of Oxford ringing out as though nothing has changed, as if the world is all the same.

Men in top hats and black coats swoop in and out with papers under their arms, one with pince-nez spectacles who looks me over as though I were a dog in a pet shop. I catch phrases here and there as they conduct conversations on the landing.

'Tragic, absolutely tragic.'

'Well, he made no provision...'

'The gambling ate it all up.'

'And then there were the women.'

'A foreigner. He made a decent fist at being an Englishman, but these Mediterranean types you know –'

'Yes, completely untrustworthy.'

'The committee funds...'

'All gone, every farthing. If he hadn't been nobbled he would have done the deed himself. He was an inch away from having his own collar felt.'

'The blackguard. And the child is nothing more than a pauper now.'

'Yes. Tragic. Absolutely tragic...'

I cannot make sense of them and I do not even try. There is only me and Pie in the world now, and everything else means nothing, counts for nothing.

12

I MANAGE TO sneak up to the attic one afternoon when Miss Hawcross has popped out to do some shopping. With the daylight, it does not seem strange and menacing at all, just a dim, dusty space full of junk.

I find my old coat lying there with a crust of brown blood on the sleeve. The cheese is gnawed down to the rind, and there are mouse droppings around it. I look up at the skylight and wonder where Luca is right this minute, and if he ever thinks of me. I could have given him more clothes, even some shoes. Pa will never miss them now.

I do not believe Luca had a hand in Pa's death. But I do not know if the world he revealed to me had any part of it either. What he said to me of the Roadmen keeps coming back, like the endless scratch of a gramophone record which has finished but is still spinning. And I do not trust the police, either.

And as for Matthew Bristol, I should like to stab him myself.

THE LOWER ROOMS are being cleared out bit by bit. We did not possess much, Pa and I, but such as there was is being pawned by Miss Hawcross on my behalf. She has given me half a crown. The rest, she says, goes on expenses. Food, lamp-oil, coal. I could not care any less. I still have Pie, and a few treasured books in my room, and I cannot imagine wanting much else. With Pa gone, it all seems rather silly, worrying about pennies and shillings. But I suppose these things are important. Because the pennies and shillings will decide what happens to me in the end.

Once the police and the coroner finish their examinations, they come to the conclusion that Pa had been stabbed to death in the early hours of the 22nd December by person or persons unknown. How clever of them.

The murder weapon was not found, and though the study had been ransacked, very little was deemed missing except for a Breguet pocket-watch.

The investigation will go on, of course, and the police will keep the file open. But there seems little more to add. Little that truly matters. I know that I should feel the need for justice, for revenge, but I do not. Pa's death seems like the end of some unfinished business which began long ago, in another country.

WE BURY HIM in St Sepulchre's Cemetery on Walton Street. There is Miss Hawcross and me and a few of the old Greeks there to see him laid in the ground. It is a plain plank coffin, and he has no headstone because there is no money to pay for one. I remember from somewhere that there should be a flower on the coffin, and I pull away from Miss Hawcross as the priest is mumbling out the words over it and the gravediggers stand by with their caps in their fists.

'"Man is born unto trouble, as the sparks fly upwards..."'

There is nothing blossoming in the graveyard, which is Midwinter-bare. But in one sheltered corner I catch a glimpse of scarlet, and in the hedge there is a holly tree, heavy with berries. I break off a spray, the leaves scoring my hands red, and set it on Pa's coffin just as the priest finally finishes.

And I feel that, more than anything, is goodbye, and I have to hide my face in my hands while Miss Hawcross grips my shoulder.

The gravediggers lower the coffin down with ropes, and then cover the open grave with a tarpaulin. As I wipe my eyes I hear them tell Miss Hawcross that there is an old tramp to be laid in on top of him that afternoon. The Sepulchre is full to bursting, they say, and the paupers, they are stacked four deep.

Pa was buried like an Englishman, but an English beggar. There is nothing Greek about it at all. The Priest is Anglican, and keeps blowing his nose, and he wears mittens against the cold.

I cannot believe that my father is in a box, and that they put him in the ground and left him there. It seems the most callous thing.

Those Committee members who have turned up do so with grim and angry faces. I catch them looking at me over the grave, and can't understand why they seem so hostile.

When Miss Hawcross tries to talk to them most turn their backs on her at once and walk away. It makes me wonder why they turned up at all. Only Mrs Gallianikos meets my eyes, and she smiles a little, and when she is leaving she touches me on the arm and says something in Greek I do not understand, but to Miss Hawcross she is as frosty as the morning.

I think Pa did something wrong before he died. Maybe it was his investments – he would talk about them from time to time as though they were vegetables in a garden. They would be thriving and blooming all the time. I was not entirely sure what that meant, but we still lived on bread and dripping for a week of every month, and it seems even to me that something was wrong about that.

I think he may have mislaid some of the money that the Committee entrusted him with, and they cannot forgive him for it. That is why the Greeks would not let us have the service at their church. He should have stayed there the night before the funeral, with the coffin open so everyone could see his face and say goodbye. The *Trisagion service*, they call it.

But instead he ended up in the pauper's corner of a country which was not his own, with the black ground stone-hard in the frost, and not a patch of blue to be seen in the sky above.

BACK AT THE house, I go up to my room at once; for Mr Bristol is here, sitting in the front room as if he owns the place – well, I suppose he does – but it seems he is here nearly all the time now.

He and Miss Hawcross have taken to sitting in the front room, which is the only place a fire is ever lit, and they talk endlessly together, and once or twice the Inspector in the trench-coat has joined them. Because the file is still open I suppose. Whatever he has to say, it is nothing which has reached me. I talk more to Pie than anyone else, and if they had caught Pa's murderer, I'm sure they would let me know.

The strange thing is that I don't greatly care. It as if my head has been wrapped in black wool, and everything is at a distance. After Pa's funeral I feel like something inside me has changed, changed in quite a huge way. It began with meeting the Romani in the wood, and placing the holly on the coffin set the seal upon it. But I cannot say what it is.

I do have this sense of premonition. The world has been turned upside down, but the turning has not finished yet. New Year is coming, and I cannot help but feel that with the new decade everything I have known will melt away.

They are discussing me, down in that front room. I will be twelve in a few days, but I am still a child to them, and so they close the door on me and the murmuring goes on behind it.

I go and sit in the study when that happens, and look at the bare shelves where Pa had his books, and the empty tobacco jar – even his pipes are gone. I set my hand on the bare boards where he lay – they took the carpet away – and I try so hard to imagine him walking through the door. He would have Mr Bristol out on his ear in a second, and would bark an order at Miss Hawcross which would leave her fluttering like a frightened pigeon.

And I cry, when I know they are not watching and cannot hear me. It is all right to cry when your father dies. It is not childish at all. I bite my own arm so I do not make too much noise, and hug Pie until she creaks.

IT IS NOT right or genteel to eavesdrop, but no-one tells me what is right and wrong any more and I have decided that gentility is not for me. So when I hear the voices in the front room rise louder I cross the hall quietly, raise a finger to my lips at Pie, and carefully lay my ear against the door.

'– out by the end of the month.' It is Mr Bristol. I can just imagine his sharp-angled face, and the way his pale eyes turn into slits under his bowler when he is agitated.

'This is charity now, nothing less, and charity is not something that sits well with me when I am doling it out to the thieves that robbed me. Near two months' rent I am owed, Miss Hawcross, and the house is sitting empty when I could have half a dozen lodgers in it. It's nonsensical, is what it is. The girl must go. I give her until New Year.'

'Surely you could let her have just one room Mr Bristol,' Miss Hawcross says, so quiet I have to strain to make out the words.

'That won't work. She's a child. She can't stay here on her own. There's no-one to look after her, and I know you have done your bit too, more than anyone maybe. But you got a job to keep too Miss Hawcross, and I know for a fact he didn't pay you since halfway through November. Charity, that's what it is, and it isn't our place. The girl is not our responsibility. You'll back me up here, Inspector.'

A new voice. It is the policeman in the trench-coat. I can smell his cigarette through the door.

'She's a ward of the state, legally speaking Mr Bristol. We've been able to trace no living relatives, and the Greek community here have washed their hands of the matter. Francis took them to the cleaners. First there was the pyramid scheme, then the shares in the steamship company that never was. He had them eating out of his hand – apparently he was quite the entrepreneur on his native heath, but his luck turned bad the last year or two. The girl has nothing coming to her but debts and writs.'

'What will happen to her?' Miss Hawcross asks.

'She's not of an age to enter domestic service. She'll go to Headington Workhouse. At fourteen she can begin proper employment, so it'll only be for a couple of years.'

'The workhouse!' Miss Hawcross exclaims, and the word itself makes me feel cold and sick.

'Unless you want to take her in. You know her better than anyone.'

'I... I can't Inspector. My circumstances will not allow it. I live with my sister and her husband. The house is chock-full already.'

'Well, there you are then. The workhouse is not so bad – you can put all those Oliver Twist ideas out of your head. I know the Master, Guy Weatherforce. He is a hard man, but fair, and his wife, the Matron, she's a good woman. It'll do the girl good to mix with other children. From what I hear, she's been alone in this house most of her life.'

'She has an insolent manner I never cared for,' Mr Bristol says. 'Probably got it from the father. The pair of them put on such airs and graces, you would think they were royalty.'

'We've been making enquiries in London,' the Inspector says. 'It seems George Francis was once a wealthy and influential man, before the fall of Smyrna. He had friends in all sorts of places, but they have withered on the vine. He banged on their doors too loud and too long it seems. The Colonial Office stopped hearing from him over a year ago. He had been trying for years to get some kind of compensation for the Greeks, but he was rebuffed at every turn, and he had, as you say Mr Bristol, a rather high-handed manner at times.

'My theory is, he gave it up as hopeless, and began living high on the Committee funds. On top of that, he owed money to people in the City, not regular businessmen or banks you understand, but an underclass of moneylenders.'

'Bloody Jews I expect,' Bristol snorts.

'A murky business indeed. In any case,' the Inspector goes on, 'I would not be surprised if that were the cause of his demise. You do not cross those men and expect to get away with it.' There is a clink of glasses.

'The poor girl,' Miss Hawcross says.

'A stint in the workhouse will do her good,' Bristol declares. 'Rub off some of the sharp edges. Pride comes before a fall, Miss Hawcross. That's in the Bible, that is.'

'Shall I tell her, Inspector?' Miss Hawcross asks.

'Best not. There's no telling what she'll do. She's a pretty little thing, but I sense a wildness in her.'

'That'll be the dago blood,' Bristol says. 'I'll bet it was dagos as did him in. They all carry knives, that sort. They'll have your eye out as soon as look at you. Not like an Englishman, who will look you square in the face and give you his fist.'

'I'll talk to Weatherforce,' the Inspector says, ignoring him. 'Come New Year, we'll get her out of here and into the Receiving Ward. You'll still be able to visit her on Sundays, Miss Hawcross. It's not a prison.'

'Can she leave of her own volition?'

'Not until she comes of age.'

'Then it will be a prison for her, Inspector. She's a bright, educated girl, and whatever her father did, she is not of the class that commonly makes up such establishments.'

'Needs must, when the Devil drives, Miss Hawcross,' the Inspector says. 'I agree with Mr Bristol. The girl has had an eccentric upbringing. By all accounts, she has been indulged. It may do her a positive good to mix with her social inferiors and have some discipline applied. I was something of a tearaway itself, until the Army knocked it out of me.'

I hear a hand thump a table in triumph, and glasses jumping.

'There you are Miss Hawcross,' Bristol exclaims, 'As prettily put as you like. It will be the making of her, I'm sure. Now stop your worrying and let us put it to the good Inspector how we are to get the monies that are still due to us. There has to be something left. A crook like George Francis will have something put by in a corner, and I says we have first claim to it, for doing right by his brat of a daughter if nothing else.'

I step away from the door and quietly walk up the hall; all the while the thoughts are running about my head like those merry-go-round horses again. What I know of workhouses I have read in stories. *Please sir, can I have some more, sir?*

And I know that the last bits and pieces of the world I knew are not to be here much longer.

I AM NOT a thief, even if they think my father is one. But the Inspector was quite right about the Devil driving and all that. Pa used to say that too.

The things I heard them say have suddenly cleared away all the black wool from my head, and I feel I am thinking clearly again for the first time since Miss Hawcross came into my room that horrible morning.

Pa is gone, buried in an English graveyard. The other Greeks have disowned us, and those grown-ups who still have anything to do with me are going to sell me into servitude. Or something like.

I could go to Jack, the way he said I should if I were in trouble, but when there are policemen involved, and a murder, and all these legal things, I feel sure that turning up on his doorstep would do nothing but start a whole other kind of trouble, and I do not want to bring that on him.

The law says I am a child and the State must look after me. But I can look after myself. Or at the very least, I have to try.

I NEVER USED to take much notice of the moon before, but now at night I find myself studying it, and gauging just how fat or thin it is. I wonder if the sight of it right now still brings the thing in Luca to the boil, and lets it out like steam from a whistling kettle. It's odd, how the way you see things changes after a time. The men in the black hats and suits frighten me more than the wolf in the attic, and the attic itself seems like a hideaway, somewhere safe from the plans the world is hatching for me. Luca does not fear the dark, because he is a creature of it. I should like to be that way too, because what goes on in the daylight world fills me with dread.

IN THE NEXT two days the house becomes like... like Toad Hall filled with weasels. Mr Bristol has admitted a series of new lodgers.

There is Mr Bartholomew, a skinny long-necked young man who takes Pa's old bedroom and makes thin porridge in the morning for breakfast and burns the bottom of the pot. He works in the University Press on Walton Street, and always has ink on his fingers.

Then there is Mr Beeswick. He is a carter with thick forearms and a big pot-belly who sets up in Pa's study and smokes cheroots and stinks out the house with them. He wears a leather apron to work, and hangs it up in the hall, and smells of horse, which I rather like. But I don't like the way he watches me as I make up my meals in the basement. And he was drunk the first night in the house and tapped his knee and told me to sit on it and I told him to go to the Devil, and he slapped his thick thigh and said I was a little spitfire.

Miss Hawcross has been in and out. She was chaffed by Mr Beeswick and looked as though she should like to slap him – I would love to have seen that. But I sense that she is already washing her hands of me, and she has an odd guilty play on her face every time I speak to her. She is Mr Bristol's creature now I think. Perhaps the two of them truly believe that Pa has secreted money about the house, like he was Captain Flint. But if he had, surely he would have used some of it to pay the rent and buy proper food at the end of the month?

In any case, there are no more lessons – so I don't suppose I will ever learn which king came after fat Henry, and I do not greatly care. Miss Hawcross has given me another half crown, and told me not to let on, as if I needed telling.

I wish I knew what had happened to Pa's watch. It had a photograph under the lid which he never let me look at, but I am sure it was of my mother. And now there is a murderer walking about Oxford with it in his pocket, who knows what she looked like better than I do.

I HAVE ALMOST twelve shillings saved up now, and I have been taking other items out of the kitchen when no-one is looking, and under my bed I have built up quite a little kit-bag of useful things. At night when the house is finally quiet, I lay them all out on a blanket. There is small hurricane lantern which I found in the garden shed. The glass is cracked, but it works well enough, and I have the oil for it too.

Matches. A tin water bottle and enamel mug. A knife and fork, and some soap and a facecloth and spare socks. The stubs of some old candles, a pencil, Pa's scarf and wool cap. And a small cloth bag into which I cram cheese and biscuits and a tin of bully beef.

It is like preparing for an expedition. I wonder what Shackleton or Scott would have included. It would be nice to have a revolver, for polar bears and other things. I miss my little knife.

I try loading in some books too, but they take up too much room in the little knapsack which holds everything. Once I have wrapped the lantern in a blanket and strapped it to the outside and have crammed everything else inside, the bag is chock-full. There is nothing for it but to leave the books behind, but I will not abandon them for Mr Bristol to pawn or paw over. They have been my friends in a way, as much as Pie has been. So I take all of them up to the attic and store them in a box.

It is a strange feeling to stand over them in that forgotten place, to see my things put away up there as so many others were in the years gone by. In some ways it feels almost like another kind of funeral.

I promise myself that I will come back for them, but I wonder how many of the people who lived in the house thought the same. Perhaps one day another girl will find her way into the attic and come across my books years from now, and wonder who it was who put them there. My name is on the fly-leaf of every one. No doubt the girl of the future will wonder who Anna Francis was, and whether she ever amounted to anything. The thought is rather horrible. I do not want to be a lost life. I do not want to be forgotten. That is what the workhouse would mean, and I simply will not have it.

It is New Year's Eve, and the 1920s are just about done. This night is my last in the old house where I have lived ever since we fled Greece.

It is a queer feeling to know that. I was five years old the first time Pa and I walked down Moribund Lane, and now

I feel more grown-up than I ever thought I would, though I am barely twelve.

I certainly feel more sensible than some of the people who are laughing and shouting downstairs. Mr Beeswick and Mr Bartholomew have invited some friends of theirs here for the evening, and they are all in Pa's study, drinking. There is a gramophone playing Blue Skies, and then Bye Bye Blackbird, and I stop to listen to the music for a few minutes on the landing.

As I tiptoe down the stairs I am crying. I can't help it and no-one can see me, so I don't suppose it matters. I stand in the hall and listen to them with their big, beery laughter in the study which was always so quiet when Pa was alive, the music crackling out of it now along with rattles of talk. I hitch up my knapsack, hug Pie close, and open the front door.

There are quite a few people walking up and down, and the snow has died back to frozen rinds of blackened slush. It still feels very cold, and I stand on the front step of the house by the open door for a few minutes. Even now, none of this seems quite real. It is not until I close the door quietly behind me and I hear the lock snick into place that I am sure I can walk on, one step at a time.

One step at a time. I wipe my face, and kiss Pie, and the straps of the knapsack feel heavy and good and purposeful on my shoulders. I get a few looks as I tramp down the road towards Walton Street, and I put a brave face on it in case someone should stop me and ask what I am about. That is the problem with being twelve. All the grown-ups think they have a right to know your business.

The music fades, I turn the corner where once Luca saw

me off, and Moribund Lane is behind me, and whatever life I had there is now in the past, as much as is the lost city where I was born. Of all my family, I am the only one left now, and I have to start making a life of my own.

PART TWO
The Roads of England

And the Lord said unto Satan,
Whence comest thou? Then Satan
answered to the Lord, and said
From going to and fro in the earth,
And from walking up and down in it.

Job 1:7

13

THE PUBS ARE busy, and there is piano music plinking out of the Jericho and people have spilled out of the front bar onto the pavement. Someone tugs on my knapsack as I go by, but I wrench free and plod on, head down, ignoring everything they say. *Drunken louts*, I think, and part of me wishes I could see their faces if Luca suddenly appeared as the wolf in their midst. The thought makes me smile, and I feel almost light-hearted as I walk north, then make the familiar turn down Walton Well Road.

Here, it is quieter and there are more patches of snow still clinging to corners and dark nooks. I start to hum Bye Bye Blackbird – it is one of those tunes that gets into your head – and the dark of the old decade's last night on Earth deepens all around me, and the chill seems to seep up out of the shadows which loom under the railway bridge, and I cannot help but feel that I am being watched, though there is not another soul around.

All of Oxford is back in the gaslight and music of New

Year's Eve, and not a person passes me as I continue on to Port Meadow and the wide darkness there, and the sky opens up above me with a few stars burning in and out of the clouds. There is no moon that I can see. But still, the notion that I am being watched, even followed, grows on me until I am turning around in my tracks every hundred yards to look back, sure that there will be a dark shape somewhere behind.

But there is nothing, and no-one is there, so I plough on doggedly, crossing the river at Fiddler's Island and then continuing up the western side of the Thames. The river is going quietly about its business, black in the night. I am in the countryside at last, and in the summer cattle graze here as they do on the common, but they are all gone now, and when I step in one old cow pat it breaks like a dinner plate under my foot, frozen and dry.

The tree-covered hills of Wytham rise up ahead.

THERE IS STILL snow in the wood, wide gouts of it pale in the darkness under the trees. Great banks of bramble and fern, all dead and dry, rise up like walls, and I pick my way in crazy zigzags, always uphill. I pass a clearing on my left, close to where Luca put his hand over my mouth and I felt his fingers against my lips. I touch my own face, remembering that more clearly than the glimpse of the wolf-shape in the dark, and it is that memory which keeps me walking.

I would feel so much better if Luca were here. This is his kingdom, this still, empty wood all heavy with darkness at the end of the old year.

I feel as though I have left something else behind along with the gaslight of the city. Pa once told me that snakes shed their skin every month, and in an odd way I think I may have too. There is a way of looking at things when you are alone in the woods at night. You see more clearly the things at the corner of the eye, and hear all the little crackling noises, the saw of your own breath, even the thumping of your heart. All so clear. It is as though on stepping out of the city an older part of the brain starts to work again. The part that remembers flint and bone and ice.

I keep hoping to see firelight in the night, and hear the drum beating and the singing, but there is only the faint rush of a breeze in the treetops and the infernal rip of briars as they catch on my clothes and knapsack.

And then something brushes against my face and scratches my cheek. I flinch away from it, imagining bats and all sorts of horrid night-creatures. But it is only the hanging spray of a tree.

No – it's not. I take a hold of it and find that I am grasping one of the twig-fashioned stars which the Romani had hung all around their campsite. I pull it free and feel it over in my hands, then look around. There is a little clearing here, and above me the stars are coming and going behind grey shreds of cloud, but still there is no moon.

I stand very still for a long time, my breath a pale cloud in front of my face. I can hear my very joints creaking. Far off, there is the scratching rattle of a pheasant in the night. I have never known a silence feel so lonely.

I can smell the ashes. I step forward until the dead circle of the campfire is at my feet. This is the place where I met Queenie and Luca and Jaelle and the rest, but they are all long gone now. The embers of their fire have been scattered. When I pick one up it breaks apart in my hand, as brittle as biscuit. I realise that I had been so sure of them again, and now that they are not here I am completely at a loss. I stand there in the appalling lonely dark, and do not know what to do.

But I cannot go back.

I take off the knapsack, unroll my blanket, and set about searching for the matches. Everything takes forever in the dark, but finally I get the lantern lit, and the bright glow of it immediately sets up a wall between me and the forest, and Pie sits watching me with the yellow light two circles in her black eyes.

Then I go about the old campsite with the lantern held low to the ground, looking for I know not what. I am rewarded by a neat pile of kindling and firewood stored in a hollow under the brambles, and I pile these up in a pyramid – that is what one must do – and use a splash of lamp-oil to make sure.

My match makes the pyramid of sticks go up with a *woof* like a hoarse old dog, and the rush of warmth is lovely – as bright and heartening as can be. I set up my own little camp, and am soon wrapped in the heavy wool blanket and nibbling on a biscuit with Pie in the crook of my arm. There is nothing better than firelight in a wood, and the flames are as entrancing as the screen in a nickelodeon. I start to feel a little better. Perhaps it will be all right after all.

And then, when I look up from the bright dance of the flames at last, there is a face on the other side of them.

I DON'T MAKE a sound. In the firelight, it seems almost that it is a mask hovering there, hanging in the dark. But the eyes blink, and it smiles, and I see long yellow teeth.

''Tis a cold and darksome night for a little girl to be out alone under the trees of the wood,' it says.

The biscuit turns to coal in my mouth. I cannot say anything. The face moves closer, and there is a spare frame, black and lean as a spider. It sinks on its haunches close to the fire and the flames make a long-eared skull of the face with two silver coins for eyes.

'This is a special place,' it says. 'It is unholy ground, not for the use of just anyone. Is you lost, little girl?'

'No,' I manage at last, and it feels like someone else speaking, calm and clear. 'I came here to find some friends. Queenie and... and the others, but they've moved on.'

It nods. 'Aye, that's what happens with their folk. They sets up for a spell, and then they gets the itch and must put their feet to wandering again. That's their curse. They was made to be like that for the evil deeds they done, way back in the history of the world.'

It raises its head and sniffs the air, and I see the black holes of its nostrils widen and close again almost to slits. It is like a man, but it is not. A withered, sickened man, perhaps, with features that look impossible even in the sinking firelight.

'You going to finish that biscuit?' it asks me suddenly.

I toss the cracker across the fire, and a long hand reaches out and snatches it from the air. It worries the morsel like a dog, and the hand which holds it has black nails.

'My name is Anna Francis,' I say. 'What's yours?'

'You don't need me to tell you my name, girl,' he says with a horrible grin. 'And I know yours already.'

'How do you know it? And who are you?'

'Bless you dear, I have so many names I've forgotten most. I have been gifted with 'em all down the years by those as loves me and those who don't. And as for you, you is the orphan child from the Old World. Your mother is long lost by the shores of an ancient sea, and your father is in a pauper's grave in Sepulchre graveyard.'

I clutch Pie to my chest. There is no warmth in the fire now, and the forest is utterly still above me, as if even the trees have stopped to listen.

'We needs more wood on the fire,' he says, and uncoils. I see him rise up, and he walks into the dark as silent as if he is stepping on velvet. There is a snapping in the blackness, and he returns with a couple of wrist-thick logs. He breaks these in his thin hands as easily as if they were matchsticks, and places them on the campfire. Then he strokes his hand through the flames the same way Queenie once did – as though he is petting a cat – and for a moment the flames flutter up green and blue about his fingers, then rise up in a flare, and in the greater light I can see his ears, as pointed as horns.

'Who are you?' I whisper.

'You don't know?' He laughs, and the sound is like an iron nail being scratched on glass. 'What do they be teaching the young these days? I declare, they think more on machines and formulas than they do on the true knowledge of the world. They blow things up, and calls it progress. They kills one another by the million, and calls it civilization.' He shakes his bony head. 'But you takes a single life, just one, and that is murder most foul, and they will pin you for that, and lay it against you the rest of your life. It hardly seems fair.

'There are men in frock coats and top hats with the blood of the world on their hands, and they eat with silver forks and white napkins every day, and they will give up their last breath in a linen-made bed whilst the ones they sent out to die lie forgotten in the earth, mouldering bones with the poppies fat and red above 'em. Ah, mankind.' He laughs again. 'It's a caution and no mistake.

'The time is coming to an end when you can wander the roads of the world as free and easy as you like, and meet a stranger across firelight. They will fence in the world entire ere they are done, the clever men of this earth, and there will no space left on it for vagabonds, and dreamers... and little lost girls running from their fate...'

He has a smile like the blade of a knife, and his eyes, when he smiles, close to two slots from which the silver light gleams, and the fire has no reflection there.

'You seek Queenie's people you say. Well little Anna, they was here, 'tis true. But they left the night your father died. Now why would that be, you think? Your boy Luca, he came scampering back into this wood as though his tail was afire.'

'You know Luca?' I ask him, and it feels as though my lips are numbing even as I speak.

'I know him and all his folk. For were they not the guardians of the secret doors? I set them there before Abraham thought of slaying Isaac. When Cain killed Abel, I was there. And the skinchangers are the Children of

Cain, who carry still that ancient sin upon them. My dear child, do I not know thee too? And do I not love thee as mine own?'

He begins giggling, a horrible sound which makes my hair bristle like the fur of a cat in a thunderstorm.

'Yea,' he says, and sweeps out one bony arm, 'Are not the least of these precious to me and mine? For I have counted the very hairs on thy head, and I know when even so much as a sparrow falls to earth...'

I feel that the night deepens when he speaks, and the sky is hidden, and in the dark beyond the firelight there are things which were not there before, writhing shadows that are fawning on him.

'How would you change your life, if you could little one?' he asks, very soft. 'What would you have different in the manner of things?'

'I would have my Mama and Pa alive, and my brother Nikos too. I would have us all living in the city by the sea again, and the Turks would never come.'

'Ah.' He raises one white finger. 'That would entail the living of another life. You cannot make such changes while you are still in this one.'

'You asked me.'

'I did.' He wags his head. 'Such simple things, love, and life. And so hard to come by in this world. What price would you pay, to have things that way, little Anna? What would you do, to have that just as you imagine?'

'Anything,' I find myself saying. 'I would do anything for it to be like that again.'

He closes his eyes. '*Anything* is just what it would take my dear. Anything and everything.'

'Who are you?'

He shrugs. 'What's in a name? You do not even admit to your own, Anna Sphrantzes. And your darling mother, she ran from the hills of her birth and forgot hers as quickly as she could. But what she carried in her was passed down. Names change, but in flesh and bone there lies a stain indelible.'

His face becomes still and grave, like that of a sober gargoyle.

'You are marked, little one. Your fate is set. You may run from it for a while, but it will overtake you in the end. It is far less taxing to give in with grace.'

He stands up, a black pole rising with that ivory-pale skull on top of it. '*Suscipiat Dominus sacrificium nostrum.*' He holds out a hand. 'Come with me, child.'

I sit frozen, and hold Pie tight against me. I want to take his hand, to have him lead me from this empty dark wood, and the empty life that is mine now. The world seems vast and cold and without light, and I even think I see kindness in his silver eyes.

But the calm, clear voice inside me which has always been there speaks clear as a ringing bell in my head. And without another thought, I repeat aloud what it is saying.

'I reject you, here, now and always; and I bid you leave this place.'

His face spasms, and his thin lips draw back from long, savage teeth, more fearsome than those of a dog. The silver light flashes out from his eyes, and there is nothing human about that face at all. He steps backwards as though I have struck him, and the white hands fly up as though to scratch the air.

'Witch-spawned bitch!' he snarls, and spittle flies from his mouth and streams down his chin. I see a black tongue stab out, as pointed as that of a lizard.

He opens his arms. The big white hands seem to float in the dark. And he looms up taller – as though his body has lengthened, or left the ground. The white face, the eyes, they glare at me, and I feel my own tongue stick to the roof of my mouth. I cannot look away.

'You dare bid me leave? Well, that is your privilege. Myself, I bid you stay,' he says, and his voice is as the hiss of a serpent.

'Stay here and rattle around in the shattered shell of your sorrowful little life. Like your worthless father, you will walk the roads of this earth until your soul is sick and weary of it, and one day we will meet again, you and I. And you will be on your knees before me, begging for what was freely offered this night.'

Just like that, he is gone. A few brown leaves skitter through the air in a sinking circle. And the night, black though it is, seems lighter, and there is warmth from the light of the fire again.

I WAKE UP in the dawn greyness, shuddering with cold. The fire is a circle of black and grey ash with one or two stubborn little red glows still worming about the embers. My nose is numb, and I rub it, and then my ears. There is a thin frosting of white on the blanket and across the fallen leaves of the campsite.

I think of my warm bed in Moribund Lane and the smell of toast, and sigh.

I do not want to cast aside the blanket and meet the cold of the morning, and there is in my head a queasy image, like the aftertaste of medicine. A vague memory or dream of the night before. Like all dreams, it seems so vivid for a second upon waking, but in moments it falls apart as I wake up properly, and it is gone. There is the unsettling image of a white face floating above the fire, but soon that, too, fades away.

I look around at the empty campsite as the light grows. The twig-stars hang forlorn and forgotten and where the earth is bare it is packed hard and tight as linoleum in the cold. There is nothing for me here. In the unforgiving grey of the winter morning, I begin to see my own foolishness. Perhaps the grown-ups are right. Perhaps I should simply do as I am told, buckle down, and get on with whatever life still has in store for me.

I am thirsty, but the water in my bottle is half frozen. I suck back shards of slush from it, and my teeth tingle with pain. I am hungry, but the thought of the biscuits I have in my bag makes me strangely queasy.

Luca spoke of a place the Romani gathered on the Old Chalk Road. He spoke of the White Horse on the Downs to the south. I remember it as clear as if he were uttering the words here and now. I'm sure I have heard of this place; I may even be able to give it a name, if I think hard enough.

Then that is what I will do. I must go south, to the high downs, to the castle he spoke of. I cannot just give up, not so close from where I started.

I stand up and stretch, then almost at once I bend low again to peer at the ground on the other side of the fire.

I was not alone in the dark. It looks as though the deer were wandering about the campsite as I slept, for dug into the hard cold earth by the embers are their cloven footprints, as though they had watched me with the dying of the fire in the night.

14

I KNOW WHERE south is. Perhaps it has to do with Pa showing me the North Star when I was very young, but I have always had a good head for directions. As I leave the dimness of the wood on the first day of the New Year I know that I am North West of Oxford, and the way I must go is to my right. I wonder if it is very far. Though I slept longer than I ever thought I would, there seems to have been little good in it, and the bad taste of the dreams I had takes a long time to wear away.

The white face, hanging above the fire with shilling-bright eyes. It is all I can recall, but it is enough to make me decide I shall never sleep in Wytham Wood again.

I tramp south, and the sun rises slow and stubborn from out of a great bank of brown cloud over Oxford, and the spires of the city are black against it, like something from a far-off past. I have no idea what time it is, but the world seems so quiet that it might be another century I have woken up in instead of another decade. The quiet road which leads to Botley is deserted, but I would not be surprised if a knight in armour came trotting down it.

Something is moving on it though. As the sun rises higher I see the long straight track more clearly, and up ahead there is a black shape walking along it towards me. In the dim winter light I cannot make out much more, but even as I watch, it goes off the road and disappears into the hedge.

For some reason that unnerves me. I clutch Pie tightly, and my steps slow. I do not want to draw even with the place where the shape disappeared, and I am half ready to take out across the fields myself, straight towards Port Meadow and the Thames again.

And then there is something behind me too. The clopping of a horse's hooves on the road, clear and loud, and the rattling of a cart. I stand there at the side of the road, feeling trapped, and cannot decide whether to go on, to go back, or to plunge into the hedge and hide.

'Whoa there!'

Too late to do anything but stand fast and see what comes. The horse and cart walk slowly up to me. An old grey horse with a white face, and blinkers and a big collar, drawing a two-wheeled wooden cart – and upon it there is a man in a flat cap smoking a pipe. He clicks his tongue a little, the cart trundles past, and he nods at me. He is an oldish man with a drawn face which has been outdoors all its life, and he wears leather leggings and a raggedy corduroy jacket with the elbows out.

He leans back on the reins.

'Have you far to go, lass?' he asks me, over his shoulder.

'Botley,' I say.

He looks down the long and empty road with the dark hedges hemming it in, and speaks around the stem of his pipe.

'Hop on then. I'll save you a step.'

I look at him, unsure, and he turns in his seat and smiles. 'I got me a parcel to pick up at the station. Happen that's where you are headed?'

'It is,' I find myself saying, though I had not thought of it until that moment.

'Well, climb up then. Morning's going by.'

I clamber up beside him without thinking more about it.

'Walk on.' The horse leans into the traces, shakes her head, and we are off. It is much more agreeable sitting up here off the road, and I can see over the hedges now.

'A Happy New Year to thee,' the man says, puffing on his pipe. 'Though it be a cold 'un.'

I say nothing. We pass the point where the black shape disappeared, and there is no gap in the hedge, just the thicket of hawthorn and stumpy ash. I wonder if I imagined it.

'G'won now,' the man says, and slaps the reins on the horse's back. The mare breaks into a trot. The houses of Botley and west Oxford are not much more than a mile ahead.

'Off travellin' are we?' the man asks.

'I'm going to see my aunt in… in' – the name comes to me out of nowhere – 'Uffington.'

'Ah. That's a tidy step for a little lass on her own. But I see you have all with you.' He nods at my knapsack. 'I hopes your mother knows what you're at, out alone at this hour.'

'She knows.'

The man grunts, and leans forward on his knees. 'There's gypsies in them there woods behind 'ee girl. You needs to watch yourself on the road, these days. They had themselves some eggs of mine, not that I begrudge a morsel to hungry folk, but you can't watch 'em close enough.'

We are back in the town now, and the streets are very quiet, but I hear the whistle of a train in the distance.

'They're all nursing a sore head this morning, the city folk,' the man says. 'Last night was the end of a long ten year, and today begins another one.' We sit in silence for a while. A motor car passes us with its headlights burning, but the old mare does not even glance at it.

'Uffington. 'Tis at the foot of the Downs. You'll be taking a train to Swindon then,' the man says.

'Yes.' I had not thought of that before now, but when the man says this, it sounds right.

'I was on a train once. Nasty, smelly things, and noisy too. Easy there you damned fool –' This to the horse, which had snuffled and capered a little as we passed a side-street. I look down it, and there is a man standing there, a tramp wrapped in rags with two eyes bright as marbles in a bearded face. He stands stock still and watches us go by, and I shiver.

We are in Oxford proper again, and there are more motor cars, and people walking up and down muffled against the cold. Normal life seems to have started again, and I can hear the shriek and puff of the trains and see the pale smoke of one hanging over the station. The man steers the horse with clicks of his mouth and little tugs of the reins, and finally brings the cart to a halt in front of the doors. Streams of people pass by.

'Here we are. Safe and sound. I wish thee well lass.'

I hop down from the cart and look up at him. 'Thank you.'

He bends over and offers me his hand. It is huge, and the palm is as hard as wood.

'I'm Gabriel,' he says with a smile. 'I see the train a huffing and a puffing for you, girl. Get thee on it, and don't look back.'

I don't know what to say to him, but nod, and walk away, towards the growing crowd of people which are going in and out of the station doors. When I look back, I see him sat on the cart smoking his pipe, the pale horse standing as still as a figure in a painting. Then I walk through to the ticket office, and he is gone.

THE TRAIN GOES south, and the carriage is half full. People in caps and people in hats and people with parcels on their knees and people yawning and people nodding with sleep, and the sun rising higher beyond the windows and the country going past outside and the taste of acrid coal smoke in my mouth. I cannot remember the last time I was this far from Oxford, and I have Pie and my knapsack on my knee and my ticket in one fist, and my other hand is in my pocket counting out the shillings and pennies I have left.

I half expect to see the black shape of a policeman make his way down the corridor of the compartment. Will they look for me? Do they even know that I have gone? I wonder if the Inspector in the trench-coat will think a runaway orphan worth chasing after.

For a few minutes I sit there with my face turned to the

window and stare out at England passing by, and think of Pa, and let the tears come while no-one can see them.

I wonder if Miss Hawcross is relieved that I am gone. Sometimes I think that she seems as lost as I am in the world. And I feel sorry for all the times I thought mocking things of her and did not attend to her lessons, but sat all sullen and slow while she whacked me with her ruler and tried to make me learn French and algebra, and which queen lost her head. That is all gone now, and I have no need to learn those things anymore, but I do wish I had made more of an effort for her sake.

I wake up from a doze and we are in Swindon already it seems, and I am barely able to leap out of the carriage behind a fat woman with a lot of cases before the whistle is blown and the train is off again in a cloud and a shriek and a volley of puffs. It would all be so much more jolly, this stealing away and traveling the country, if only there was someone to share it with. As it is, there is only Pie and me, and we are getting wry looks from people on the platform.

I walk out of their stares and in the waiting room there is a map on the wall, and lines of roads and railways all over England like the veins in a leaf. I see names there I have heard before, but they are only names with no memory to paint them.

I was on a battleship once, which traveled the high seas all the way from Greece, but the thought of getting across a single English county leaves me bewildered. I feel very small and alone and lost, and I know that I smell as though I have stepped out of a bonfire, and cramps are knuckling at my tummy, hunger I suppose.

Perhaps the people jostling by think I am a gypsy, for I

am all smoke-smudged and ragged, and there are still bits of briar in my hair which I try to tease out when I think no-one is looking.

I had begun to think of myself as English, my Greekness quite gone, but I realize now as the people look at me that I am not and I never was. My very face is different from theirs. No matter how much French I learned or how many kings and queens I memorized, that was always going to be true.

Well, hang them. I have to go east now, out of the towns again and into the open country, the blank spaces on the map that the roads avoid. That is my place now. It will be woods and firelight from here on in, and sleeping on the ground and smelling of woodsmoke.

So I begin walking. As much to get away from things as to get towards them. And it is easier, in a way, to do that, for it means that every step is progress. 'If you do not greatly care where you are going, then it is impossible to be lost,' I tell Pie.

But I am brought up short outside the station all the same, wondering which way to go. As I stand there a well-dressed man goes by, and as he passes he gives me a quick glance, frowns, and then flips a sixpence down on the pavement in front of me before walking on.

I pick it up. So this is what it is to be a beggar.

Well, sixpence is sixpence. I pocket it and walk on.

WHAT A DREARY place. I pass lines of red-brick houses all crammed together, and people hurrying without a word for one another. An omnibus goes past, crowded and bright with an advertisement for Bovril.

Guinness makes you strong. Camp Coffee, drunk by men in kilts. Craven A cigarettes. Pond's cream for a glowing complexion. The world is brown and grey except for the colours on the hoardings. I wonder if Louise Brooks uses Pond's cream. I wonder if she has ever slept on the ground and watched a fire in the night.

The cramps spike up in my middle and make me pause and gasp a little. I wonder if it is something I ate yesterday, but all I remember is nibbling on a biscuit. The mere thought of food makes me feel sick now.

There is coal smoke in the air here, rising from the chimneys in yellow streams. On one wall an ancient ragged poster has a soldier with a huge moustache who is pointing at me. You, it says beneath his glowering face, as though he is accusing me of something.

East is where the sun rises, and while there is no sun to be seen here I know by the sky where it is hidden, and I tramp along with that lighter cloud in my face. I pass factories as I go, waste ground and broken glass and tall chimneys, lorries with flapping canvas tilts, pubs still closed with their windows like blank painted eyes.

A little brown and white dog goes snuffling past me in the gutter, raises his head as I go by and looks at me with the sweetest, most hopeful face; but as I slow he twitches away as if expecting a blow and runs off with his tail down. Another orphan, I suppose. I wonder if I will ever look as frightened and hungry as he does. And I feel a sudden blast of hatred for all the people who walk past him without so much as a glance or a kind word. What a horrible place. How horrible the people. And the pain in my stomach comes and goes in stabbing waves.

I have no time to be sick. There is nothing to do but keep walking.

At last, I leave behind the streets of little houses and the hanging reek of coal smoke. There is open country ahead, on my left flat and wide; on my right the road skirts a series of hills, all joined up and spotted with copses and woods. It travels to the horizon, the high ground, and as I trudge on the sun comes out from under a gravel-grey cloud, and the light falls on my face as if to show me the way.

My spirits lift a little. I see a signpost – Wanborough – and the road takes me up along the side of the ridge, and I am rising with it, and to the north the vastness of the country opens out under the sunlight, patched with woods and villages, all quiet with distance.

Far, far off to the north-east, I can make out the spires and towers of Oxford, just for a moment while the light is clear. I am almost walking back towards it, but it looks so far in the distance as to be a different kingdom entirely, a far place removed by the miles and miles of quiet countryside in between. For a second I am so intensely homesick that I feel almost short of breath.

And the clouds roll over the sun again, greying out the splendid view. I tuck Pie in the breast of my coat, grasp the straps of my pack, and labour up the steepening slopes.

Near the top of the rise there is a crossroads where a road comes down from the hill and then arcs across my path and extends out into the distance, as straight as a ruler's edge. The slope drops off steeply to my left, and there is a scattering of bare trees where the ways meet, and a single, squat stone as tall as a gatepost but much more massive.

And sitting upon the stone is a black shadow, a man. With the light behind him I cannot make out his face until I am closer, and I brace myself to say good day – but a hundred yards from that he leaps easily off the stone and begins walking towards me. And a few yards after that I see it is Luca, and I begin to smile and quicken my pace.

He stops as I draw close, and I see his thin face, and long nose, and he holds up a hand. I am so happy to see something familiar in the world again that I almost break into a run, but the pain poking through my stomach keeps me at a slow walk and I am panting as we come together.

'Here's a fine thing,' he says, and he pats me on the shoulder. 'Off on our holidays, are we?'

I bend over, clenching my eyes shut, trying not to be sick. 'How are you here? How did you know?'

'Bless you girl, everyone is out looking for you. Thank your luck it was me as found you first.'

'Why... why should you be looking for me?'

'Queenie said we must. We knows what happened to your Da. It was the Roadmen did that, she said, though we had been watching the place. They must've got by us, and your Da opened the door to 'em... I'm right sorry, Anna, for what happened. We should have stayed closer.'

'I don't understand.'

'Let me take that sack o' yourn. You look white as a snowdrop.' He peels the knapsack from my back and slings it over one shoulder as lightly as though it were stuffed with cotton wool.

'The Roadmen? Why would they hurt Pa?' I am bewildered, but so glad to lose the weight of the pack.

'Queenie'll tell you. She knows. She had us all out

watching the roads. She read things in the fire, and saw you was meant to be with us. You's got the Old Blood in you, girl – on your mother's side I suspect. I'm here to take you to the camp. We're up on the Old Chalk Road, the Ridgeway. It's a bit of a step, near eight or nine miles. Are you game?'

I manage to smile at him. A great relief runs through me, as welcome as hot chocolate on a cold day. I am not alone, and I am no longer lost. Someone else is here now who knows where to go.

'I'm game. I want to go to Queenie. There's nowhere else now. They were going to put me in the workhouse.'

Luca takes my arm, staring at my face all the while. A flash of anger lights up his eyes. 'Workhouse my arse,' he growls, and his fingers squeeze tight. 'We'll sort you out, Anna. We'll keep you hid from the peelers and the Roadmen. You're to be family now, Queenie says.' He pauses. 'You are special, like. I ain't sure why, but there it is.'

We walk on, but Luca turns me around until we are on the long straight road which is running up the hill. 'Up here,' he says. 'This was laid down by the ancient Romans, this track, and if we follows it up the ridge it leads to the Old Way our folk has been using for time out of mind. One good haul, and then we're up on the high downs, and can look down on the whole world.'

But I feel faint, and now there is a wetness between my legs, a stickiness. I look down, and see there is a thin line of blood running past my knee. My legs buckle, and Luca takes my weight.

'Lord, girl, you're not well.'

'I have to… let me sit down.'

The road is deserted. I reach down, and my hand comes up bloody. I stare at the blood in astonishment and fear. 'Luca, I'm hurt.'

He stares. His mouth opens and closes. 'Let me get you summat for that.' He begins rummaging in the knapsack, and comes up with a woolen sock.

'Here, use this.'

'Luca, I have to see a doctor.' I feel a rising panic. I don't see how I could have hurt myself there, in that place.

'This your first time?'

'What do you mean?'

He puts the sock in my hand. 'All women bleed, with every moon.' His face is reddening. 'It's a normal thing. It means you ain't a little nipper anymore. You is a woman now. Here – soak it up.'

'Soak it up?'

'Use the damn thing, girl.' He stands up and turns away.

I do as he says, tucking the sock inside my knickers. 'Will it stop?'

'Takes a while, a few days.'

'Days?'

'So I hear.' He rubs the back of his neck. 'Didn't no-one ever tell you this?'

'No.'

He shakes his head, looking down at the wide countryside below. 'T'ain't nothing to worry about. It's a womanly thing. Means you're grown up, in a way.'

'How horrible.'

'Don't be looking at me to tell you more. It's not a man's business.' He bends and takes up the knapsack once more, still not looking at me. 'When you're ready, we'll go on.

Queenie and Jaelle can tell you all about it. T'ain't my place...'

He rubs his long nose, and coughs. 'Well?'

I stand up, feeling very odd. I feel even Pie is looking at me differently, or I at her.

'All right then. Perhaps I'll feel better walking.' Irritated, I say, 'You can look at me now.'

He glances back. 'Well and good. Follow me, then.'

'But not too fast.'

He growls a little. 'Aye, right.'

WE SET OFF again, me trailing behind him as we make our way up the side of the ridge. Close-cropped grass, and a cold wind which strengthens as we get to the top. The view opens out even further, but I am not attending anymore. I feel as though my body has somehow betrayed me. More than that, I feel there is a barrier between me and Luca now, as though I have been set down on the other side of an impenetrable dark hedge and there are no gaps in it and never will be again.

We turn off the long straight Roman road, back into the face of the sun, and there is a last, steep slope which has me gasping and bent over.

'This is Fox Hill,' Luca says, not looking back. He sounds positively jaunty, and I envy him his quick, even stride that eats up the slope without obvious effort. I am like a little worn out slug in his wake, and the space widens between us as he strides ahead.

We are at the top at last, and I can see the line of high hills and plateaus extending out to the east for as far as the eye can see. A different world.

This is empty country, not like the Oxfordshire I have known, though I'm no longer sure which county we are in. The wind is cold and raw, and there is nothing to break its path up here. At another time it might be bracing and the view would be worth the chill, but right now I am almost dismayed at how strange England looks to me. I had always thought of it as a country with close horizons, but this is something else entirely. Wide open and vast under the sky. It is a land for wandering sheep, and the riding of horses, and it seems immense even in the grey light of the winter morning.

Luca looks up at the sky, and scans the hills like a jackdaw, quick and sharp. 'We has four hours or a little more 'til dark,' he says. 'I wants us to be up with the others afore then. 'Tis an evil time o' the year to be traveling the Old Roads. All sorts turn up on the track, not just the Romani. The dark turn o' the year brings out all manner of weirdness from the earth and the deep woods, and things that were sleeping wake up, and takes to the hills and the tracks and wanders where they pleases.

'This is the fastest way to go, and there ain't no villages or houses on the way. 'Tis open country, bare and empty, and we is easy seen, up here. We has to set a good pace.'

He looks me in the eye for the first time since offering me the dratted sock.

'You up for this, Anna?'

'Yes. But stop running ahead of me. I'm not going to stare at your back all day.'

He grunts, but gives a half smile. 'Well, then.'

We walk on, side by side this time.

206

THE HIGH RIDGE seems a place taken out of time. To the north, I can make out the roads and villages of the world I know, a vast plain of them. And if I peer to my right I can see the rumpled folds of the hills go down into farmland and trees; but ahead there is only the grass and the stone-grey sky, the earth going up and down in enormous waves and swells, and nothing to measure it or break the spell of its emptiness except a few lonely clumps and dots of trees and the occasionally isolated barn.

I could have loved this place once, when Pa was alive and there was the old house to go back to, and a fire and a bed for the night. But now it only brings home more clearly to me all that I have lost. I feel that I have stepped outside anything that could be normal and ordinary, and the knowledge is not exciting at all. I feel sick and afraid, and I hug Pie to me and kiss her cold face. She is all that I have left now from that other life.

The sky breaks open in a bright blue maze and the cloud shadows shift across the face of the hills, tawny titans racing upon the wind. But the sun is westering, and our shadows are no longer behind us, but in front, and growing longer. I huddle in my coat and fight the pain in my middle and I want to talk to Luca about it, but that would not be right or proper it seems. And I know I am so snail-slow compared to him and I am holding us back, but there seems nothing left in my legs but weight to drag.

'Idstone Hill,' Luca says quietly. 'Won't be long now 'til the Long Barrow.' He glances at the sky. 'That is no place to be when the dark is thickening.' He touches me lightly on the arm. 'You gots to go faster, Anna. We can't be this side o' the Barrow if the light fails.'

'I thought you liked the dark – what have you to be afraid of?' I snap at him.

'There's worst things in the dark than me and mine,' he says. 'At this time o' year, they says the Devil hisself goes up and down the old ways and paths, looking for lost souls to claim.'

'What rot!' I say. But even as I do, I feel a queer kind of sick feeling spread all through me, and I see again a white face hovering over firelight in the night.

15

The sun fades as we travel, and if I watch it for any length of time I can almost see it sinking down the sky. I start walking faster.

'What's the moon doing tonight?' I ask Luca. I have almost forgotten, in the strange rush of the day so far. I know it is important, but the significance of these things is still soaking in. There are train timetables in the world, and Bank holidays. And now there is the moon to wonder after too.

''Tis growing,' Luca says. 'Half full, and a year's-end moon too.' He takes my hand, and I almost jump at the warm touch of his fingers. My own are cold and stiff.

'At this time o' the year, 'tis hard to fathom how it will go with my kind. The urge is there, plain as day, but maybe it can be fought, and maybe not.' He looks at me and smiles. 'That is part o' the fun of it.'

He does not look as though he is having fun. 'How did this come to be?' I ask him.

'It is as it was,' he answers, almost automatically. 'There bain't be no gainsaying it. This is nature, Anna. T'ain't nothing we can do about it.'

'Do you wish it was different?' I ask him.

'Sometimes,' he says shortly. 'But no sense crying over milk as has already been spilt.'

THERE ARE WOODS up ahead on both sides of the track, and as we approach them so Luca's pace slows, and he begins to breathe more quickly, and his hand tightens upon mine. He keeps looking at the sky, and then he tugs me on until I am almost trotting and Pie is bouncing in the folds of my coat. The sun is well down in the sky now, a meagre, miserly sun, January at its selfish worst.

Luca stops in his tracks, looking at it. 'The Long Barrow is up in yonder trees,' he says, and his face has lost its ruddy health. It looks like parchment stretched over bone.

'You has to hang on to me Anna, whatever you see. Don't you be leaving go of my hand. You hear me?'

'I hear you,' I repeat. I catch his fear the way you can catch a yawn. I do not want to see what it is that can make someone like Luca afraid.

We walk on, more slowly now, and Luca is placing his feet on the pale chalk of the track as carefully as a dancer, while I clod alongside him. The evening darkens – I cannot believe how quickly the light seems to sink out of the sky, like wine pouring out of a bottle. And the trees grow close on either side. Beech and birch, and Scots Pine, overhanging the track and deepening the shadow. There is not a bird to be heard, just the faint rush of air in the branches overhead. We are in a wood which is stark and bare, and still it holds the gathering dusk in its grip. And on the left I glimpse something else through the trees, a great dark shape rising up out of the ground. It is a mound set in its own clearing, and surrounded by old beeches that are taller than houses.

I slow as we approach it. 'Keep up,' Luca says in a whisper. But my feet feel heavy, and it is as though there is a great cold stone in my stomach which wants to drag its way down through me to the clay and chalk of the path.

There is a light off in the trees, a flicker of fire by the black bulk of the mound, and as we creep on I am sure I hear the ringing tap of a hammer on metal.

We are level with it now. Fire leaps up in a red flag of flame and shadows are going back and forth in front of it along with the rhythmic tap of the hammer. Something large blocks out the light as completely as a curtain for a second, and I clasp Luca's hand until our bones quake together and feel that I have to stop, that I cannot move another step. But he pulls on me, breathing hard, and something deep and liquid and animal-like comes out of his mouth, a low snarl. I tear my eyes away from the mound and see the light in his, as silver as the moon but washed with green. And his lips have drawn back from his teeth like the face of a frightened dog.

I think I hear a horse whinny, and the stamp of its hooves seem to echo in the very earth below us. I cannot drag my gaze away from the mound and the flicker of fire. The silhouette moves across it again, and it is man-like; but just for a second I am sure I see a rack of antlers on its head.

We stagger on two steps, then three more, and I can feel the weight in my bowels lift a little, but just as we are about to get by I hear a new thing. It is a low sobbing, someone in pain at the side of the track.

And in the trees there I can make out the tumbled outline of a fallen stone, a megalith twice my height. The weeping comes from it, a sound to wrench the heart.

'Luca –' I whisper.

'Walk on.'

''There's someone –'

'Walk on!'

He has my hand in a grip I cannot break, and my arm feels limp as rope as he tugs on it. I crane my head around, searching in the dark. And I think I see someone lying on the ground by the great fallen stone.

No – he is half under it.

As we go by him the sobbing rises to something like a wail, an awful agony. A voice is talking through the sobs, saying things I cannot understand. It rises to a screech, and then bursts into a cackle of mad laughter.

The moment we are past the stone the laughter stops. As does the tapping hammer. It becomes easier to walk on, to stride normally again. It is as though we have managed to wade through a river and are on dry land once more. Luca's harsh breathing begins to ease, and his awful grip on my hand loosens a little.

I look back when we are a hundred yards further on, when the dusk seems lighter and the trees less close. And I see a black shape stark against the pale chalk of the track behind us. It comes out of the trees and then disappears into them again, a worm of black shadow.

The light is gone now and the winter night is full upon us. When you are outside from dawn to dusk the shortness of the daylight is almost frightening. I can see why men reared up the great stones to celebrate the turning of the year and the long slow haul back into the bright seasons.

'What was that?' I ask Luca quietly.

'It was an ancient thing,' he answers, and his voice is as hoarse as though he had been shouting. But his eyes are dark and normal again.

'Some say that the Smith-God hisself lives in the barrow, and they calls that place Wayland's Smithy. There is something there, and it is old as these here hills, and I do not care to go near it.'

'The thing that was crying –'

'You hear the weeping and the laughing on a winter night at the turn o' the year, and sometimes close to Midsummer too. The Smith's apprentice, 'tis said, pinned under a great stone in punishment for slacking at his work.

'Queenie says a great battle was fought here once, on the plain north of White Horse Hill. The last of the old folk who had been here since time began won a bloody fight against the incomers from the east, and they was led by their high king, Arthur, who rode a white horse and had it shod by Wayland hisself before the fighting began. Badon, that battle was called, and it was the last time the old folk of Britain won against the men of the east.'

'King Arthur,' I murmur. It is all too much. I am walking in the dark of a fairy-tale, caught in a strange story that no-one should have to believe is true.

Luca stops and stiffens, and he raises his head to sniff

the air. Then he looks back along the pale track, and his fingers tighten in mine once more.

'We gots to hurry, Anna. There are things awake tonight, things walking on the Downs we have no need to see.'

'I thought I saw –'

'Come on.'

I stagger as he lunges forward at almost a run, my knapsack bouncing on his back.

There is only the pain and the tiredness. They seem to muffle all the marvels of the night. We leave the trees, and the world opens out once more, a huge stretch of downland with the white track snaking across it. And the grey light grows until I can see my way quite easily and I realize the moon has risen and is rising up the sky as swiftly as the sun went down it such a short time before.

I feel a vague but powerful sense of some great prehistoric rhythm, as regular as the tap of the hammer in the barrow. As though the high downs are part of an immense timekeeping device which runs silent and unknown at the heart of an old, forgotten world.

The land rises steeply before us again, and there is a hill ahead on our left with the first stars blinking into life above it.

'Whitehorse Hill,' Luca says. I can see sweat shining on his forehead in the moonlight. 'There's an old castle up on the top, Uffington castle they name it. 'Tis but a bank and a ditch in the grass, made by the peoples who was here before the Romans. All that is sacred ground, to my folk and to the Roadmen too. If we can make it up there, they'll likely leave us be for a while. This is their country, Anna. They set their mark upon it in the old time, carved out the

White Horse before even Arthur fought his battle, back when men worshipped the sun and the moon. And maybe things before even that.'

'I saw a shape,' I say. 'It looked like a man with antlers on his head.'

'Don't speak of it. And pray to your god that it stays where you saw it.' Luca knuckles his eyes. 'We just got to get to the hill, to the old castle. T'ain't far now. Put all else out o' your head.'

'Will Queenie and the others be there?'

'I hopes so. 'Tis a great place to watch the land on all sides. Not a shrew could move upon the grass within a half mile of it without getting seen.'

'Then they can see us coming.'

'That's what I'm hoping.'

Luca stares back down the track.

'There's no-one back there, now,' I say.

'The Roadmen can hide themselves like snipe when they've a need to. And they have beasts as do their bidding. Hawks, and owls by night. Come on. No good standing still.'

The slope steepens again, and when I look down I can see the white sludge of wet chalk has plastered my feet. It is getting colder, and the stars seem ice-bright, while the moon keeps rising silently up the sky and there is not another light to be seen in the world that lies below. As if all of England is empty and deserted and we are in some other era before gaslight and motor-cars and steam trains.

A bank looms on our left, and Luca is frowning now as we plod up the hill to the top. We stand up there on the roof of the world and he helps me up to the top of the dyke and there is nothing there within the turf ramparts except an open, empty space.

'They ain't here,' he says, and he wipes at the sweat on his face again and the light of the moon leaps out of his eyes as he blinks.

He looks south along the ridge which continues from Whitehorse Hill.

'Uffington Down, Kingston Down, Woolstone Down,' he says, as though he were repeating the words of a song. 'They wouldn't go there. There's farms in the valleys below, and too many a coming and a going, even by night.'

He turns. His breath comes out in a hot cloud.

Looking east, the track continues and the land begins to fall again before rising to a lesser height in the distance. There is a black line of what must be woods to the right of the track, down in the dip between the heights.

'Boxing Hare Wood.' Luca exhales, and I see even in the moonlight that his breath is coming and going in a cloud far greater and denser than mine, as though it is puffing out of a steam engine.

'Where are they?' I ask him.

'They didn't stop here after all, or we'd see some sign. There ain't so much as a fire-scar on the grass.' He bends and runs his hands along the turf, like a blind man reading Braille. ''Tis frosting fast. This night will be cold. We has to find them.' He casts about at a crouch, almost on his hands and knees. As he draws away he looks like some beast snuffling on a scent. 'Someone has been here, but they didn't stay long,' he says. 'There's prints of feet. They stopped and looked out a while, if I know anything.'

'Queenie?' I ask.

He shakes his head, and straightens. 'One or two, no more. And they wore boots. 'Tis my guess the Roadmen was here, ahead of us, watching the track. If my folk saw 'em, then they would have gone on down from here.' He points. 'East. Boxing Hare is yonder long wood down in the valley, good for camping. Someone'll be in it, either my folk or the others, but we can't just stroll down and take a look.'

He runs his hands through his hair. 'You'll be safe here. They won't come at you in this place. I'll go take a looksee in the valley, sniff around the wood and see if Queenie is there.'

'You're leaving me? What about the Roadmen?'

'You'll be all right here, Anna. You can bet they know we is somewheres around here already. They been following us all day.'

I hug Pie. 'You're leaving me.'

'Won't be for long. You sit tight and quiet. Don't be leaving the circle, and stay off the track.'

He lopes up the side of the bank and takes off his threadbare coat and tosses it to me. There is steam rising off him, rising from his neck and his bare forearms. He turns and smiles, and the light is burning bright in his eyes and I see his teeth shine, and it seems that his face has changed, become longer, the bones even more pronounced.

'Are you… are you changing?' I ask him.

He says something, but it is not words I know, not words at all, as if the inside of his mouth can no longer make English. Then he bounds down the side of the bank and out of sight.

I scrabble through the stiffening grass and watch him go down the long open slope. He moves incredibly fast, sprinting upright, then in something like a crouch. In the uncertain moonlight I cannot be sure if he is on all fours before he is no more than a black dot on the pale track, speeding away into the night.

I sit there on the lip of the ancient dyke. I think of Achilleos and wily Odysseos, and the monsters they faced and overcame; but there is no comfort now in recalling the old stories Pa told me. They belong to another world, sunlit and hot and shimmering with the din of crickets in the grass, the sound of the sea.

This place is dark and bare and stark and I am shivering under a cold moon and there is not a sound except the wind coursing over the turf and even the streak of a falling star cannot bring it to life. It feels like a hidden place, though it is right here in the belly of England.

Perhaps men know that; perhaps they have always known it without thinking about it, which is why in this crowded little island it has been left alone, the time here measured in some way that is wholly different to the streets and railways and parks and gardens down below. It is not a wilderness; it is the opposite. A place where man has made some connection with the slow beat of the earth's heart, carved his marks all across it in worship and wonder, and then left it alone as the reasons for his own awe have become lost and forgotten.

Stupid thoughts. I hug Pie close, and listen to the sound of nothing in the night.

THE MOON IS high in the sky and I am shuddering with cold. I was asleep, for how long I don't know, but my teeth are chattering and the grass crunches with frost as I reach out for Luca's jacket and pull it tight across my shoulders. Pie's face has dew frozen upon it and my legs are numb below the knee. I try to flex my toes in my galoshes and wonder if I could even stand up. But the cramps in my stomach have bled away, which is something. I think of toast, and the kettle singing, and wish I was back in the tall old house in Jericho, which was never warm but was never as pitiless as this.

Then I hear noise upon the track, and all thoughts of Jericho and the cold are instantly gone, and I do not even shiver as I lie full length on the rime-stiff grass and peek over the edge of the bank.

A familiar noise; the clopping of a horse's hooves and with it the clattering trundle of wheels coming up the hill to the edge of the dyke. I stare. A horse and cart, the animal leaning into the traces as it hauls its way up the hill – and a dark shape upon the seat of the cart, slapping the reins on the horse's rump and clicking the way horsemen do out of the corner of their mouths.

I want to jump up, for I think I know who it is, but I also want to wait until I am sure. Before I move they draw level with me, and at once the shape on the cart reins in.

'Whoa there.'

He turns in his seat, and scans the bank while the pale mare mouths her bit and shakes her ears, her breath coming out in hot clouds full of moonlight.

I want to stand up, but my feet are numb. I want to speak, but something stops me.

A match flares, and I see the face of the man on the seat of the cart as he leans into the flame and sucks it into the bowl of his pipe. It is the farmer, Gabriel, who gave me a lift to Oxford station in the morning that seems already a long time ago.

Before I can make my mouth open, a shadow leaves the grass at the side of the track, not twenty yards away, and strides over to the cart.

'My Lord,' it says.

'Well?' The pipe burns red in its bowl, lighting up Gabriel's face with every draw.

'They are in Boxing Hare Wood, all of them. They have sigils up around.'

'Their watchers?'

'Out wide, but coming in. Watching no longer.'

Gabriel smokes in silence, until his head is wreathed in it. 'Then they know more than we,' he says, and sighs.

'The boy has been abroad, the skinchanger – he passed me on the track below not an hour ago, alone and moving fast.'

'The boy has heart,' Gabriel says. 'I like him. A pity he is what he is. Even on Port Meadow, he stayed his hand until forced.'

'That went awry. We picked the wrong men for the job. We are truly sorry,' the dark figure says.

'Sufficient unto the day is the evil thereof,' Gabriel says, and he puffs on his pipe a while. 'The girl is on this road, that much is sure. I set her on the way myself, guided her steps, and your people followed her past the Long Barrow. I do not quite understand how we lost her...'

'It is my fault, Lord. The barrow was open. The Smith was at work...' The words hang there in the dark.

'I know,' Gabriel says.

'I had to work round it. I lost ground, and followed the boy, but she was no longer with him. They must have split up. She is alone now. She has to be.'

'She is here, brother, upon the Old Road within a scant mile or two of where we stand – you can be sure of that. Alone or no, she will find her way to them – we can be sure of that too, now.'

'The barrow –' the man on foot begins.

'It was open. That is all there is to say.'

'I thought there was something else, Lord.'

'Do not speak of it. Not to me or anyone. To name it is to give life to shadow. Time enough for that.'

The dark figure bows. 'What is it you wish of us?'

'Watch, and wait, for now. I came here as a beater, to flush out the birds, and now it seems they have flown faster than I could wish. The boy was quick off the mark. Watch the road. Mark everything. When the time comes, we will move.'

'How will we know –?'

'I will decide. What happened in Oxford was perhaps inevitable, but it was not our finest hour. There will be no more hasty interventions. We are in our own country now. The crux of the matter is upon us. We must be patient. Do you hear me, brother?'

'Always, Lord.'

Gabriel nods, and the red glow of his pipe bowl lights up his face from below as the breeze catches it.

'I will turn back. The hills are busy enough tonight, and I want to watch at the barrow for a while. This is the lightless dawn of the year, and our powers are not what they might be, whereas they have the strength of the dark and the season within them, and all manner of things are stirring that should be asleep. I want no more blood, brother. Our folk must stand back until the time comes.'

'Some take it hard –'

'They will obey,' Gabriel snaps. 'Mind the road.'

The dark figure at the side of the cart bows deep. Gabriel clucks his tongue and slaps the reins on the back of the horse, then begins guiding the cart back down the hill. It tilts and sways in half-frozen bumps and ruts and begins rattling back into the west. The dark figure watches it go, and then silent as a hunting cat it glides back up the track to the east and cuts across country, disappearing into the quicksilver darkness.

16

'THEY'S THERE ALL right, in Boxing Hare Wood,' Luca says when he returns, panting and grinning like a dog in summer. I can feel the heat coming off him. I think I could almost warm my hands at it.

'Well, that's good,' I say, trying to stop shivering. It is more than cold. It is an ache at the heart.

The kind farmer who let me ride on his cart is one of them...

I am wondering if there is anyone in the world I can truly trust. I am even beginning to ponder if Jack and Mr Ronald are part of some great conspiracy. The utter strangeness of it all would be almost funny, if I were not sitting here in the middle of nothing and nowhere, staring at a boy whom I know to be more than that, right here – in the black heart of a winter night so cold I wonder if Pie's porcelain face might crack.

This is an adventure, I tell myself. More frightening and real than anything I could ever have imagined. Invariably uncomfortable, Jack said. Well, he was speaking the truth about that, at least.

'The Roadmen were here,' I tell Luca. 'They stopped right in front of me. They were following us the whole time.'

His grin closes. 'You sat tight? Did they see you?'

'No. They didn't know I was right by them. I heard them talking, but they didn't see me.'

'Then that's all right,' he replies, very calm. 'Did you not know they watch everything, Anna? They's everywhere. It's all we can do to fox them for an hour or two.' He smiles. 'But I'm back now. You're a right sharp, you are, not a flat at all. Queenie is right – you got our blood in you and no mistake.' And he reaches out a hand and strokes my hair, just for a second. But it makes my blood thunder in my ears.

'We have us a couple more miles to go, that's all, and then you'll be sat down with us, and the fire is going, and there is stew in the embers, and you need worry no more,' he says.

'Luca, why are the Roadmen so set on following me?' I ask him, and I am genuinely puzzled. 'What is it about Pa and me that is so important to all of you?'

He looks at me blankly. 'They harry and hunt us, girl, us and all the Romani. It's been going on for more time than anyone can recall. You're one of us now, so they hunts you too.'

You're one of us now – that warms me. But it is not enough.

'They killed Pa,' I say, and the words drop like stones out of my mouth.

He nods. 'That they did. They have their own secret

ways, the Roadmen, and they don't mind spilling blood when it suits them. Now come, girl. We gots to go.' He half-rises.

'He let them in. He opened the door for them. Like they were someone he knew,' I say stubbornly.

'Most people open a door when it's knocked,' Luca says, impatient now. 'Get up Anna.' He lifts my rucksack. 'It ain't far now girl, and this is no place to linger.'

'What will the Roadmen do to me if they catch me, Luca?'

'Why –' He blinks. 'Why, they are the Roadmen, girl. They hates our kind.'

'Your kind.'

'You is one of us too Anna – don't you listen to me? I swear, that doll o' yourn got more sense than you.'

'Because Queenie says so.'

'Aye, because Queenie says so! She's my ma, and she never speaks false, not to me nohow. If Queenie says I'm to bring you in, then that's what I do.'

My heart falls, a horrible plummet in my chest. 'So that's the only reason you're doing this – because Queenie said so – that's why you're here with me.'

'Yes – no! God rot you girl, we don't got the time for this!'

We clamber up the bank, and Luca stops there for a long time. He takes my hand and sniffs the night air again, and his head swings back and forth like a hound seeking scent.

'Aye, they been here all right,' and his tone is hushed. 'Him o' the pale horse was on this very spot. Why'd you not tell me?'

'You didn't ask,' I hiss back. 'I thought the Roadmen were all tramps and the like. How was I to know?'

He sways back and forth like there was a wind on him. 'He was here his very self. Girl, you scare me. This ain't right. There is summat else to all this; I knows not what.'

'What do you mean?'

'Just you hang on to me and get ready to run if you needs to.'

'But Luca... he said –'

We are off, and Luca is dragging me in his wake once more.

WE RUN TEARING through the moonlight, and my galoshes become hot and slippery on my feet and I can barely keep up, for all that Luca has my knapsack bouncing on his back again. I stumble and trip, but every time I do his grip on my wrist yanks me up again. Once I go to my knees, and I cry out as I feel a flint gash one open. Luca does not even speak. He bends, looks at it, and then takes my arm and hauls me on again with blood trickling down my shin and into my sock.

I no longer know what all this is about, but whatever it is I know it has a grip of me now and will not let go, no more than Luca will let go of my hand as we pelt downhill towards the long wood on the right of the track.

It is a mile or two, he said, but it seems so much longer. I am hungry and thirsty and last night I slept in a wood alone and all day I have been walking, and I am so tired and bewildered that I just want to sit in a quiet, warm room for a while, just curl up with Pie and let the strangeness of the world leave me be.

We stop at last, and I bend over, trying not to be sick.

The cramps are coming and going in my tummy again, and between my legs it feels horribly sticky and chafed. Luca is breathing hard too, and I see the strange dimensions of his face shift with every passing shadow of the moon. I do not know what I will do if he changes into the wolf right here in front of me. That would just be too much.

He shakes my shoulder gently. 'Look, Anna,' he says, pointing.

I follow his finger and see we are only a few hundred yards from the treeline now, and there is a tiny light coming and going in that darkness.

'That'll be Jaelle, with a lantern,' Luca says with a smile. 'All is well, now. One last dash, and we can get you beside a fire.' He looks at me with that strange face of his and I see his nostrils widen into black holes.

'You need to wash, girl.'

'You think I don't know that?' I snap. I bend and rub my throbbing knee.

'Your blood is on the air,' he says, his gaze ranging back up the hill behind us.

I know it. I can smell it myself. 'Let's go,' I say. I am so tired I just want to get it over with. 'But not so fast, Luca. I can't run another step.'

'All right.'

We walk on down the long open slope that is amazingly bright under the moon. Luca catches me when I stumble and the heat of him makes me shiver, and I feel the hard bunched cords of his arm, and his nearness makes me a little dizzy for a moment. This is what they mean in the books when the heroine swoons, I thought. I always thought it was such rot, but it turns out to be true. Of course, the heroine has to be hungry and thirsty and tired beyond measure too. And bleeding – let's not forget that.

'Look to your left,' Luca says quietly.

I do, and instantly shrink back against him. Standing like stones in the moonlight are one, two, three – half a dozen shapes black and silent not two hundred yards away.

The same on the right. And more behind us. They look as though they have been standing there forever, but in fact they must have just sprung out of the grass.

'Roadmen,' I whisper.

'Aye. I never seen so many together before. Walk fast, Anna, and look ahead.' He puts his arm about me and propels me forward more briskly.

The Roadmen stand still and quiet while our progress sounds ridiculously loud on the chalk track. I never thought I would be so glad to see a wood loom up in the night again, but as we draw near the line of trees so other shapes step out of the darkness, and the light moves with them. For a terrible minute I am sure it is a trick, and more of the Roadmen are luring us into a trap, but then I hear a girl's voice, quick and sharp.

'Move along Luca! Are you blind?' I remember the voice. It is Jaelle.

'The little maid is hurt and tired,' Luca retorts. 'Give us a hand then.'

I see Jaelle's beautiful face above the light of the lantern, but it is severe and drawn now, and her black hair falls like a hood around it. Beside her other Romani men are fanning out, and they carry cudgels and knives. I shudder at the sight of the cold blades.

She holds the lantern up and peers down into my face,

and sniffs. Her eyes widen a little. 'Anna,' she says, and smiles. 'You has changed, since last we spoke.' She sets a hand on my shoulder. 'Come – you'll be safe with us, little one. The enemy will not touch you now.'

Into the wood we go, and the moonlight is broken into a million little wandering pieces by the trees, and Jaelle and Luca support me, one on either side. The wood is more open than I thought, and dry underfoot. We turn right and follow it downhill. Beeches, I think, and some ash, and a big glossy holly which catches the light and shines like wet glass. Then there is more light ahead, a fire, and people around it, and a lovely smell of cooking meat.

A bulky figure stands there with the flame-light behind it, and I see silver shining on its forehead and glimmering in its eyes. It steps forward with its arms open, and becomes stout old Queenie with a wide smile on her face. She embraces me, and I sink into her arms with a sigh, and it is such a relief to stand still, to feel the running is over. For now at least.

She raises my head in her hands and looks down at me.

'Anna me dear,' she says, 'You is most welcome.' It is a lovely smile she has, and for a second I can see that she must have been as beautiful as Jaelle once. I just wish that her long teeth did not look quite so much like fangs.

17

THERE ARE FIFTEEN or twenty of them around the fire, men and women mixed. They are all ages from twenty to sixty it seems, and they all have the windburnt, bony faces of people who have been living out of doors for a long time. I never remarked on it before, but there are no children. Luca is by far the youngest here.

Jaelle sits by me as she did in Wytham Wood, and I am handed a tin bowl full of stew and a wooden spoon. I am very hungry, but it will be a race, I think, to see if hunger or tiredness wins out tonight. As I spoon the food down – it tastes dark and gamey this time, like kidneys – so Jaelle dabs at my gashed knee with a wet cloth and clucks every time I wince.

'T'ain't bad,' she says. 'These things always looks worse than they are.' She stops and stares at me as I am eating, until I have to stop. 'You done had your first bleed Anna, ain't that so?'

I feel the heat creep into my face, and can only nod. She

pats my arm. 'That's nothing to be ashamed of, girl. Means you are a woman now, well on the way to being growed up.'

'I need a bath,' I tell her in a low voice. 'It's filthy and feels horrible.'

Queenie draws near with a wide can of steaming water.

'No bathtubs here,' she says brightly. 'But we'll see what we can do for 'ee.' She looks me up and down, and her face becomes solemn. 'We is all daughters o' the moon, Anna. We feel the waxing and the waning of it in our bodies the way no man ever can. 'Tis our gift and our curse. We brings forth life, but must bleed for it. Blood must be paid for everything. Open your legs.'

'What? No!'

'Do as I say girl. You needs to be washed.'

I look at the others around the fire, my knees clamped together. 'But they will see!'

'No-one will look near us, I promises you that,' Queenie says firmly. 'Now you do as I say.'

She pulls aside my sodden knickers and peels off the wool sock, handing it to Jaelle. The younger woman takes it and sets it in the fire. I smell the blood on it as it burns. Then Queenie wipes me down like I am a little baby, and dries me, and hands me a clout of linen.

'Use that. 'Tis a heavy bleed for one so young. You'll change it again in the morning.' She strokes my cheek. ''Tis a wonder you were able to keep your feet at all today.'

'She's white as a daisy,' Jaelle says.

'Eat up,' Queenie tells me. 'I'll make some tea as will help. But you needs rest, more than anything.'

'What about the Roadmen?' I ask. 'There are I don't know how many outside the wood.'

'You don't be worrying about them curs,' Queenie tells me. 'They won't come nigh my fire, not on a night of moon.'

I am too tired to really care, my mind fuzzed over like a barley sugar left in a coat pocket. I see Luca across the fire, and will him to look at me, but he is busy talking to that horrible rat-faced old man, Job. He has brought me here. Maybe that is all he ever meant to do. Queenie says. I don't know why I keep looking at him, or why it should seem so important that he not ignore me.

'Drink this,' Jaelle says, offering me a tin cup. 'There's wholesome stuff in here. Mint and dandelion and Angelica root, and feverfew for the aches and pains.'

I sip the hot liquid cautiously. It tastes like minty mud, and Jaelle laughs at the face I make.

'Every drop, girl. That's real medicine that is, as good as any bolus you buy in a shop. It'll settle you, flesh and bone.'

I drink it back. The warmth is welcome, at least. Jaelle strokes my hair. 'Such a pretty girl,' she murmurs.

Sleep starts to sink down on me like the curtain at the end of a play. I am blinking and yawning, and the tin cup clinks aside. Jaelle stretches my old blanket over me.

'Lie here now, Anna, and take thy ease. There ain't nothing in the night to worry 'ee, not no more.'

'Why am I here?' I ask her, blinking.

'Don't you be worrying about that now my sweet. Sleep. Sleep, Anna.'

My knapsack is here beside me, and Pie too. She looks so out of place, like something left abandoned by a passing child. I hug her; I feel the same way myself.

I thought that when we came here and found Queenie

and the others again I might feel as though I could belong. But instead it feels more like I stepped off a cliff that day I walked out of the old house on Moribund Lane, and I have been falling ever since.

Too tired even to stay afraid... I yawn, and watch them go about their business around the fire. One woman is sewing, though how she can see to do it in the firelight I have no idea. Another is scrubbing out some pots with a bunched handful of grass and a third is slicing up meat on a tree-stump, licking her thumb and smiling.

Men come and go across the campsite, and drop bundles of wood down beside the embers. One of them carries a small axe, another a billhook. For the first time, I see that they have made a series of hurdles out of chopped saplings interwoven on upright stakes. These are set up along one side of the fire, either to help reflect the heat or to hide the light. Hanging from the hurdles are little dangling bodies. I see rabbits there, and squirrels, and a cock pheasant with the feathers reflecting back the firelight like jewels. I wonder if the Romani have guns, to shoot these for their food. I have seen none, and I don't want to. Knives are bad enough.

My head sinks back, too heavy to lift. Above me, five pointed stars made of twigs are dangling all over the campsite. Like Christmas decorations, I think hazily.

And I suppose I sleep at last, with my old blanket around me and Pie, and my feet pointed at the fire.

IT IS LONG into the night, and I think I am awake. I open my eyes above the edge of the blanket and my face is stiff with the cold. The fire has died down into red embers and low flames that grasp feebly at the blackened wood. Everyone is sleeping, and so quiet is the night that I can hear the breath of the sleepers. I look up, and above the trees the stars are glinting and sparkling like frost, millions of them. They gather in an arc that carves clear across the sky. I look for those that Pa taught me, but the familiar ones seem lost in the welter, a vast span of spangled light. I never imagined there could be a night sky like this.

I stand up, and the blanket falls from me and I step as quick and quiet as a cat around the fire. I feel light as a dragonfly dancing on the air.

Luca lies with a blanket up to his chin and an old wool cap on his head. He looks much younger while asleep, all the lines faded out of his face. But I can see others beneath the skin, as though his flesh has too much bone beneath it, and the black hair at his nape continues in a line down into the collar of his shirt. He looks as doll-like as Pie in the night. If I raised him up I almost think his eyes would spring open and there would be nothing but black glass in the sockets.

The wood is long. It streams along the slope of the down for more than a mile. But it is narrow, too. I step through it without a single twig so much as creaking under my feet and look out to the west, where the land rises up to Whitehorse Hill.

There is a fire burning up on the hilltop, high and bright.

THE OLD YEAR has died and the new one is begun, but the dark still lies heavy and cold across the world, and winter hangs deep in the night. I begin walking uphill. I am barefoot, coatless, but I feel no chill. Looking at my arms I see the frost glitter bright upon them, yet my breath makes no cloud. I walk with huge, easy strides, eating up the ground, and in no time at all I am on the hilltop on the eastern edge of the ancient hill-fort, and the bank rises up before me like a wave frozen in the grass.

The fire is crackling and roaring and there are shadows dancing around it, but it seems almost that the light flows through them. It is like seeing the sun dappled through the leaves of a living tree. There is no sound but the click and rush of the flames.

And beside the fire there is a pale horse, and on its back is the man who called himself Gabriel. But he is no Oxfordshire farmer now. He sits naked on the horse, and his white torso is daubed with circles and sigils of red clay, and on his head are the antlers of a great stag, and in his eyes is the same light which burns in the distant glimmer of the stars.

'Daughter,' he says to me. He holds out his hand, and in it I see a sprig of mistletoe, the berries upon it as bright as pearls in the moonlight.

18

In the earliest red glow of the morning the camp comes awake, the women first. I lie and watch muzzily as Jaelle bends and blows at the grey ash of the fire, and feeds the sparks she raises with dried grass and bark which she takes from a leather pouch. Then she sloshes water around in a tin and sets it by the growing blaze, and bit by bit she builds the fire again until it has light and heat once more.

I get up with the blanket around my shoulders, and crouch by the flames for a second. My stomach feels almost normal, but my knee throbs and there is a black scab of blood on the wound.

'Don't pick at it,' Queenie says from a mound of rugs on the other side of the fire. 'Why must young 'uns always pick at these things?' Then she turns over and pulls a blanket over her head.

'Queenie ain't much of a lark,' Jaelle says, grinning.

Someone walks past me and dumps a dead rabbit at my

feet, making me start back in shock. The little eyes are wide open.

'Think you could gut and skin that?' a voice says. I look up and it is the old man, Job, sneering down on me from his hairy rat-face.

'Well?'

I touch the rabbit – still warm. 'Is it dead?'

Job laughs, a horrible wet sound. 'You ain't much use, are you? Is it dead!' He snorts with contempt and walks away.

I leave the fire and the rabbit. I want to pick up Pie, but somehow I can't after that – not in front of these people.

Luca is standing on the eastern edge of the wood. Beyond the trees the land is open and rises slowly to the horizon. And the sun is just above it, still stained red from its rising. The light is cherry-bright on the grey trunks of the beeches and there are birds singing all through the wood, a glory of sound.

Luca turns and glances at me irritably. 'You make a lot o' noise.'

'It's not like walking on a carpet.'

'You got to pick your way more careful, like. And keep looking all around, all the time. That way you gets to see things that ain't common or everyday.'

'What like?'

He is staring out at the sunrise. He points across the open fields. 'Out there, come spring, you'll see the hares come, if you sit quiet enough. They jump up and prance and dance and box each other, mad as March. 'Tis a sight to see. That's how this place got its name. We calls it Boxing Hare Wood for 'em, though the name ain't on no map. Hares is sacred animals, creatures tied to the moon. Some o' the Romani hunt 'em for sport, but not us – not my kin. We sets traps for rabbits and squirrels, and we'll take a pheasant or a pigeon, but not a hare. They's things of beauty.'

It seems an odd thing for him to say, and as he speaks he has almost a kind of wonder in his voice. I sit beside him in the dead brown bracken.

We watch together as the morning grows. At last I say, 'Are they still out there?' It is not hares I speak of, and he knows it.

'They's always out there Anna, like rats in the hedge. Sometimes close, sometimes just a lonesome man on the track miles away.'

The answer is not enough for me. 'Luca, who is the man on the pale horse?'

He frowns, and looks down at his hands. 'He is the leader o' the Roadmen. He's more than that, too. He comes and goes like some ordinary man in the world, but he's…' He trails off.

'What?'

'I shouldn't be speaking of it.'

'Speak to me. I won't tell anyone. I want to know.'

Luca's face screws up in a scowl. 'He is the Great Hunter. A fallen angel, some say. He is death, Anna. When he appears, it follows on after him like a cloud o' crows follows the plough.' His voice drops. 'They says he and the Devil, they do compete for lost souls. He is to be fled from, always.' He turns and looks at me.

'Remember that. He ain't some farmer on a cart. You is in the Old World now, and nothing is what it looks like.'

He reaches out a hand and touches my face; and we sit like that, just for one moment, while the sun rises out of its bloody bed in the east and the light climbs higher up the trees.

THERE IS TEA for breakfast, and a kind of flat cake which the women bake in the ashes of the fire. Bannock, Jaelle calls it, and it sits heavy in the stomach. When they are done I help them haul up water from the little stream which runs down at the bottom of the wood, and they douse the campfire in a whoosh of sharp-smelling steam. Then we all go on our hands and knees and break up the warm wet embers in our fingers and scatter them, and the men rake dead leaves over the scar, and everyone packs up.

'Where are we going?' I ask Queenie as they all begin to troop out of the wood and onto the track again.

'Does it matter?' she asks me with a smile. 'You don't always got to be going somewhere, little one. The journey is what counts. Soon enough, we'll be scattering again, and some of us will go one way, and some t'other. Best thing is to taste the time together and enjoy it. Come sowing, the family will be all over the country working here and there, and we'll be bent-backed with the labour o' the birthing year. Right now, the land sleeps, and we can walk across it as grand as kings. The crops is yet to be planted, and the beasts are all in the byre. Winter is hard, but in winter we is as free as we can be.'

'What about the Roadmen? How do we stay clear of them?'

'You might as well ask how we stay clear o' the rain.

They is part o' the world just as we is. Sometime there is a storm, and sometime there is shelter to be had from it, and sometime not. We takes it as it comes.'

It is not much of an answer, even to me. But I see that I will not get anything else out of Queenie for now. As we move up the track she and Jaelle have their heads together, talking quietly, and I can't quite pluck up the courage to eavesdrop.

WE WALK EAST along the old track, a close gaggle of ragged people with burdens roped to their backs. I scan the surrounding hills and downs as we go but the countryside seems empty, to me at least. Nothing moves in the bright chill of the morning but us and a few distant birds, and as the day grows the flight and pursuit of the night before seems almost like a dream, a moving picture left behind in the dark of a nickelodeon. Life is normal again, or as normal as this new life can be.

We come to a crossroads on the height of a tall down, and turn north along a real road. It leads off the ridge and plunges steeply downhill with a thick wood on our right and a village straddling the way ahead.

'Blowingstone Hill,' Luca says, striding along beside me with that tireless pace of his. 'And that is King's Stone village. Queenie – tell her about it – she loves the stories, this one.'

The older woman looks down at the country below. 'There's a great stone with a hole in it, and some can get it to sound a note, if they've the lungs of an ox. An old king blew through the stone to summon his soldiers for a great battle with the people o' the north, long ago. They say those as can raise a sound from the stone is a future king of England.'

'Have you tried?' I ask Luca.

He grins. 'I ain't never going to be no king, Anna. That's for sure.'

We are down from the ridge now, and the land has become ordinary, the little roads and woods and villages of the heart of England. We turn off to the north-west so the sun is behind my right shoulder, and tramp through Uffington. The company splits up here, some going ahead, some falling behind.

'Shouldn't we all stay together?' I ask Luca.

'There's folk would not take too kindly to seeing two dozen of our kind walk past 'em in a bunch,' he says. 'One twitchy old maid calls in the peelers, and before you knows it they is packing us in a Black Maria and it's away to a workhouse, or the cells. Best to come through these places a trickle at a time.'

'That's not fair.'

'That's the way o' the world, Anna. You wants to stay free and clear of ordinary folk, then you got to be careful about it.'

We walk on. The roads are quiet. I count half a dozen motor cars and a single horse and trap before midday. We walk through Fernham, Little Coxwell, and Great Coxwell, and it comes on to rain. A steady, chill up-and-down kind of rain that patters on the head and shoulders. I am glad of my galoshes now. I think of all the times I sat in the hall in Moribund Lane and watched the old Greeks come through the door shaking the wet off themselves, Pa pumping their hands and rattling away in Greek and English. And the fire burning in the front room. And I would give anything – anything – to have that back again.

It has not been such a long time I suppose, but I feel so very different from the little sulking girl who just wanted to be left alone. Even Pie is not the same. She is packed up in my knapsack now like any other kind of baggage. I miss her and I do not. I miss being able to talk to her as though she was a real person. I think that is over and done with now. But she is still all I have left of a far distant world, and I will never part from her.

I am glad of the rain. I hate people to see me cry.

THE LAND RISES once again. I am rather grumpy now because the wet has soaked through my coat and I can feel it cold on my chest and it is dripping from my fingers. Pa's old cap keeps the worst of it from my head, but his scarf is as sodden as if I had thrown it in a ditch and trodden on it. I think about sleeping out of doors in this, and my heart is down in my galoshes with my poor numb toes.

Luca appears beside me, bobbing up like a Halloween apple. For some reason he is smiling. 'It gets like this, and I just starts to thinking about the fire at day's end,' he says, and nudges me playfully. 'Don't be fixin' on the here and now. We'll sit around it tonight and all be wet and miserable as sin together, and I'll bet you anything you like you can laugh about it then.'

I have to smile back.

Then I look up at the slope rising ahead. It is a low hill crowned with trees. It looks somehow important, and I can't say why.

'Is that where we're going?'

Luca wipes the rain out of his eyes. He sobers. 'Seems so.'

'Does it have a name? They all have names.' I nudge him back. 'I bet you know.'

We splash along. Luca does not seem to want to talk any more. In fact he has drawn away and pulled his cap down to shield his face from the weather.

We are all bent into it, lashed by it, the January day closed in around us like a wet fog. I wonder if I have said something wrong.

'Badbury Clumps, they names that place round here.' It is Jaelle. Her black hair is plastered like seaweed over her face and her skin is as white as Pie's. She looks as though there is no blood in her at all, but she is peering up at the looming tree-topped height with an odd light in her eyes.

'Our folk still uses the old name for it. We calls it Badon Hill.'

THERE IS A shallow bank with a wood inside, tall beeches again with still a few coppery leaves clinging to them. The wood floor is flat and open. The trees make the patter of the rain even louder but it seems somehow quieter within, like being in a shed with the rain on the roof. I take off Pa's hat and look up. We must have walked ten or twelve miles this morning, and already the day is drawing in. Once again, the normal world beyond pulls back, and there is only the dark sky and the rain and the wood, and the cold wet earth underfoot. Ageless things.

I shall get used to it I suppose. I hope I do. I hope it is not always this hard.

One by one, the rest of them trickle in. Queenie is not here, which is odd since I have never yet seen her more than ten feet from Jaelle's side. There is little talk; they all seem to have been here before and know what to do.

I stand there dripping and watch them, for despite this morning I don't feel as though I should just pitch in with the rest. I don't know quite what to do. Not yet.

It is the women who do all the setting up. The men seem to drift away into the trees. I don't know if they are hunting, or seeking firewood or water, or perhaps even guarding us. But the women need no help from them. And Jaelle is a wizard when it comes to getting the fire lit.

She clears a space down to the earth before laying a little carefully made bed of twigs. Then she produces a fistful of timber from the leather pouch under her coat. I half want her to start striking flint and steel, but it is a match which does the trick, and more of the women step forward with sticks and little branches that they produce from under their clothing as though they were hoarded treasure. They have been carrying them all day it seems, and I feel horribly guilty. I did not know. I wish someone had said, and I would have done the same.

The fire sputters in the heavy drops which are cascading down from the trees above. Jaelle bends over it, and blows on the guttering flames, and passes her hand over them as though she is stroking a cat. The light flashes, startling me. It blows out blue and green, and catches in the wood at last, rising bright and clear.

It is dark enough now for it to cast shadows. In the bright yellow light of it Jaelle meets my eyes and smiles, and shakes her hand as though it hurts her.

Old Job turns up and he has a billhook which he uses as quick and deft as a knife, and he slashes and hacks at some green wood and stabs it into the ground. A spit, all white wood and grey bark, in its own way a little sculpture.

Soon there is a can of water hanging over the fire, and I can just begin to see the sense of what Luca was saying earlier. I always thought that firelight in a wood was a fine thing, one of the best things. But here and now it is more than that. It is all that makes it possible to look into the prospect of the night ahead. Without it, the misery would be overwhelming.

I hear hacking and chopping in the wood out of the light. More of the men come in with bundles of firewood, and they dump them before walking away again. The women pile them up next to the flames, and some of the greener limbs begin to ooze bubbled sap with the heat, while from the more rotten wood the insects begin to crawl like rats leaving a sinking ship. Beetles and woodlice and all manner of crawling life, all scurrying away from the flames.

But I am so glad of it. I take off my coat the way most of the others are doing and hold it before the flames. Not to dry it – that would take too long – but simply to warm the wetness it holds.

There is very little talk. I hear them speak in their own language, and wonder if I shall ever have to learn it. *Un, deux, trois...* I hope not.

'It'll clear afore morning,' a voice says beside me. It is Queenie.

She seems to have appeared out of nowhere. The rain has soaked her and covered her in bright-lit drops. She looks as though she is dressed in gems, and her face is shining with water. She appears much younger than she did trudging along through the day and unlike the rest of us, she doesn't so much as shiver once. I can see Jaelle in her face, and Luca too. I wonder who their father is, and if he is out here with us somewhere in the gathering January dark.

'You has many questions, little one. I sees 'em in your eyes,' Queenie says, and sits down before the fire, waving a hand for me to follow.

She has a smell about her, thick and musty. It reminds me a little of the smell of the attic, but is more powerful than that. As I take my place beside her, so the others seem to fade away A long burning stick is lifted from our fire to light another, and I am sure the woman who takes it bows to Queenie as she backs away.

'This is Badon Hill,' Queenie says. 'It is our place, as Whitehorse Hill belongs to the Roadmen. All this part of England is as deep in magic and myth as the mind of a child. The great battles of the long ago past was fought here, in the White Horse Vale, and before that, the stones was raised and the old signs was carved into the earth itself. Avebury, down to the south and west of here – it were the heart of worship once, and the sun was bowed to. But before even that, men knelt to the moon, for the moon is tied to the making of life, and the cycles of the Great Mother.'

Queenie looks at me, and for a second it seems almost as though the weight has fallen from her face, and she is as lean-boned as Luca.

'You is part of that now, child. With the first running o' your blood, you is become a woman. And the moon moves in you, even as it does in Luca there. Just in a different way, is all.

'In the oldest of stories, the Great Mother was a mare, a she-horse. She gave birth to the stars theyselves. But men took the horse and used it in their wars, and made the stallion their symbol, forgetting the old truth of it. So the Roadmen, as they would become, carved the white horse on the very face o' the hills to mark their power.

'And the people that worshipped the moon, they faded into the shadows o' the world. Men bowed to the sun for the seeming power of it, but even that was twisted into the worship of the Christ-man, who came later.'

Her face tightens, becomes angry.

'And his followers conquered all with their lies, leaving the Old World in the darkness, 'til it was nothing more than myth and memory.

'Beltane, they stole and made into the feast o' their god's death and rebirth, twisting the ancient truth. Samhain, they took to pray for their dead, and it became Hallow's Eve. Imbolc and Lughnasa, they names for their saints. All this was taken from us by the followers o' the Christ-man, until only a tithe of what was once known across the whole o' the wide western isles is kept. By such as us. A people as is vanishing, year on year, until it comes down to a last few, wandering the downs and scratching for a way to get by.

'That is all we are now, child. But it don't mean that we do not still hold the truth in ourselves, the knowing of what is at the heart of it all.'

'How do you know all these things?' I ask Queenie, awed.

'They was passed down, mother to daughter, from the time we first came to this land.' She looks up at the sky, and smiles. 'There was some of our folk as wandered here from the ancient east when the stones was still buried in the grass, waiting for men to wake them. We been here ever since, longer than those as calls themselves English. When the first of our kind arrived the soldiers of the Eagle was still half a world away, and the trees was like a green sea from Chester to Dover.

'But we keeps ourselves to ourselves, and our blood pure. Most of us anyways. It's true we dwindle, year on year. There ain't many left now. And fewer still as has the gift that Job and Luca has been given.'

Here Queenie pauses. She looks into the fire and I think I see a shade of sadness cross her face.

'That takes a special kind o' making. The skin o' the wolf is not just there for anyone to wear.'

She falls silent. I sit and wait in my steaming clothes while the others go about their business around the camp. There are three fires now, for everyone is soaked and needs to dry out. The men are fashioning wooden frames to hang their wet things upon. I see Luca patiently sharpening the end of a stake, while beside him Job is slashing at the dead bracken and gathering it together for bedding. He looks across the fires at Queenie and then at me for a second, and I can't help but wonder why he despises me so. It is as plain as day across his face.

'There is another line of power, some of it belonging to our people, some of it not,' Queenie goes on at last. 'A different gift that runs only in the womenfolk. There was a great Queen once of this country, in ancient days, who rose up against the soldiers of the Eagle and tried to cast them out. Her name was Boudika, and she had it, though she weren't of our kind, not entire.' She sets a hand on my knee and taps the healing scab there lightly. 'I suppose to you, little one, a witch is someone in a pointed hat who rides a broomstick.' She chuckles.

'I suppose so.' I think of Hansel and Gretel, and any number of other fairy tales.

'Are you a witch?' I ask her.

'I am.'

That takes me aback. Queenie watches me, and the firelight is yellow in her eyes. She is smiling.

'So... can you cast spells?'

'I can.' Her eyes widen, and a frightening change comes over her face. She raises a hand and stabs the fingers out in a star.

There is a burst of laughter behind me, and Jaelle rubs the top of my head. 'Ma, what are you playing at?'

Queenie grins.

'She's just funnin' with you, Anna. You got to take a pinch of salt with what Ma comes out with sometimes.' She leans down and kisses Queenie on the cheek, and Queenie pats her face.

The air blows out of my mouth. I breathe again. 'You were just joking.' I am both relieved and oddly disappointed.

But Queenie is grave now. 'I was and I wasn't. There's such things as witches, Anna, but they ain't what you been taught in your books and stories. They are those as has the old magic o' the earth buried deep in them. They don't need no spells, or black cats or gingerbread houses. In them is the same power which was put in the stones by the ancient peoples. In the faraway lands they helped build the great pyramids, and some of them was queens o' Egypt. That is my blood, and Jaelle's too.

'And it is in you, child.'

I am dumbfounded. 'Are you saying I'm a witch?'

She nods, and takes a hold of my hair and tugs on it a little, swaying my head.

'I knows some of the old names of the womenfolk your power might be from. Cassandra and Clytemnestra for two. Medea for another. Your mother was a witch, Anna, from a line as old as mine. I smells in it your blood.

'If you goes back far enough, you'll find a single woman at the dawn of the world, walking cross Africa with the first men to hold flint in their hands and crack fire out of it. She is mother to us all. Epona, the Bronze folk called her, but she has as many names as there are tongues spoken across the Old World. We is part o' that line. We partake in that power. And you can't deny it.

'You has bled now, and are a woman, and that power is waking in you.'

'I don't know what any of this is about,' I say. 'I don't know why the Roadmen are after me, or why you have taken me in.' I pull my wet coat closer about me, suddenly cold despite the fire. There is something in my pocket which scratches at my fingers, a twig or something. 'I don't know why they had to kill Pa,' I say miserably.

'He was your protector, so he had to be done away with,' Queenie says. Her face hardens. 'With him gone, you was cut adrift in the world. The Roadmen wants to end this line, Anna. It is a rival for their own powers. 'Tis a struggle that has been going on for as long as there are women and men loving and hating one another.'

'It's about good and evil?' I ask, thoroughly confused.

''Tis more complicated than that.' She sighs. 'And simpler

too, like the coming and going o' the seasons. Winter gives way to spring. Summer dies and in the dying it turns to autumn. The world is made new by it, but sacrifices got to be made to make it happen.

'Most folk know nothing of this; it passes them by like the rain on the window. But for us, out here, it is everything.'

'I ran away to keep out of the workhouse,' I tell Queenie. 'That's all I know.'

She looks closely at me, and finally nods. 'Happen that'll do for now. I done said enough for one night. That pretty little head o' yourn must be fit to bust with all this.' She sets her hand upon my head and shakes it again. 'Right now, you needs to get dry, and eat. This life is hard for those who ain't born to it.'

It is. Harder than I thought. It is all very well to daydream about campfires, and stars by night, but I see now – I feel now – the weary labour of it, and the effort it takes just to make a way through the day.

'Get some sleep, little one. I shall watch over thee, and soon there will be food to eat, and the fire will be hot and high, and we will talk some more, perhaps.'

PERHAPS IT WAS a spell, perhaps not. But I do sleep, despite the bustle of the camp, for I am bone-weary.

Queenie's words run through my head and conjure up strange pictures, half-dreams and imaginings.

In my sleep I see a vast, dun-coloured plain covered with yellow grass and dotted with strange, swollen trees. A tiny group of people is walking across it, skin burnt black by the sun. They are tall and very thin and near naked, and they carry long flint-tipped spears. A woman walks out in front of them, and she has eyes blue as cornflowers in her dark face and breasts flat as empty pockets, but the men all defer to her and she looks at the shimmering horizon and strides on tirelessly, the dust of the hot earth rising round her feet.

Then the world changes, and it is the familiar one of long grass-covered slopes and broad-leafed trees, and rivers wide and brown.

Another plain, but this one is rich and green. Men are at work upon it, hundreds of them, and the haze of woodsmoke rises into the air. They are dragging huge stones from the riverbank, crowds of them heaving and sweating and carrying earth and setting down a roadway of rolling logs. The great megaliths inch forward over the grass towards a circled mound which is bristling with timber scaffolding. They scar the earth as they are hauled onwards, and the skin of the world is ripped away to reveal white chalk and brown clay, and the sharp edges of broken flint.

Strangely, I hear the beat of hooves on the turf, but there are no horses here. And the men chant at their work in a language that is wholly unknown and achingly familiar, as if it were words I should know, or once used myself.

The sun is gone, and all is in darkness. I am in a forest now, and when I look up I can see the limbs of the trees black against a star-bright sky. And there is a moon in it, bright and full. The forest is thick and untended and the trees within it are giants of their kind. Oaks with trunks wider than a dinner-table. Great ash with wrinkled bark. Berry-bright rowan, and holly dark and shining under the moon.

Things move in the wood, padding from shadow to deeper shadow. I see eyes reflecting back the were-light, and I can smell them. A great wolf looms out of the darkness and lopes towards me on soundless paws, but I am not afraid. It comes so close I can feel the heat of its breath, and I run my fingers through the harsh prickle of its fur, and that touch is pure delight in my palms.

The wolf lies down at my feet and I lie with it on the fallen leaves and the deep-smelling earth, and I feel the heat of it down the entire length of my body and I grasp its fur in my fists and pull it close. Above us, the moon is quicksilver-bright against the branches of the ancient trees.

19

'THEY'VE GONE,' OLD Job says.

'Is you sure of that?' Queenie demands.

'Damn it woman, if I says they is gone then it is so. There ain't a hair nor a scent o' them between here and Coxwell village. Luca – you tell her.'

I open an eye. The fires are blazing high and everyone is gathered about them. Job and Luca stand before Queenie, who sits on the frayed carpet of her bedroll as if it is a throne.

'It's true, far as I can make out,' Luca says. 'I went north as far as the river, but there ain't nothing to be seen.'

'Tracks?' Jaelle asks them. She is seated on Queenie's right.

'Some, but they was old – yesterday's. Could be they is in the deeps o' Badbury Forest, but if they are, they found some way to get there without so much as bending a blade o' grass.'

'They'll not go near woods, not at this time o' year,'

Queenie says, batting the idea aside with a wave of her hand.

'Maybe they gave up,' Jaelle says.

'Maybe. But it don't feel like that.' Queenie ponders. 'All right. We stands watches tonight, as usual. Tomorrow we heads north to the river and crosses at Radcot Bridge. 'Tis time to be away from the Downs and the open country. Where there's more common folk around, they is more cautious.'

''Tis a lot o' trouble for a black haired bundle who don't know her arse from a hole in the ground,' Job growls.

'I'll judge if that be so,' Queenie says, very quiet. She and Job stare at one another. Then Queenie points at Luca. 'You want him to be the last of his kind?'

'You know that ain't it,' Job says. His grey beard twitches.

'My way is the only way,' Queenie goes on, her voice lowered so that I can hardly make it out. 'So she's young – well I was no older. Does you remember that, Job?'

'You was one of us. She ain't. She's a city brat, spoiled and soft. She'll not stay with this life, no matter how you works it.' The old man turns away and mutters something inaudible.

'What are you two on about, Ma?' Luca asks.

'Never you mind boy. The moon is rising fat and white. 'Tis almost time you wore the other face.'

Luca nods. 'I feel it coming. I been bottling it in for hours.'

'Job?'

The older man runs his fingers through his beard, not meeting her eyes. 'Aye, 'tis time all right. Mayhap that's why the Roadmen give up the chase. They was on our backs most o' the morning, and then they drew off, like...'

He kneels down beside Queenie. I try so hard to look asleep, and watch them through slitted eyes, the firelight flashing out in white wands. I know that I am not supposed to hear any of this.

'I don't feel it like I used,' Job says in a whisper to Queenie, and there is something like a sob in his voice. 'My days is near done, sweetheart. You knows it too.'

Queenie strokes his face. ''Tis the price that is paid.'

Job clears his throat. He flashes a look at me and I lie, breathing soft, eyes closed now. But my heart is hammering fast.

'Does she have no idea what she's about?'

'Not yet.' Queenie's voice is suddenly a sharp hiss. 'And don't you be thinkin' o' telling her.'

'She'll be all right.' It is Luca's voice. 'She got more heart than many a grown man I've run across. I'll look after her, Ma.'

'You're a good boy, Luca. See that you does.'

After that, I hear the sounds of them settling down again, the clink of metal and click of wood, water being poured. I lie puzzling it out in my head with the firelight a golden bloom on my closed eyes. I wish I understood more. But I suppose it has only been a few days.

I remember my strange dreams, and I am quite sure they were not my own. They feel more like someone else's memory.

I would lie on – I am almost dry now, and not hungry at all. But I have to go to the toilet, and try as I might that urge cannot be wished away. I open my eyes and yawn and stretch, and make a great business of showing I am awake. I find Queenie and Jaelle smiling at me. Of Job and Luca there is no sign.

I stand up and begin stepping out of the firelight.

'Where you off to, dearie?' Jaelle asks at once.

'Just have to –' I open my hands and make a face. She nods.

'Don't be straying too far now. No need to be bashful with us.'

I feel a pressing need to get away from their eyes, almost as pressing as the other thing. It is a relief to walk out into the darkness under the trees. The air is much colder away from the campfires, and the moon is coming and going in the middle of a wrack of broken cloud. It lights up every hanging raindrop.

I keep walking despite the growing urgency of my need. I wonder what Pa would make of me now, or Miss Hawcross. I wonder if anyone at Moribund Lane misses me at all. I suppose not. I am only an orphan to them, a bother, a trouble. Barely a person at all. At least these people seem to think I am important. I don't know why this is, but it is rather a nice feeling not to be someone just underfoot. I may not be able to gut and skin a rabbit yet – I must get Luca to teach me – but I am wanted here, at least. I have not felt that for a long time.

I am in under the deep beeches now, and I like to think I am moving quietly. But there is a sound off in the wood I cannot account for, a strange snuffling and grunting. I head towards it. Perhaps it is Luca. Luca the boy, or Luca the wolf. He will not hurt me either way – I am sure of that now. Pa used to say that a little curiosity was a dangerous thing. He was probably right – but what is life without it?

I see a thing thrashing on the floor of the wood, and dare not go closer. There is an awful whining noise that neither a man nor an animal should be able to make, and the thing rears up and then falls again. It rolls and writhes, before collecting itself. It is kneeling now, a man, and as I watch he begins to undress. It is old Job.

I see him peel off his jacket, his trousers, his shirt. He grunts and groans, and doubles over as if in an agony of cramps, but finally he has his clothing piled at the foot of a tree, and naked, stands up to stare at the moon with his head thrown back.

I cannot say when it begins, or how, but he drops to all fours, and as he does the white of his skin has darkened, and his back arches like that of a frightened cat. I hear a deep snarl which has no business coming out of a man's mouth, and as his head whips back and forth long black ears spike out upon it. There is a sharp crack, and Job's face seems to explode outwards, and a snout pushes through the bones of his face while he shudders and groans.

And before I can take another breath the man is gone altogether, and the wolf is there.

It is huge, grey as the moonlight and white on the muzzle, and it rears up on its hind legs for a second, as if remembering the man it was, before leaping off into the trees.

It lopes away towards the wood's edge, and the villages at the foot of the hill beyond. And watching it go my heart is all a hammer again, and a cold shiver goes through me as I think of the sleeping people in their beds below, totally unaware of what is padding around their doorsteps in the night.

The normal world has gone once more, and the old, strange earth which Queenie described to me is here.

But some things remain the same.

When I am sure he is well and truly gone, I squat and pee at last, the steam rising round me, and it is such a relief. Then I begin to turn back for the camp.

But as I do I hear a strange sound in the night, completely out of place. I stand stock-still, listening. The night is so still and silent, as if everything has frozen in place under the moon. And it is so cold that any noise seems to crack out louder than it should.

A ticking noise.

It is coming from the little bundle of clothes at the foot of the tree. I walk over to it with my breath clouding in front of my face, not quite able to believe my ears. I kneel down.

The clothes stink, of sweat and smoke and the flesh of an old man. And the ticking is so loud.

So familiar.

I look around at the dark trees, guilty as a thief. Then I root through the bundle.

The first thing I find is my penknife, the one Pa gave me. I stare at it, astonished.

But there is something else, heavy and solid. I pull it out of the coat pocket, a disc of metal in my palm.

It is Pa's beautiful Breguet watch.

It trembles in my hand, for I am shaking all over now. I press the stud and the lid clicks open, and there is a picture inside. I can almost make it out in the moonlight, but not quite. I know it is my mother.

A shocking rush of pain runs through me, and I clench the watch shut again in my fist.

THE STRANGE THING about grief – how for a while it backs away, and you think it had become part and parcel of the makeup of your life. It becomes a kind of aimless pain, unfocused, just another toothache.

But every now and then it will lunge out of the shadows and grab you by the throat. And there is no way of knowing when that will happen.

And after a longer while still, you think about the person you miss, the one who is gone, and it is as if there is a wall of glass between you and the memories of them, as though your mind were protecting itself from the pain. It goes that way from day to day, and you think that is the way it will always be. But the wolf is still there in the darkness, waiting. And every so often it will spring out into the light, and you will feel its teeth in your throat.

THE TEARS COURSE down my face and I wipe them away at last. I do not think I have made a sound. I put the watch in my pocket, and I feel again the scratch of the twig in there against my fingers.

They killed my father. Job killed him. Not the Roadmen, or Gabriel, or some people up from London. These people – Romani or gypsies or whatever they are - they murdered him.

And all my world has just been thrown up into the air again.

'THAT WAS A fool thing to do, keeping that trinket. I had not known he did that,' a voice says.

I am so startled that I spring away from the bundle at the foot of the tree and fall to my side. I scrabble to my knees with my fists clenched.

It is Queenie. She is standing not ten feet away in the darker shadow of the tree. Her eyes shine.

'You was not meant to know this, little one. A little knowledge can hurt a body. Now you knows something that should have gone into the past without another word.'

'Job killed him, didn't he? Didn't he?' My voice rises. *Please tell me it is a lie.*

But Queenie shrugs. 'I suppose so.' She looks at me, and there is such a bitter, twisted expression on her face.

'You killed him,' I spit at her. 'Murderers. You killed Pa.'

'We did,' she says, and walks slowly into the moonlight. 'If we had not, then I tells you true child, someone else would have. Your Pa was feckless, angry, a lost soul. He was on his way out. We was just there to give him the final push.'

'But why – *why*?'

'To get you, of course.' She bares her long teeth. 'We wants you, Anna. We needs you among us. You belongs here. If you had not shown up in Wytham Wood that night, then you would still be going to the workhouse, maybe not this year, but in the next, sure as houses. And in time, you would have been as lost as your Pa was, a scullery maid one day, or a seamstress if you was lucky. Now you has the chance to be something else entirely, someone important.

'Your father was no good, Anna.'

'That's a lie! It's all been nothing but lies from the start.' My throat is throbbing with rage. I can barely think, I am so full of it.

'No. I have not said a word of falsehood to you, apart from who it was killed your Pa.'

'Was Luca in on it?'

Queenie's eyes flash. 'No! He is as innocent as the morn. It was Job alone. Luca thinks the same as you did up until you chanced on that there watch. There is no murder in that boy, little one. His heart is pure. You has to believe me on that one thing, if nothing else.'

She is telling the truth. Or she is the greatest liar ever made.

'But you sent him to me.'

Again, the twist in her face, like pain.

'I did. He is my only son, and he does my bidding. That don't mean he has not his own wants and likes and loves. And he loves you, Anna. 'Tis plain to see.'

Even that cannot dim the fury, the rising hatred. But it breaks some wall in me, all the same.

'What do you want of me?' I whisper.

Queenie kneels down in the dry leaves of the wood, a bulky woman wrapped in a blanket with silver coins shining in an arc across her forehead.

'Job and Luca is the last two of their kind in England. That line has gone back to the days before history was set down and recorded, but now it is near its end.

'Job is near done, his life burned up by the gift he was born with. Soon it will be Luca alone. After him, there are no more. And a wondrous thing will have been taken out o' the world and lost forever.

'To make a skinchanger, a skinchanger must lie with a woman as has the pure blood in her – the witch-blood which is nearly gone to dust now, in this land at least. I am of that blood, as is Jaelle, my daughter. You has that blood in you too, Anna. The power o' the moon runs in your veins. There ain't no denying your nature.

'To keep the gift in this world, one o' them has to lie with you. That is why you are here. Dearie, you have bled and become a woman. That too happened for a reason. You must lie with Luca, and bear his child, That way the ancient bloodline can be brought to life once more.'

I stare at her, disgusted, horrified. 'I'm too young.'

'I weren't much older than you when I had my first born. But the Roadmen killed him, my beautiful boy. I lost three more, in birth or before it, and then Jaelle came along, and Luca, my last. He was born with a caul over his head, and I knew then that he would live, and be the one to continue the line.'

I scrabble to my feet. 'I won't do it, not ever. You can all of you go to hell. I'll go to the police – I swear to God I will. And Job will hang for what he did.'

Queenie rises also. 'You are so young, you don't know what is right and what is wrong in this life, child. It ain't all fairytale black and white.'

I fight the stupid tears. 'Murder will never be right. I know that much.'

Queenie shakes her head. For a moment I think there are tears in her eyes too.

'You ain't going nowhere, child.' She steps towards me, and all of a sudden the moonlight makes round silver lamps of her eyes and her mouth is twisted and I can see her teeth long and brown over her lower lip.

'Don't you touch me!' I feel the knife in my pocket, and I draw it out and click the blade open. 'Don't you dare!'

I can hear voices from the camp, and there are other shapes coming through the trees now. I turn to look –

Queenie lunges at me, quick as a striking snake. She seizes my arm, and there is a horrible strength in her. I am pinioned, and I cannot pull free. Looking at the penknife, she laughs.

'What – will you cut me now, dearie?'

Her other hand comes up in a swing and slaps me hard across the face, smacking my head to one side.

'Don't you dare spring no blade on me.'

The rage rises up in me like lit petrol.

Without another thought, I stab the knife into her forearm as hard as I can, and she utters a shrill yelp and lets go of me.

Then I turn and run.

20

It is like running from Luca on Port Meadow but oh, so much worse. For I hear them back in the trees, and I know Jaelle's voice as it rises in outrage and fury, and the others are gabbling too, men and women both. The voices grow into a chorus, as bright as fire in the night.

I run as fast as I ever have in my life with the bloody knife in my hand and Pa's watch bouncing in my pocket, and all I can think of past the fear is the fact that Pie, poor Pie, is left behind me in their camp, bundled up in my knapsack, and I shall never see her again now. And as I run I am weeping, and the sobs hurt me as they tear in and out of my throat.

Whatever they want of me they shall not have, and I will run all the way to Oxford if I have to, and turn myself in and tell the police everything. I do not care if I end my days in the workhouse, because there are worse things – I know that now. They say I belong to their world, but they are lying. I won't have it – any of it.

There will be no more campfires, and boys who turn into wolves, and white horses, and the moon will be nothing more than a light in the night sky. I don't care if I have to run all the way to the North Pole, but they shall not have me.

I don't know in what direction I am going, but it is downhill, and I am out from under the trees and running down a wide open field with more woods in front. The land seems dark and empty and I speed up as I hurtle across the grass, my coat billowing out behind me and the chill air aching in my lungs like it has blades in it.

I can hear them behind me. They are hallooing to one another like huntsmen on the trail of a fox. I pelt onwards with no idea in my head except to get away.

BUT I CANNOT just run forever. I cannot even run for many more minutes; there is a stitch in my side and my socks have come down in my galoshes and are bunched around my toes.

I hiccup, and as if that is enough to tip some balance, I trip and tumble and roll over in the grass, the breath thumped out of me. I kick off the rubbery galoshes and am barefoot, but I am not cold now. One second I crouch there on hands and knees, and then I am up again, running even faster now, and when my bare foot comes down on a hidden stone in the grass the pain of it is scarcely felt.

Into the trees again. I slow down to try and get some breath back. The roots and leaves are like knots and needles under my feet, and jabs of pain spear up my legs. The wood is open, not like Wytham, and I can still jog along clutching my side. I am running along the flank of a hill, following the contours through the wood – but soon it is open fields again, hedges and bare furrowed earth.

Where have all the lights gone? The world is dark, as if I am alone in it but for those chasing me.

I cannot go much farther. Once I stop, and have to bend over and vomit, and up comes the stew they served me earlier.

I am stumbling and staggering across the ploughed earth like a drunk. The soil is frozen stiff and when I trip and go down again it feels like falling onto heaped stones. I look back, and I see the light of a lantern on the edge of the wood behind, not a quarter of a mile away. The moon is high and bright and leering at me, an enemy. It casts my own shadow black before me, rippling over the furrows. There are clouds in the sky, coming in from the north.

Oh, Christos, help me. God, help me now.

I start running again, though the pain in my side is a sharp shriek and my feet feel bruised and gashed. There is open country ahead, perhaps a mile of it, and just for a moment I glimpse the moon-bright glitter of water. A river. My mind dredges up what Luca said about running water. There is nowhere else to go, anyway.

I stagger on, through a hawthorn hedge, the thorns scoring my face and hands and legs. Then over a barbed-wire fence, and into ankle-turning ruts where a tractor has mashed its way. I break through the ice of a puddle and my foot goes in the freezing water and the bite of it nearly makes me cry out, but I grind my teeth on it and pick a way through the ruts and the deep holes cows' feet have made when the earth was soft and wet. It is like playing a horrible kind of hopscotch, and it eats up the last strength I have.

I have to stop. I cannot go on. I must have covered several miles, and none of it on a road or path. Perhaps I have a few minutes' grace –

I totter into the base of a hedge and draw myself in there. I want to curl up in a ball and close out the world, but instead I lie panting and stare out at the night, and the panic comes and goes in my brain like a bobbing silver balloon.

I have never been so afraid, not ever, not even when we were on the burning quay and Pa was holding my face tight against the awful howling grief as Mama was taken away.

And then I hear, clear as a train whistle, a high, lonesome howl in the night. It is the sound of a wolf. I have never heard one in my life before, but I know what it is as surely as night follows day.

And another answers.

It is a terrible thing to hear, alone and exhausted in the darkness. I understand now all the fairy tales, those that talk of the dangers of the deep forest, and the beasts that lurk there. All those fears were true. I know them now. I am in the middle of one such story, and all I want is out of it.

I take Pa's watch out of my pocket and click it open. I cannot see the face in the lid, just a blur.

'Mama,' I whisper. I think of her, and Pa, and my brother Nikos, and I wonder how in the world I ended up here, so far from home, cowering under a hedge in an English winter and waiting for the wolves to catch up with me.

'Now you understand,' a voice says.

And I am not at all surprised to see a white face before me, hovering in the dark.

Strangely, I am not as afraid of him as I am of the wolves

howling in the night, though his eyes shine like shillings, and his ears are as pointed as those of a hairless dog.

'I do understand,' I say quietly. And I run my sleeve across my face.

He smiles. 'Dearest girl, did I not tell you that it would be so? It is the way all desperate things end. And you are far too young for this. It is not right that you should have to shoulder such things on your own. And sweetheart, you are very much alone.'

There is a smile. I know it is there. I can feel it like ants crawling across my scalp.

'All you have to do is take my hand.'

And he holds it out to me.

I fight back the tears, and the hiccupping sobs that are crowding out my breath. I almost reach for it.

Then I hear the ticking of Pa's watch. And I cannot believe how loud it sounds – louder than the beat of my own heart. That is my life, ticking past.

It is not much of a life, all things considered, but it is my own, and I am beholden to no-one for it, not anymore.

I owe the world nothing, and whatever the world gave me it has taken away again. I do not even have shoes to wear, or Pie to hug.

And that knowledge is suddenly a terrible relief to me. Whatever else happens, I am free.

'No,' I say to the thing in the night. And I wipe my eyes on my sleeve again.

The eyes sharpen, and an edge creeps into the hemlock voice.

'Do you know who I am, child?'

'Yes, I know.'

'Then you know that I can give you what you want. It is here for the asking.'

'It wouldn't be real, whatever it is you think you can give me.' My voice shakes a little. 'I won't take anything from anyone. Not now. And if I die I want to go to heaven, and meet them all again. In the meantime, this is me, here, and it is all I am. And you can't have it. No-one can.'

The hand is withdrawn, and the silver eyes stare at me – so cold – like there is an arctic waste blowing behind them.

'I have seen brave strong men who do not have half the heart you possess, girl,' the thing says. It hunkers down before me, its knees level with its ears.

'And that is what makes you so precious to me. You are a strong soul, full of your mother's courage. And your father's failings have only made you stronger. How fine you are.' He reaches out the white, long-fingered hand once more, and I feel his black nail trace down my cheek, as chill as the point of an icicle. 'We will let it go at that for now. You have some life yet in front of you; it may be minutes, it may be years. But when you come to the end of it, I shall be watching. I will always be there, for there is something of me in your blood. You will find that to be true, in time. For now, I bid you good luck with the wolf.'

And he is gone, the after-images of his bright eyes hanging in the air for a second. And my heart is still thumping as loud as Pa's ticking watch.

BUT I HAVE my breath back, and though I feel heavy and tired still, the stitch in my side has gone and the suffocating fear has drawn back into its dark hole.

I can think again. I know I cannot just lie here. They'll find me, sure as anything.

I crawl out from under the hedge and straighten up. I have lost my bearings, and I have to look up at the sky and find the Plough, the Pointers, and the North Star just as I was taught. The cloud is thickening now, but it has not yet touched the moon.

North is where I must go, to the river. After that, I have no other aim in mind, and no idea what to do. But I will not just lie down and wait for them. I will not give up.

I start to hobble on again – my feet are almost completely numb, and they are covered in mud and the black shine of blood. Just as well they're numb, I think. I don't want to look at them too closely.

There is blood on my face too, and my legs. The hawthorns scratched me good and proper.

I touch the knife in my pocket. They tried to steal everything from me and make me one of their own. But they shall not have me, not even for Luca.

I must get to a police station, or at least to a town. Who would have thought that the heart of England could be so huge and empty in the dark?

I AM ACROSS the furrows of the ploughed field now, and through another hedge which strips hairs out of my head and covers me in fresh scratches. But it is open pasture after that, and along one side of it there is the sound of running water, a little stream flashing bright under the moon. It must run to the Thames in the north. The slope is downhill, and I follow the stream and get my second wind, jogging along through withered grass that has the frost beginning to sparkle across it like a carpet of crushed glass.

I stop to look behind me every so often. The lantern has disappeared now, and there is no more hallooing and shouting in the night. Perhaps they have given up. Perhaps I have lost them. I want to believe that, but know it is not real.

There is a clump of buildings on my right with tall dark trees growing around them, but not a light to be seen. The whole world is asleep. It has turned its back on me. I blink back tears, swallow down the panic. Queenie spoke of a bridge. Perhaps I can find it. I wish I had a map. I wish –

The wolf howls again, so much closer now. I feel a thrill of absolute terror go through me, as cold as it someone had tipped a glass of water over my head.

I start running again, as fast as my numb bloody feet can go. I am travelling over an open plain of flat land with lines of hedges running across it, the river lost again.

There is a wide track, rutted and full of frozen puddles, and my feet follow it without any more thought. Perhaps someone, somewhere in this empty place is awake, and will open a door for me and then shut it against the night. Perhaps –

I hear a snarling behind me and I twist to look, but then something smashes into my back and I am knocked to the ground, sprawled across the track.

I lie dazed for a second, but then catch my wits and roll onto my hands and knees – it is right there with me, the wolf, and I can smell it and feel its heat.

Its jaws fasten on the collar of my coat and it half-lifts me off the ground like a terrier shaking a rat, and its hot slobber runs down my neck. I twist in my coat, and see a bright, raging eye and try and get my elbow at it, but the thing is moving too fast. It drops me, and then clamps its jaws around my ankle and I scream out at the pain and the crushing vice-grip of the teeth. Then it begins to drag me up the path, and the stones tear at the back of my legs. I kick my bare heel into its face. Nothing works; it is not going to let go.

It is over. I am going to die here, tonight. The wolf will have me, in the end.

But not without a fight.

I reach into my coat pocket for the little penknife – at least I might be able to hurt it first – and instead my hand comes out with a ragged twig, and there is something shining upon it.

The wolf opens its jaws and snarls at me, the black lips drawn back from its teeth. Its eyes are as yellow as lemons and full of hate and triumph.

This is Job, white-muzzled, grey-backed. The older wolf, the man who murdered my father.

My terror flits away, and in its place there is that boiling rage, the same which made me stab Queenie. I hobble to my feet, staggering like some drunk chucked out of the Jericho.

'Come on then – are you afraid? What are you waiting for, you rotten, filthy old man. Come and get me!' And I bare my own teeth at it like I am an animal too.

The wolf springs, maw agape.

I thrust out my hand, and my knuckles are ripped open by the thing's teeth as my fingers plunge into its hot mouth. It knocks me on my back, but I thrust my arm out stiff, and my hand goes deeper, fighting the twist of the tongue. The jaws are trying to snap my hand off, but half my arm is down the wolf's throat now, and in that hand is the twig from my coat pocket with its pearl-bright berries.

It is a mistletoe sprig. The sudden knowledge of that floods me with defiance and hope, like some remembered dream.

If what Luca told me about it is not true, then I know I will be dead in a few seconds.

The wolf chokes, and shakes his head until I think my arm is going to break. It rolls off me but I follow it, hugging the great head with my free arm and jamming the mistletoe as deep down its gullet as the fingers of the other can force it. I have never felt such hatred for anyone or anything in my life before. I am snarling like the wolf itself as I hang on, and the animal's teeth saw into my upper arm like knives, shredding my coat and the flesh beneath. But I will not give up or give in.

The wolf gives a horrible choking squeal and the paws scratch at me and the hind legs come up and kick me in the stomach.

I fall free of it, gagging, my right arm covered in blood and slime above the elbow. But the mistletoe is still in the wolf's black throat.

The beast yowls as though it is being burned, and thrashes around in agony. It beats its head on the ground and claws at its ears with its forepaws.

If I did not know who this was and what he had done, I think I would pity it. It looks as though it is burning up from the inside – gouts of hot breath billow out of the jaws like steam from a whistling kettle.

And it changes. The fur shortens even as I watch. The paws splay out into black-nailed fingers. The long muzzle snaps in with a crack of bone. There is a naked old man writhing on the track now with blood trickling out of his mouth, and he is clawing feebly at his bearded face.

I watch him die. It is a terrible thing, but I do not look away for a second. I did this, and I have to see it out to the end.

Our eyes meet, and there is no more hatred in his, just a wild fear. He reaches out a hand towards me, but I stand motionless with blood trickling steadily off my fingers.

'The Devil will come for you now,' I say quietly to Job. I look up at the black and silver sky.

'He is not far away. I have spoken to him already tonight.'

Job gargles blood. His eyes stay fixed on me, until they freeze in place. Then he slumps back, rolling onto his side.

That much is done, at least.

I nudge the body with my bare toe and it is like prodding a raw pork loin. He is dead meat now, no more.

'That's for Pa,' I whisper.

Job killed my father; now I have killed Luca's.

I killed someone. The enormity of that is too much to take in right now. I have committed the greatest of all sins, and yet I feel no sorrow or remorse. Can I ever be forgiven?

I cannot bring myself to think on it.

THERE IS NOTHING for it but to go on. I turn back towards the north and the cloud darkening the night's horizon. I am too spent and sore to run – I can barely hobble. My ankle is swelling up where Job bit it, and my right shoulder feels twisted and torn; that hand is so slimed with filth that I wipe it on the grass and don't care to look at it any more closely.

But I keep going. One hundred yards. It feels like a mile.

I peer behind me, and see the body lying white and still on the path behind. Even skinchangers can't come back from the dead.

Two hundred yards. Three hundred.

I haven't gone much farther when I hear a sound that freezes my blood once again. The other wolf. It sets up an awful tearing howl that is utterly different from all I have heard before. It is grief and fury mixed, and it rises up almost to a scream.

I do not look back. Luca has found his father, and in a few minutes he will find me, and it will all be over. No matter what he feels for me, he is one of them. He is the enemy, and I have hurt him worse than I ever knew I could.

My ankle buckles and I go to my knees, the breath sobbing in and out of my mouth. I cannot go on. It hurts too much. I do not even have it in me to crawl.

Half the sky has darkened with black cloud now. It is pouring out of the north like a carpet, and ragged outliers of it are passing over the moon. When that happens the world becomes blue-dark and hidden.

But when the moon comes out from behind those tattered sails of cloud the world lights up in silver-grey. Back and forth the light goes, and the wind is quickening. There is a weather-change in the air.

I do not want to look back and see the eyes of the wolf coming up the track. I stare north instead, and see a bright sparkle of running water come and go in the fitful moonlight. I was so close. Not that it would have done me much good. I can't swim, and the thought of how cold that river must be...

I almost laugh at my own stupidity.

The devil takes the hindmost, Pa always said. Well, he was right. I just wish it did not have to be Luca. He is the only friend I think I have ever had.

At last I turn, still on my knees. He is here.

The great black wolf is only yards away, padding soundlessly towards me. Its eyes are bright as mirrors under the moon, and it walks in a cloud of its own breath.

'I'm sorry Luca,' I say to it. 'He was going to kill me. He killed my Pa. Queenie lied to you. It wasn't the Roadmen, it was Job. He murdered my father, and Queenie told him to do it.'

The tears course down my face. I can't help it. I look up at the sky, and wonder what time it is. I take out Pa's watch and click it open. It is after three.

I realize something, a forgotten fact from another world.

'This is my birthday. I am twelve today.'

I look at Ma's face in the lid of the watch, clear now in the bright moonlight. She is beautiful. I knew she would be. I know her dear face, now that I see it for the first time in so long. And the memories the photograph sends soaring quite take my breath away. The tears blind me.

The watch is ticking away my life, as it ticked away those of my parents. I close it and hold it close to my heart.

I will be with you soon.

The wolf is almost on me now. It moves as slow and careful as though it is stalking a deer, instead of a lame little girl.

'Don't make it hurt too much,' I whisper.

21

Kneeling, this wolf's muzzle is level with my eyes. It is beautiful and fearsome beyond anything I have ever imagined out of the pages of a book. Larger than the wolf-Job, its fur shining black as sin.

Queenie was right; Luca is a wondrous thing, one of many marvels that most people in the world cannot even guess at.

I find myself wishing I could tell Jack about all this. There is a Devil after all; I have met him. So there must be a God, too, and that knowledge is incredibly comforting. It does not all end here. I think it would comfort Jack too. I think he wanted to believe in something even more than I did.

The story has a power all to itself, he once said.

But what if the story is true.

The wolf is growling, low in its chest. It is truly something, to not be afraid at this moment, my last on Earth.

It pads forward, panting. I close my eyes.

So close I can feel the prickle of its fur.

And it stops there.

The wolf is huge and warm and dark, and I feel the heat of its breath on my face. It does not move.

'Luca,' I say, my voice all broken and hoarse, and I cannot seem to help myself, but plunge my hand into the thick coarse coat, the glorious darkness of it.

The beast shudders at my touch. Then it lowers its head, and the great snout nuzzles my neck, and licks at the blood there. It gives a whine, like that of a family dog.

I burst into tears, and hug the wolf, my bleeding arms barely able to encircle the massive neck.

'Luca, I'm so sorry,' I sob. And the great wolf stands there and takes my weight as I lean into it, and I hear its heartbeat deep in its chest and the warmth of it, and I feel like I could stay like that for ever.

IT STARTS TO rain. I feel it cold on my nape. The wind is getting up and rushing through the hedges and moaning over the open fields.

I hear something different below it, another noise on the track behind me. The wolf is looking at it. I turn around, recognizing the sound even as I do.

Hoofbeats, an unshod horse trotting down the track.

And I see him towering there.

The pale horse slows to a walk, and it throws up its head and gives a thundering whicker, tossing its mane like a wave. Upon it sits a thing of majesty, a broad-chested man daubed in red clay with the antlers of a great stag rising up out of his hair, and the light of the stars in his eyes. He and the pale horse seem immense, tall as a tree, and as they step forward, so the wolf in my arms sets its ears back and snarls.

And the man on the horse speaks, a deep voice with a lilt to it like music.

'Leave her be, skinchanger. It is not for you that I am here.'

The horse comes to a halt beside me, and lowers its muzzle. For a second it is on my cheek, bristle and velvet-soft. The man looks down at me and smiles.

'Gabriel,' I say. And I want to bow my head, but I cannot take my eyes from his face. The wolf backs away growling, and my arm falls from its neck.

Other, faint noses in the night, growing louder. Voices. The rest of Luca's folk are finally catching up with us.

'Go back to your people,' Gabriel orders the wolf. 'Tell the witch she has failed.'

'No!' I shout, finding my voice again. 'He's my friend. He wasn't going to hurt me. Luca, don't leave me.'

The wolf stands there, teeth bared, a sing-song snarl rumbling out of it. The pale horse stamps its hoof and becomes restive.

'Your place is not with them, child,' Gabriel says. 'It never was.'

I look at the wolf. It stands there, teeth half-bared, the growl rumbling in its chest. I want to hug it again, the way I once would have hugged Pie – or different – but the same. I don't know. But I know I cannot bear to see the beast that is Luca leave me. I glare up at the majestic figure, and meet the star-cold eyes.

'I don't care. He forgave me, don't you understand? I killed his father and he forgave me for it – I know he did.

I won't leave him. He's –' I choke. 'He's all I have now.'

Gabriel frowns, and for a moment his face looks terrible, frightening, like the statue of an old god.

'There can be no splitting of such loyalties. I will allow this friend of yours to choose, here and now. His own people. Or you.' He looks at the wolf. 'Skinchanger, I offer you this choice only once. There is no time, and no way to go back once the thing is done.

'You stay with her, and you shall have my friendship. You go back to your own people, and you must let them know that they are to leave her be, now and forever. If they harm her or dog her footsteps, then I will unleash my brothers of the hunt upon them, and I will harry them day and night across the whole length of the kingdom.'

The wolf stands there, blinking. Finally it walks back up to me and pushes its nose into my chest.

Gabriel nods. 'Very well.'

I sag. The pain is rising in me now, and I see that I am kneeling in a pool of blood. It is pouring down out of my fingers in a black stream.

There is a swooping blackness that fills my head for a second, and when it passes I find I am up off the track, astride the pale horse before Gabriel, and an arm hard as oak is holding me there. I struggle for a second, on instinct alone.

'Hush now, child. I mean you no harm.'

Black figures crowding down the track, and the swinging glow of a lantern. A woman's voice rises up in a shriek, and the sound makes me shiver and squirm.

'Let us go,' Gabriel says quietly 'They have their dead to mourn.' And the tall horse turns under us and begins walking to the north, towards the river. The wolf trots alongside silent as a shadow.

The pain grows less. The warmth of the horse and of Gabriel makes me almost drowsy. But my blood is trickling down the flank of the great animal. I am leaking at the seams, and I do not greatly care.

'Am I going to die?' I ask.

'Yes, child.'

'I killed a man back there. I have that sin on me.'

'It was no sin, to fight for your own life. Your soul is clean.'

'I don't want to go to hell.'

'Nor shall you. That test you passed also.'

My mind is slipping in and out of the night. I look down at the wolf trotting faithfully beside us. Then I feel the change of gait as the pale horse slips into a canter, picking up speed, its mane flowing out like white flame in front of me.

For some reason I think of the horse on that last day on the docks of Smyrna, galloping wide eyed and on fire through the crowd, and somehow it seems almost as though things have come full circle. This horse I am on shall take me out of the world with it. And I shall see them all again, Ma and Pa and Nikos.

I am not thinking very clearly. I must have dreamed. But I am sure that we are moving even faster now, the horse galloping under me with a motion as regular as the rocking of a boat. Luca the black wolf keeps pace with it, loping tirelessly beside us.

And we are not on the ground, but soaring through the air, and the whole wide land of England is spread out under me in the moonlight, the hills and woods and rivers and the tall stones and the ancient barrows. It seems almost for a second that I see a shape, a pattern to it.

'So beautiful,' I say, trying to keep my head up, my eyes open. It is my own country, the place of my heart. I know that now. I belong here at last.

22

So it was a dream I suppose. It certainly felt like one.

I lie and watch the shadows on the ceiling come and go. A dark wood ceiling, and the sunlight is fretting across it, a breeze stirring lace curtains and letting the light in and out.

For a long time, all I am is a pair of eyes, a single sense. All I do and all I want to do is watch the shadows above me come and go.

I am alive. For some reason I am surprised. I watch the play of light and shadow above me and try to make things add up in my head.

My other senses begin to work as well. I am in a bed, on clean sheets and with a patchwork blanket lying upon me, bright as a toddler's finger-painting.

I can hear birdsong outside the window, and I think a motor car in the distance. And somewhere close there are footsteps coming and going on a stone floor, and the clink of plates.

And I can smell baking bread. The homeliest smell in the world. It must be Mrs Bramley, down in the kitchen.

I turn my head – my neck is very stiff – and tucked in beside me in the bed is Pie, eyes closed.

I reach out and touch her white face. Her dress has been washed and has come up like new, except where the burn-marks remain. My shoulder aches. I leave her be. It is so much easier to simply lie here, to simply –

I raise my arm again and see it is bandaged in white linen, the knots neat and tidy.

The dream flutters in and out of my head. I look around the room, at the washstand with its basin and jug, an old wardrobe in a corner, a picture on the wall – a framed tapestry, a bible quote:

And behold, I am with thee, and will keep thee in all places whither thou goest, and will bring thee again into this land; for I will not leave thee until I have done that which I have spoken to thee of.

I TURN MY head. 'It wasn't a dream, was it Pie?' And despite the pain that stabs through my shoulder, I take her in my arms and her black eyes open and close as if to agree.

The door opens, and in comes a tall, ruddy-faced woman with her grey hair up in a bun. She wipes flour-dusted hands on her apron and smiles down on me.

'Well, thee's awake at last. Now that's just champion. How do you feel, me dear?'

I stare at her. 'I don't know where I am.'

'Don't thee be fretting on that. Just know that you is safe and sound here with us. There ain't nothing to worry about, Anna.'

I believe her. She has a good face, broad and kind.

'Was it all real then?' I ask. Some things I remember, and some I forget, and some I don't want to remember ever again.

She leans over the bed and touches me lightly on the forehead.

'The fever is down. The poison is out of thee at last. You will be well now, child. All shall be well. Lie quiet now, and I'll bring thee some soup and bread.'

LATER, SHE FEEDS me spoonful by spoonful, a rich broth full of leeks and pearl barley, and she breaks off pieces of warm bread for me to chew, putting them into my mouth one by one. I don't mind, for my arms hurt every time I raise them.

The sun wears round, and she lights an oil lamp in the corner and turns the wick down low. I look at the passing daylight outside the window and shivers go up and down my back as I think of the frost on the Downs, the chalk track, and the camp on Badon Hill.

And every time I close my eyes, I see the yellow stare of the old wolf.

I sleep, Pie's head next to mine, and when I wake up again the curtains have been drawn and the room is quite dark except for the lamp, and there are voices in the house. I haul myself up until I am sitting, and find I am dressed in an old-fashioned striped nightshirt, and there is not a part of me that does not seem to be scratched or twisted or bruised in some way. There is a thicket of black stitches on my right arm, like intersecting lines of marching ants. I can feel bandages on my feet, like thick socks, and my toes are throbbing under the blanket.

And my hair has been cut short. I run my fingers through it, more astonished by that than anything else. It has been trimmed back to the nape of my neck. I wonder what I look like. There is no mirror to tell me.

Clumping footsteps, and the door opens again. This time it is a face I know.

Gabriel.

He stands there with a pipe in his mouth, and he is the farmer on the cart again who once gave me a lift to Oxford Station.

But if I stare hard enough the other thing is there also. The creature with the stag antlers which rode the pale horse. A kind of king.

He takes the pipe out of his mouth and meets my eyes with a quirky smile. 'Aye,' he says quietly. ''Tis a lot to take in.'

He sits on the bed beside me and pats my knee.

'Ask me,' he says simply.

'Where am I?'

'You is in Aldgarth Farm, in Yarnton, north o' Oxford.'

It sounds so ordinary. I almost want to laugh at him. After everything, after all that has happened, there is still Oxford, and women with kind faces, and soup, and Pie next to me in the bed – a real bed, with clean sheets. It does not seem quite right that such things should be, not after the sights I have seen in the night. Not after I have...

'Did I die?' I ask, very quiet.

Gabriel's face becomes grave.

'You are here, and alive and well, my dear. Our doctor stitched you up, and so far as he knows you was bit by a dog.'

My head whirls. Now I do laugh, but I am close to tears at the same time.

'I don't know. I don't know what I am, Mister Gabriel, or what's to become of me.'

'Know this then; this is my home, Anna, and now it is yours too, for as long as you wish.'

That throws me. I feel a rush of relief, even a kind of happiness. I don't want to be homeless anymore. Being an orphan is bad enough.

'Thank you – it's very good of you,' I say carefully. And then the question pops out, 'Who are you – who are you really?' My voice drops as I speak. It feels impertinent, but I have to – I have to know.

Gabriel looks at me solemnly.

'I am the last of a long line o' folk that has been here since this land first became an island. There is in me a power, a memory. I am the guardian of the last bits and pieces of the Old World.' He shrugs. 'And I am Gabriel Alden, with thirty acres to farm and a living to make.'

It doesn't help, not really. But I know one thing. Something I have to say.

'You saved me – didn't you?'

'You saved yourself, girl, not once but twice.'

I shake my head, remembering without wanting to.

'What am I, Gabriel?' I ask him quietly.

'Ah.' He laughs. 'Now there's a harder question. They thought you was a young witch, those you were running from. Me, I'm not so sure. There is a bloodline in you I can't quite fathom.'

'Perhaps it goes back to Troy, and Agamemnon – or Odysseos,' I say, grabbing for old straws.

'Perhaps it does, Anna. That is something we shall have to ponder out in time. But I would not be dwelling too much on it now. You has had enough o' the Old World for a while, and it will always be there waiting for you.'

I am not sure I am so glad of that.

Then I lift up Pie. 'How did you get her back?'

He chuckles. 'That there doll was left at the gate by persons unknown. A peace offering I thinks you might call it. The travelling folk are licking their wounds. They made their play, and it went bad on 'em. They has scattered again, I hear. Most of 'em are moving into the west. I don't think we'll see 'em in this part o' the world for a while to come.'

I think on this, and finally say the name that has been in my head all this time.

'What about Luca?'

Gabriel nods, and a certain grimness comes into his face.

'Boy! He cries. 'Get in here!'

My heart is fluttering as the door creaks open and Luca puts his face around it. He looks paler, and is lean as a rake, but he half-smiles as he shuffles in.

We stare at each other. Gabriel looks us both up and down. 'Not much to say, eh? Set thee down, boy. I'll let the pair of you alone. Supper will be on the table soon though. Don't be tiring her – she ain't on her feet yet, nor near it.'

'How long have I been here?' I ask Gabriel.

'Three days. My Mary has been watching over you morn and night, and this one has been in and out like a jack in the box, when he ain't out in the fields with me. You had some bad infection from all the bites and scratches and whatnot. And there was so much filth in your hair Mary had to crop it off. But it'll grow again. You are young, and whole, and you'll have a few scars, Anna, but in time you'll be as right as rain.'

He leans over and kisses me on the forehead.

'Don't be lettin' any night frights and noises worry you, not in this house. There ain't nothing out there in the dark that can touch you no more. I promise you that.'

Then he leaves the room, clapping Luca so hard on the shoulder that the boy staggers.

Luca is wearing a shirt and breeches that are far too big for him, twine for a belt, and a flat cap screwed up in his hands as though he is wringing out a sponge.

The cat gets my tongue for a long drawn out minute.

'You look like a boy,' Luca says at last.

'I do not!'

'Your hair, 'tis shorter than mine.'

I run my hand over it. Not a sleek bob, just a shorn sheep look it seems.

'Well, I don't care.'

'Nor me either,' he says, and smiles.

I start to giggle. On impulse, I hold out my hand. He stumps over to the bed and takes it.

'I'm sorry for what happened,' I say.

'T'ain't for you to say sorry,' he replies gruffly.

Perhaps there are other things we should both be saying, but I know neither of us wants to hear them, not right now. This moment here is enough.

His hand is cool on mine and the touch of it dizzies me a little.

'How long are you going to stay?' I ask him.

'As long as you,' he answers, and colour floods his pale

face. 'That's to say, as long as you want.' He drops my hand and clears his throat. 'That Gabriel, he has plenty o' work to do about the place, and I have a room of my own out back, and there's horses to work up, and fields to plough for the spring sowing...' He trails off.

'He was your enemy,' I say.

'That's what I was told,'

'We were both told a lot of things, I suppose.'

'That we were.'

We look at each other.

'I want you to stay,' I tell him. 'You're the only friend I have in the world.'

He slaps his cap on his thigh. 'I will then.'

'Well that's all right.'

Suddenly we are both grinning at each other like fools.

'Boy!' the woman's voice calls out. 'Supper is ready. Make sure thee washes thy hands.'

Luca bends over and kisses me on the cheek. Then he straightens, face flaming, and pads out of the room.

I lie back in the bed. I laugh again, for no reason at all.

Or perhaps it is because I feel that I have finally come home.

Acknowledgements

THIS BOOK WOULD not have come into existence without the faith and patience of Ben Smith, to whom I owe a great debt of gratitude.

And acknowledgements are also due to Liam Arbuthnot, Darren Turpin, and the other members of the Old Forest Social Club, for reading over the manuscript and encouraging me when I was unsure if I was barking up the wrong tree altogether.

And finally, none of it would have been possible without the love and support of my wife Marie, who is an inspiration to me every day.

'One of the very best writers of fantasy around'
Steven Erikson

Paul **Kearney**

A **DIFFERENT KINGDOM**

Michael Fay is a normal boy, living with his grandparents on their family farm in rural Ireland. In the woods—once thought safe and well-explored—there are wolves; and other, stranger things. He keeps them from his family, even his Aunt Rose, his closest friend, until the day he finds himself in the Other Place. There are wild people, and terrible monsters, and a girl called Cat.

When the wolves follow him from the Other Place to his family's doorstep, Michael must choose between locking the doors and looking away—or following Cat on an adventure that may take an entire lifetime in the Other Place. He will become a man, and a warrior, and confront the Devil himself: the terrible Dark Horseman...

WWW.SOLARISBOOKS.COM

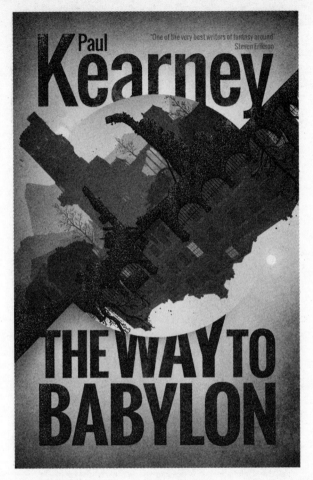

"One of the very best writers of fantasy around"
Steven Erikson

Paul KEARNEY

THE WAY TO BABYLON

Michael Riven—a successful author and former soldier—has fallen off a mountain. Broken in both body and mind, racked with guilt and loss by the death of his wife Jenny, he withdraws into himself in the rural hospital where he painfully recovers. His readers are desperate to know what will happen next in the fantasy world of his stories, but neither writing, nor living, are of interest to him anymore.

But there are others seeking the scribe out. Men of Minginish have begun a quest to rescue their blighted homeland, and have come between worlds. Riven will be asked to travel to a land both familiar and terrifying, which he once thought his own creation. The author must take up the companions of his stories—grim Bicker, fierce Ratagan and sly Murtach—and find a way to mend what was sundered.

 WWW.SOLARISBOOKS.COM

Paul Kearney

'One of the very best writers of fantasy around'
Steven Erikson

RIDING THE UNICORN

Warder John Willoby is being pulled between worlds, disappearing for minutes at a time from the prison and appearing in the midst of a makeshift medieval encampment before tumbling back. That, or he's going mad, his mind simply breaking apart. It's clear, to him and to his family, it must be the latter.

His wife can barely stand him, and his daughter doesn't even try; he drinks too much and lashes out too easily. He isn't worth anyone's time, even his own. But in this other world—this winter land of first-settlers—he is a man with a purpose, on whom others rely. A man who must kill a King so as to save a people. With a second chance, Willoby may become the kind of man he had always wanted to be.

 WWW.SOLARISBOOKS.COM

Follow us on Twitter! www.twitter.com/solarisbooks

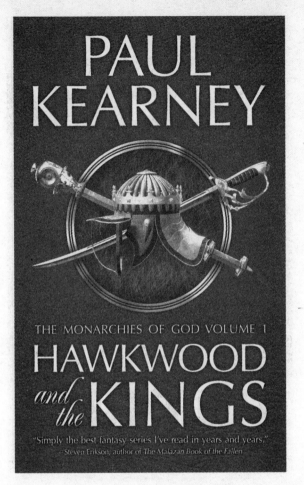

PAUL KEARNEY

THE MONARCHIES OF GOD VOLUME 1

HAWKWOOD and the KINGS

"Simply the best fantasy series I've read in years and years."
–Steven Erikson, author of The Malazan Book of the Fallen

For Richard Hawkwood and his crew, a desperate venture to carry refugees to the uncharted land across the Great Western Ocean offers the only chance of escape from the Inceptines' pyres.

In the East, Lofantyr, Abeleyn and Mark — three of the five Ramusian Kings — have defied the cruel pontiff's purge and must fight to hold their thrones through excommunication, intrigue and civil war.

In the quiet monastery city of Charibon, two humble monks make a discovery that will change the whole world...

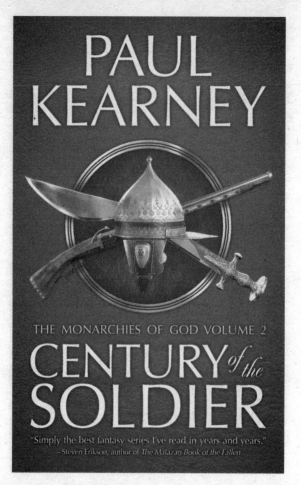

PAUL KEARNEY

THE MONARCHIES OF GOD VOLUME 2

CENTURY *of the* SOLDIER

"Simply the best fantasy series I've read in years and years."
– Steven Erikson, author of *The Malazan Book of the Fallen*

Hebrion's young King Abeleyn lies in a coma, his capital in ruins and his former lover conniving for the throne. Corfe Cear-Inaf is given a ragtag command of savages and sent on a mission he cannot hope to succeed. Richard Hawkwood finally returns to the Monarchies of God, bearing news of a wild new continent.

In the West the Himerian Church is extending its reach, while in the East the fortress of Ormann Dyke stands ready to fall to the Merduk horde. These are terrible times, and call for extraordinary people...

WWW.SOLARISBOOKS.COM

Follow us on Twitter! www.twitter.com/solarisbooks

PAUL KEARNEY
THE TEN THOUSAND

"One of the very best writers of fantasy around."
Steven Erikson

The Macht are a mystery, a people of extraordinary ferocity and discipline whose prowess on the battlefield is the stuff of legend. For centuries they have remained within the remote fastnesses of the Harukush Mountains. Beyond lie the teeming races and peoples of the Asurian Empire, which rules the known world, and is invincible. The Great King of Asuria can call up whole nations to the battlefield. His word is law. But now the Great King's brother means to take the throne by force, and has called on the legend, marching ten thousand warriors of the Macht into the heart of the Empire.

WWW.SOLARISBOOKS.COM

Follow us on Twitter! www.twitter.com/solarisbooks

PAUL KEARNEY
CORVUS

"One of the very best writers of fantasy around."
Steven Erikson

Twenty-three years after leading a Macht army home from the heart of the Asurian Empire, Rictus is now a hard-bitten mercenary captain, middle-aged and tired. He wants nothing more than to lay down his spear and become the farmer that his father was. But fate has different ideas. A young war-leader has risen to challenge the order of things in the very heartlands of the Macht, taking city after city and reigning over them as king. His name is Corvus, and they say that he is not even fully human. He means to make himself ruler of all the Macht, and he wants Rictus to help him.

WWW.SOLARISBOOKS.COM

Follow us on Twitter! www.twitter.com/solarisbooks

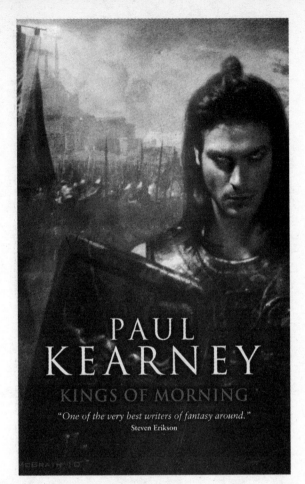